DIRTY LITTLE MIDLIFE MISTAKE

HEART'S COVE HOTTIES
BOOK 3

LILIAN MONROE

Cover design: Qamber Designs
Editing: Shavonne Clarke
Proofreading: Jane Beyer

Published by Method and Madness Publishing PTY LTD
PO Box 168 Subiaco, WA, Australia 6008

Print ISBN: 978-1-922986-43-6

ONE
CANDICE

IF SOMEONE WERE to tell me that today I'd kiss Hollywood heartthrob and certified silver fox Blake Harding, I'd laugh. And laugh.

And laugh.

Yes, my café is the official caterer on set for his latest movie. He's filming a movie in my hometown, and he's presumably eating the food I bring to set. If the stars were to align just so, I might catch a glimpse of his world-famous lips.

But I haven't actually *seen* him.

So to kiss him?

Ha.

Nope.

Not in a million years.

First of all, he doesn't know I exist. I'm a forty-six-year-old widow, yoga teacher, part-owner in the local café, and mother of an angsty teen with an unhealthy love of black eyeliner. He's...

Well, he's Blake Harding! He dates starlets and supermodels. The average age of his lovers is somewhere between my daughter's sixteen (nearly seventeen! When did that happen?) years and my forty-six, and, if I'm honest, it's closer to Allie's age.

According to every gossip magazine in existence, Blake Harding's love life has a revolving door of gorgeous, thin women begging to be photographed by his side. I, on the other hand, don't have a love life. I have a revolving door of dramatic teenage crises and mile-long to-do lists. In his world, I'm a lowly grunt on set who scurries in with trays of food then scurries out.

People like him don't kiss people like me.

I don't kiss *anyone*.

If you were to tell me that in fifteen short minutes, Blake *freaking* Harding's lips will be on mine while he crushes me to his gorgeous chest, I'm sorry, but you need to stay calm and put on this lovely straitjacket. Maybe take a mouthful of assorted pills while you're at it.

Moving on.

Being in charge of catering on a movie set is a lot less glamorous than I thought it would be. For the fifteenth day in a row, I pop the trunk on my black Ford Focus hatchback, throwing my ponytail over my shoulder before grabbing three stacked trays of food. Assorted sandwiches, salads, pastries, coffee beans, tea bags—it's all here. It only took hundreds of hours of preparation and a few extra grey hairs on my head to get this contract fulfilled, but so far, so good.

For the past two weeks, I've been delivering food to set twice a day, every day, and been mostly ignored while I do it. That's fine by me—it's the most profitable contract the Four

Cups Café has ever won in its eighteen months of existence. We have just over two weeks of catering left, and once it's done I'll finally be able to rest. Well, until the Heart's Cove Fringe Festival starts a few weeks later. But I'll have at least a day to myself. Hopefully.

My friend and business partner, Fiona, grabs another stack of trays from the trunk and lets out a breath. "They sure do eat a lot."

"The more they eat, the more they pay." I grin at her, wiggling my eyebrows. "And the more they pay, the more vacations we can take."

Fiona laughs, and the two of us set off in the direction of the set's entrance. The security guard glances at the badges hanging around our necks, then nods for us to enter through the gap in the fence. We walk over plastic cable covers on the ground, along a sidewalk toward the huge white catering tent.

Craning her neck to see what's going on behind the cameras, Fiona stumbles over her feet then catches herself with a yelp. I snort, giggle, then clamp my lips shut when we get death stares from the crew.

"Quiet," a woman with frizzy black hair hisses. "They're rolling."

"Sorry," I mouth, then glance at Fiona and cringe. Her eyes twinkle.

"Action!" someone yells in the distance.

By the time we walk through the flaps to enter the catering tent, the center of my back is damp with sweat. I wipe my forehead and let out a sigh. "Has April always been this warm, or is my internal thermometer all out of whack?"

Fiona snorts, dabbing the back of her neck with a paper napkin. "Don't even get me started."

"We had to turn the air conditioning on last night for the first time. I've never turned it on this early." I unpack the trays of food while my thoughts drift to my husband. He would have patently refused to turn on the air conditioning in April. I smile at the memory. The little things sometimes slip from my mind for months at a time, then come roaring back. He hated sleeping with the A.C. on, even when I was sweating buckets beside him. Said it made his throat dry, and for someone with lung problems, anything that impeded his breathing was a problem.

Turning on the A.C. last night was really nice, even if it did make me feel oddly guilty.

Someone runs past the tent at full tilt, and Fiona pokes her head through the opening before glancing at me over her shoulder. "It's all so serious," Fiona whispers. "Whenever I see behind-the-scenes stuff from movies, everyone is always laughing and joking around. That's false advertising as far as I can tell. No one remotely looks like they're having fun."

"Maybe romcoms are particularly solemn to shoot."

"I thought I'd at least get to see the back of Blake Harding's head by now," Fiona mock-grumbles, her lips tugging at the corners. "What's the point of being on set if you can't rub elbows with Hollywood's Sexiest Silver Fox?"

"Careful." I arrange croissants on a plate and set it down. "Grant wouldn't like to hear that you have your eye on another man."

"If Grant could be here to meet Veronica Taylor, he'd drop everything and sprint over." She checks the coffee carafe, sniffs it, grimaces, then starts making a fresh pot. "We watched *Take Me to Paris* last night and he said, and I quote, 'Veronica Taylor could take me to Paris any day.'"

I laugh.

Fiona's eyes soften as she shakes her head, a smile teasing over her lips. She's thinking of Grant. Her gaze lands on the glittering, emerald-cut engagement ring on her finger, and I know she's swooning internally. I'm happy for her, even if my heart does squeeze into a painfully tight ball.

I touch the ring on my right hand for a moment, then force myself to drop my hands and keep working. It's coming up on three years since Paul died, and although it didn't come as a surprise, it still hurt like hell. I moved the ring over to my right hand before the one and only date I've been on since Paul passed, which felt significant but appropriate. I haven't moved it back.

"Ready?" Fiona arches her brows and jerks her head toward the tent's entrance. "I hear people talking, so it's probably safe to exit."

"Lead the way." I smile at my friend and let the remnants of grief ebb away.

We exit onto the concrete footpath and I take a deep, cleansing breath of fresh air. We live in Heart's Cove, a town on the northern Californian coast nestled amongst redwoods. In early April, the weather is starting to warm, trees are just starting to bud, and the promise of summer warmth is heavy in the air.

I love Heart's Cove. Paul and I moved here when we were in our twenties, when he got a job with a local architecture firm.

We never left. We had our daughter Allie, bought a house, and grew deep roots of our own. When Paul died, there was no question that Heart's Cove would remain my home. I could never leave this place, even if Allie decides to spread her wings in the not-so-distant future.

Fiona's eyes gleam. "What do you think about sneaking over there and seeing what a film set looks like?"

"We shouldn't."

"Oh, come on, Candice. Live a little."

"When did responsible and strait-laced Fiona turn into a rule breaker? Have you traded places with Simone?"

She just grins and jerks her head. "If we circle back around the food tent, we can watch what they're filming from the side."

"Now I know where Clancy gets her rebellious streak."

Fiona just laughs, grabs my hand, and leads me around the tent. Clancy is Grant's daughter and Fiona's unofficial stepdaughter, at least until the wedding. Seeing the three of them together, though, you'd never guess they aren't related. They're as much a family as Allie and me.

We weave through a few trees, squeeze between two bushes, and end up beside big lighting equipment and cameras. There's a commotion happening to our left. My eyes flick to the distinctly purplish face of the movie's director, Mark Yelina. He's about to explode, and the poor, dark-haired production assistant looks like she's trying not to break down and cry.

"Go and get her!" Mark shouts, pointing to the distant trailers housing the talent. "We can't afford to wait any longer."

"She won't come out of her trailer, Mark. I don't know what to do."

"Tell her that if she values the four million dollars she so expertly negotiated for this role, she'll get her ass out here before I fire her."

"Uh-oh," Fiona says. "You think he's talking about Veronica Taylor?"

"I don't know what other female actor would be paid four million bucks," I mumble from the corner of my mouth.

The production assistant's lip wobbles. "I swear, Mark, I tried. Ms. Taylor said her horoscope predicted she'd have a bad day, and she can't leave her trailer in case a catastrophe happens. She won't listen to anything I say."

"She said—" Mark chokes on his own words, splutters, then spins around and looks at one of the producers. "Her *horoscope?*"

The producer, a woman in a silk blouse and pencil skirt, shrugs.

"Jill, you said she was easy to work with." Mark's face turns a deeper shade of purple, his ears bright red. Uh-oh. Not good.

"I said she was perfect for the role," the producer, Jill, responds. "Her agent said she was easy to work with."

"I'm going to kill her. No, I'm going to kill her agent, then I'm going to kill her." Mark clenches his hands into fists.

"I don't think his skin is supposed to be that color," Fiona says through her grin.

I struggle to keep the smile off my face. "Stay and watch the fireworks, or make a hasty escape before someone notices us?"

"Hasty escape, definitely," Fiona says. She takes a step back just as my eyes snag on another person standing on the opposite side of the clearing.

Holy hotness.

Blake Harding is walking toward set like he was sent down from heaven just to make women ruin their panties. He's not a man. Men don't look like that. My jaw drops open as he walks into view, arms hanging by his sides, his pose relaxed yet alert. He walks like he's never had a care in the world, like he's in complete control of his surroundings. He moves with careful, focused grace, and I understand why women flock to him. One look at him, and it's impossible not to think of that body moving in more intimate ways.

Taller than I expected, Blake has thick, dark hair with a sprinkling of salt in his pepper. Deep laugh lines bracket his mouth, with just the right amount of stubble lining his square jaw. He's masculinity personified. Eyes the color of coffee grounds sweep over the assembled crowd, a smile teasing over his full lips. He thinks this is funny.

"Candice," Fiona hisses. "Come on."

I stand there, staring at the sexiest man I've ever seen, immovable as a concrete wall.

Blake rubs his hand over his jaw, a brow arching as he faces Mark Yelina. He's wearing low-hanging jeans and a tight, white T-shirt with a blue button-down shirt layered on top of it, every button undone. He looks like he'd be at home on a couch somewhere, sipping a beer and watching a game—and the couch would thank Blake for the honor of supporting his perfectly formed ass.

"We can't afford another delay. We've only got two weeks before we wrap up." Mark whirls, pointing to Blake. "We're filming this scene with or without her. You need a stand-in?"

Blake shrugs. "Sure. Easier than professing my undying love to empty air."

Mark scans the crowd, his thick brows pulled low over his eyes. Fiona grabs my arm and yanks me back just as Mark's gaze lands on me.

Oh, no.

No, no, no.

Uh-uh. Nope.

This isn't happening.

"You!" He thrusts his index finger at me.

No.

Every single person turns to look, including Blake Harding. His eyes crash against me, and I stumble back. *Whoa.*

He focuses on me, and I feel like the only woman in the world. His gaze snags on mine, then drops to my lips before climbing back up to meet my deer-in-headlights stare. His eyes hold pure power, pure male heat, and all of that blazing intense focus is pointed at me.

I might pass out. My feet move backward, as if the weight of Blake's gaze is too much for my body to handle.

Fiona catches me with a hand on my arm and reverses my direction. Instead of pulling me back toward safety, she pushes me forward. Toward the cameras, and lights, and people...and Blake.

"She's got the height, hair color, close enough build. Get her the right clothes and let's do this." Mark whirls on me. "You capable of standing on a mark and not moving?"

Somehow, my mouth moves and my vocal cords make noise. "Yeah."

"Good. Caitlyn, get her dressed and ready. Let's go people, we haven't got all day!"

A tornado of activity erupts. A honey-blond woman dressed in black hurries toward me, a nervous smile on her face. "I'm Caitlyn. Wardrobe. Let's get you dressed."

"Okay." Goodie. My voice worked again.

From there, I'm thrust into a tent and stripped. They give me a flirty summer dress to slip over my head while someone attacks my hair. I keep my hair long and usually in a ponytail. It's pulled down while someone heats a curling iron, going to town on my head.

"Don't worry, your face won't be in the movie. We just need the clothes and hair to match for certain shots where the back of your head might show." Caitlyn smiles at me, wrapping a chocolate-brown braided belt around my waist.

In less than five minutes, I'm ready. Caitlyn leads me back out of the tent and toward the mass of people and equipment, and my already-overworked heart starts going into overdrive.

It's so, so different being on this side of the cameras. Half a dozen lenses are pointed at me, with more lights than I ever imagined necessary on full blast. There's a gazebo to my right, decorated in lush flowers that definitely had to have been imported specifically for the movie. Nothing else is in bloom this time of year.

Blake Harding sits on the gazebo steps, his elbow resting on the top step while his long legs stretch out in front. There's something in his eyes, in the way he watches me approach, a tiger ready to pounce. His eyebrow twitches as he takes in the sight of me in this dress, then his head tilts ever so slightly.

Micro-movements that speak more than words. He makes a deep, yawning void open up in my stomach as heat gushes through my veins. If one *look* from him can do this to me, what effect would a touch have? A kiss?

Why the hell am I thinking about kissing Blake Harding?

"All right, places, people!" Mark bellows behind me. I'm thrust onto a mark on the ground, yanked around, and told to stay still and say nothing.

Easy enough.

That is, until Blake stands, his eyes heated. When those deep, dark eyes sweep over my body from head to toe, it becomes very, very hard to stand still. I fight the urge to fidget. My body is melting to a puddle of goo. His tongue slides out to lick his lips as he watches me, his body relaxed and easy as he crosses the distance between us.

God, I love the way he moves.

"Ready?" Blake growls low, his hand sliding over my waist. The touch sparks heat between my legs, the warmth of his broad hand making my head spin.

I nod, because what else am I going to do? Blake Harding is touching me. A literal Hollywood movie star's hand is holding my waist. His big, broad chest is shoved up against my face, his depthless coffee-ground eyes laughing as he takes me in.

"Pretend you love me." He winks.

"That's beyond my acting abilities, I'm afraid."

A delighted chuckle falls from his lips, and oh, I want to make him laugh again. I want to feel that chuckle in my *bones*. His hand gives me a little squeeze, which makes the space between my legs spasm. "That's hurtful." He pouts, eyes laughing. "What's your name, gorgeous?"

Well, isn't he a charmer? I pretend I'm immune but in reality, my whole body flushes. "Candice."

"Candice," he says, and I nearly swoon at the sound of my name on his lips. "I'm Blake."

"I know."

His grin widens, affording me a glimpse of his perfect, white teeth. That smile could cause traffic accidents.

"What exactly are we filming right now?" I ask while someone fluffs my hair, another person nudging my feet apart a few inches.

Blake's eyes glimmer. He opens that sinful mouth to answer, but another voice cuts in before he can speak.

"Camera ready?"

"Ready!" another voice calls out.

"Roll sound."

"Sound is speeding."

A woman in worn running shoes hustles up to us with those clickety-clackety stick things they use in the movies—go figure—calls out the scene and take number, then snaps it next to my face. I jump.

"Action!"

And then my whole world turns on its side.

TWO

CANDICE

THE FULL FORCE of Blake Harding's charm hits me like a high-speed train. His eyes, which had been beguiling a moment ago, turn to molten chocolate. Wow.

"I've wanted you from the moment I saw you, Hayley," he says, and I don't even care that he didn't say my name. For all intents and purposes, I am Hayley. I'm the character in this movie. Candice no longer exists. I'm the object of Blake Harding's desire. His voice is deep, rugged, and it pulls at the deep, feminine core of me. "I'll never let you go. I'll always be there for you, even if you push me away for the next hundred years."

He leans toward me—

"Cut!"

His hand falls from my waist as he turns away from me. Disappointment slams into me, and it takes all my focus not to topple over onto the grass.

"You've never been one to forget your lines, Blake," Mark

calls out, one ear covered by a headset as he stares into a monitor in front of him. "'I'll always be there for you, even if you push me away for the next hundred years. I can't stop protecting you, Hayley, it's not in my nature,'" Mark reads out, then arches a brow at Blake.

"Got it," Blake answers.

They call the commands to each other, snap the sticks, then Blake's molten-chocolate gaze is on me again, the heat turned up to full blast. I'm going to need new panties after this.

"I've wanted you from the moment I saw you, Hayley," he says, and although he's already said it once, my heart still jumps. No wonder he's the star of every swoon-inducing romcom to hit the big screen. The man is a maestro. He hits his lines, then slides his hand around my waist, tugging me forward. My body is all too happy to comply. I crash into his chest, catching myself against the soft fabric of his shirt, curling my fingers ever so slightly against his strength. He's all male power, and being so close to him makes me forget everything. His other hand cups my jaw, his face angled slightly. All I can see is him. His face. His chest. His hands on my body.

Holy mother of unholy acts.

It's for the cameras. Right. We're being filmed. Not for me. This isn't for me. Still...

This is...a lot. I'm breathless, waiting for the next line to make my heart thump.

"Push me away, but I'm not letting anyone hurt you. Not now, not ever." A voice that's nothing more than a growl. Words that make me want to melt.

This man is hot as blazes, and his lips are close enough to

kiss. I'm going to faint. How did I get here? How did this happen?

Then Blake's fingers tighten against the nape of my neck, his other hand sweeping across my back, and he pulls me tight to him. A hard, male chest crushes my breasts, muscular biceps caging me in. My thighs brush Blake's. His fingers curl into my hair, he tilts my head up, and he's *right there*. Those famous lips are an inch from mine, and they're gorgeous. Beautifully full on the bottom lip, perfectly formed, slightly open. His stubble looks raspy and delicious, and I find myself licking my lips.

Something changes in his gaze when I do. Dark chocolate turns heated as he watches the movement of my tongue, his body turning so, so still and hard against me. His hand tightens on my nape, his other arm pulling me impossibly closer.

Every inch of me is pressed against every inch of him, and let me tell you, it feels *good*. Better than good. I've never been so close to someone so incredibly masculine, so powerful, so damn *hot*.

The heat in his gaze flicks to my eyes, and another subtle shift happens. He makes a decision. I see it the moment it happens. Heat turns to want, and want turns to action.

Then Blake Harding kisses me.

I—

Whoa.

His lips are soft, demanding, perfect. He nips my bottom lip and draws a gasp from me, then sweeps his tongue into my mouth as soon as my lips drop open. He tastes faintly of mint, and it tastes good. Really, *really* good. I find myself softening, melting against him, my hands clutching his shirt as my legs wobble. But he doesn't let me fall. He curls his fingers into my hair and holds me against his body, deepening the kiss like nothing else in the world is as important as my lips against his.

I've never been kissed like this. Never, ever, ever. Not like he needs to kiss me to survive, like he wants me so bad he can hardly keep himself together.

Being caged in his arms is heaven, as if nothing else in the world can get to me. The hand on my nape curls, fingers digging into my skin as he tugs my hair to pull my head exactly where he wants me. I'm putty in his hands. Moving how and where he pleases like I was made for that exact purpose. His other hand shifts higher, wrapped all the way around my back while his fingers brush the side of my breast. Another spasm happens down below. A low growl rumbles through him as my body turns pliant and needy in his hands.

This isn't a kiss. This is a conquering. Blake Harding is kissing me like the world is ending. Like he's been walking through the desert and I'm his first taste of water. Like he needs to kiss me in order to *live*.

I never want it to end.

But distantly, faintly, I hear rustling, voices. One word in particular said once, twice, three times—

"Cut! For the love of God, Harding, cut, damn you!"

We fall apart, gasping, and I stare at the perfect male specimen before me, mind reeling. His chest heaves, his eyes slightly bewildered as they follow the movement of my hand as it reaches my mouth. My lips are damp, swollen, thoroughly ravished.

I take a step back.

"Candice—" A pleading rasp. Blake reaches for me, then lets his hand drop.

That kiss...it rattled something in my mind. I can still feel it, taste it. My body's burning. I'm going to fall over.

I want to do it again.

No, I don't. I don't kiss men. I'm not ready to kiss anyone. I can't. It's not right. Paul died three years ago. It's too soon.

But my lips are bruised and my heart is hammering, and Blake Harding is staring at me like he wants to eat me. I tear my gaze away from him and stare at the director. "Are we done here?"

Mark Yelina, Golden Globe-winning, Oscar-nominated director, stares at me for a beat. "We got it." He clears his throat, and I scurry back to the tent to put my own clothes on. When I exit the tent, I don't look in Blake's direction. I don't want anyone to see what that kiss just did to me. Especially not him.

"YOU *WHAT*?" Simone screeches after Fiona and I get back to the café, and Fiona helpfully informs the whole room of my quick but successful career as a Hollywood movie stand-in.

"It was hot," Fiona says, eyes twinkling.

"He was just acting." I ignore the heat building under my skin and stride toward the espresso machine. The Four Cups Café is busy for a Wednesday midmorning, and almost everyone in the shop is staring at me. Half of Heart's Cove heard Fiona announce that I kissed Blake Harding, which means all of Heart's Cove will know about it by sundown.

"Girl, that wasn't acting. Did you see his face afterward?"

Fiona turns to Simone. "Rattled to the bone. Like his whole world had just imploded. He was in shock."

"Damn right he was." Simone grins at me while I do my best to ignore her.

A weird mess of emotions rises inside me. Trying to tease them apart is like trying to unbake a cake. Add one part guilt for kissing someone other than Paul, one part pure, red-hot lust, two parts confusion over the violence of my body's reaction, then throw them into a bowl with a pinch of vague embarrassment. Bake at three-fifty for forty-five minutes, and you get whatever the hell is going on in my head.

"I'm going to need the whole story," Simone says, leaning against the counter as I grind some coffee into the portafilter. I need a double shot of sense knocked into my head.

"Same." Jen emerges from the kitchen, a streak of flour across her cheek. "Blake Harding?"

"It was nothing. They asked me to stand in for a shot. No big deal."

Yeah, no big deal that it was only the second kiss I've had in three years. No big deal that it was the first kiss that made my body feel like it was on fire. And when I say first, I mean *first*. As in, first of my life. No big deal that I want to do it again.

That's some sort of betrayal, isn't it? Paul passed away so recently. I shouldn't be ready to move on. I loved my husband. We knew there was a possibility he'd die young, and we prepared for it. I still chose to make a life with him. How could I move on so soon? How could I move on *at all*?

I busy myself steaming milk, hoping the sound of the

espresso machine will muffle the thousand questions being hurled my way.

"...and there was tongue. I'm telling you, it was too hot to put in the movie. Blake Harding looked shellshocked when they broke apart. The director yelled cut about a dozen times!" Fiona's flushed, her eyes shining. "Blake. Freaking. Harding!"

A collective swoon washes over every woman in the coffee shop, and a few jealous looks are thrown my way. I keep my eyes on my jug of milk, swirling it a few times before pouring it into the waiting espresso. Coffee will fix this. Coffee fixes everything.

The thing is, Fiona is right. That kiss was insane. The way his hand curled around my neck. How his chest was so impossibly broad, so perfectly muscular, so solid and hard against me. How I felt like I belonged in his arms, and I never wanted to leave. I wanted more. When his lips were on mine, and his hands were splayed over my body, I wanted to tear my clothes off and beg him to take me. I wanted sex. Hot, sweaty, dirty sex.

It was a perfect kiss. It was hot. I'll dream of it, I already know.

But I'm *not supposed to kiss anyone*.

My first sip of latte is delicious, and my shoulders drop a fraction of an inch. Coffee definitely helps.

Then the coffee shop door bangs open, and Dorothy rushes through. Along with her twin sister, Margaret, Dorothy owns and operates the hotel in town. She's the definition of a free spirit, and I want to be her when I grow up...whenever that is. Sure as hell hasn't happened yet.

Her eyes jump to me in an instant, and she throws her arms

straight up in the air, screaming as she jogs in place. "Candice kissed Blake Harding!" Her flowy, giraffe-print wrap blouse flutters as she bounces up and down, a new streak of purple in her hair shimmering in the sun that streams through the windows. But it's Dorothy's smile that hits me most. With lips painted bright red, she throws her arms to the side and squeals again. "Just *wait* until Eli hears."

"You don't need to tell Eli," I protest uselessly. She's probably already called him. The two of them have been joined at the hip for nearly a year. "Eli doesn't care."

"Eli most certainly *does* care." Dorothy giggles, hooking her arm through Simone's and tugging her close. "This is the best bit of gossip since you and Wes tried to sneak around."

"We weren't sneaking around." Simone rolls her eyes.

Everyone snorts. Even me. Simone just grins.

"Mom!" Allie crashes through the café door, eyes wild.

"Why aren't you in school?" I put my hands on my hips.

"Study period," she explains, then throws her arms to the sides. "Blake Harding?"

Oh, for crying out loud.

Groaning, I drop my head in my hands. Excited chatter fills the café, the door opening and closing as more and more Heart's Cove residents make their way to where the action is.

The action being me and my traitorous lips.

Then, after I turn my back to the room to take another sip of my latte, wishing I had something stronger to drink, a hush falls over the room. The hairs on the back of my neck prickle, and I stare at the wall, craning my ears.

I don't like the sound of this. Not one bit.

Someone clears their throat. Dorothy. "Candice, honey, there's someone here to see you." Her voice is strange. Muted. I've never heard that from her before.

My heart thumps. No. No, no, no.

This can't be happening. Today is a dream. A nightmare. I'm going to wake up any second.

But as I spin around, I know this feels way too real to be a dream.

Blake Harding is standing in my café, eyes of melted chocolate staring at me like I'm the only woman in the room. A thrill pierces my stomach at the sheer intensity of his gaze. He stares at me with such focus, like his entire existence depends on what I'm about to say.

"Hi," I squeak. Lovely. Such eloquence. Hope he wasn't too attached to his entire existence.

"Candice," he says, and my ovaries do a little jig. How can he make my name sound like it's the most beautiful thing in the universe? No wonder he has a new woman every week. The man is sex incarnate.

"You...want a coffee?"

He blinks, then looks at the huge espresso machine to my right. Recognition flits across his face as if he only just realized he's in a coffee shop. Clearing his throat, Blake (freaking) Harding combs his fingers through his hair and causes a collective female apoplexy by the sheer sensuality of his movements.

"Sure. Maybe we could have a coffee together somewhere where we can...talk?"

"Do it!" Dorothy hisses in a stage whisper. "For the love of God, Candice, *do it!*"

I throw her what I hope is a withering glare. She just grins maniacally and gives me an encouraging nod. Simone gives me a thumbs-up from behind Blake's back. I flick my gaze back to Blake and feel every muscle inside me tighten. He's doing that thing where he stares at me and makes me feel like no one else exists. Dear Lord. I'm in trouble.

"Cappuccino," he says with a slight, cheeky, sexy, playful grin. He knows exactly what he's doing. Blake Harding is a player, and he's set his sights on me.

I'm *not* going to fall for it. Oh, no. Not me. Sure, we shared a scorching kiss. I'll share a coffee with him, too, but I'm not going to do anything else. I'm not a fool. It's too soon.

Mechanically, I start grinding beans. This will all be over shortly. But when I lock the portafilter into the espresso machine and press the button to extract the coffee, the door bangs open again.

"Margaret!" Dorothy calls out. "Finally. You heard about this?" She jabs her thumb at Blake, then at me.

"Never mind that," Margaret says, breathless. Her normally tidy hair is falling out of its bun, spots of red shining bright on her cheekbones. "Candice, you have to come. Your house is on fire."

THREE
BLAKE

"KEYS." I hold out my hand toward Candice as soon as we step outside the café. She stares at me, not understanding, so I wiggle my fingers. "Give me your keys."

"I'm fine to drive."

"You're white as a sheet and trembling so much it looks like your legs are about to give out. I'm driving. This your car?" I point to the black hatchback parked in front of us.

"I don't—"

"Let him drive, Mom."

I spin around to look at the curly-haired blond girl standing behind Candice. *Mom.* Her teenage kid. Shit, Candice has a kid.

What the hell am I doing here?

When we kissed, I wanted more. I followed her into town even though Mark told me he'd rip my balls off as soon as I returned. I asked her for a coffee date like some lovesick teen. All because of what? A kiss?

No. Not just a kiss. That wasn't just a kiss. It woke something up inside me, something that I thought was long dead.

I've kissed women. If I'm honest, I've kissed lots of women—but none of those kisses felt like *that*. No woman has ever reacted to my touch the way Candice did.

When I wrapped my arms around her, she didn't just soften. She *melted*. It felt like she let go of something deep within her. For those few moments, she gave a part of herself to me. *To me*.

And I took it.

I forgot about the movie, about Veronica's ridiculous tantrums, about Mark yelling at us, about the tight filming schedule we've all been rushing around to keep. None of that mattered because when I kissed Candice, she became mine in a way I'm not ready to give up.

It's been a long, long time since I wanted to keep a woman by my side. Seventeen years, to be exact. In the depths of my heart, I might even admit it's been longer. That's just how long it's been since I've had the guts to try.

But she has a kid. And her house is on fire. And judging by the people currently jumping in cars to follow us to her place, she has an established place in this community.

That kiss felt too good to ignore though, and I need to know if there's something behind it. It's been a long, long, *long* time since I've wanted to know more about a woman, and I want to know more about Candice.

The teenage girl crosses her arms and stares at me, her eyes brilliant and blue as if she can read my every thought. I hold her gaze for a beat, then turn to her mother.

Candice reaches into her purse and drops her car keys into my outstretched hand. "It's not far." She points down the road in the direction of the movie set. "Head that way and hang a right at the lights."

We climb into the vehicle, the girl sliding into the back seat as Candice takes the passenger side. She clasps her hands so tight her knuckles turn white, and before I know what I'm doing, I'm reaching across to slide my palm over hers. Her hands open for me, fingers intertwining in mine. I feel her soften beside me, and something else clicks inside me.

I like being the man who makes her soft. She gives herself to me in these infinitesimal ways, but I feel it. I *feel it*. And I want more.

"It'll be okay," I say uselessly, knowing full well it probably won't be okay, but needing to say it anyway.

"So you're as much a hero in real life as you are in the movies?" the girl says from the back seat with more than a pinch of sass. I check the rearview mirror to see her eyebrow arched high, her arms crossed.

"Not quite, no." I flash a grin that slips off my face in an instant.

If only she knew how far I am from heroic. My life is one tragedy after another, most of them of my own making.

I pull my hand away from Candice's and immediately miss the heat of her skin against mine.

My head is reeling. I don't get attached. I don't pursue

women like this, unless I'm trying to get them on their back. Why does this feel different?

I shake my head as I drive, hoping to clear my thoughts. I rushed over here after *one kiss*.

That's crazy, right? The last time I felt this out of control was when I met my first wife. I was nineteen years old, and I married her six months later. We divorced at twenty-one, and it broke something fundamental inside me. I was young and dumb and naive, and what happened afterward made me retreat. It made me doubt myself.

I tried again in my thirties, but it wasn't the same. That marriage lasted six years, but it ended in worse shape than the first. That's when I vowed not to go down that path again.

Now, nearly thirty years after the first time, seventeen years after the second, lightning strikes again and burns that vow away.

Candice directs me down leafy residential streets toward the plume of black smoke marring the sky. We turn the corner to see neighbors huddled on the other side of the street, hands over horrified mouths, as the fire department fights the blaze.

"Holy shit." A breathless whisper from the back seat.

"Allie, language," Candice says on autopilot. Her own eyes are wide, hand on the car door, knuckles once again bone-white. She nearly falls out when I open her door from the outside, and I realize she hadn't even noticed me getting out of the car and moving to her side.

Hooking my arm around Candice's shoulders, I help her from the vehicle and head for one of the police cruisers parked a short walk away.

The deputy takes his hat off when he sees Candice. His eyes flick to me, recognition flitting across them, and then return to Candice. "Mrs. Viceroy."

A breathless huff, and Candice answers softly, "For crying out loud, Joe, how many times do I have to tell you to call me Candice?"

The deputy cringes. "Candice, I'm sorry. I can't let you get any closer. The fire department is doing all they can."

"Do they know how it started?" She's trembling against me.

The man shakes his head. "We'll know more when the fire's out and the forensic team can do their investigation."

"Candice!" I turn to see half a dozen cars parked behind Candice's, with what looks like the entire clientele of the café streaming from the convoy. The elderly woman who told Candice about the fire emerges from one of the cars with a woman who looks remarkably similar—a sister, maybe—and a grey-haired man with a shiny bald spot on his head. I've seen them all at the hotel. The two women own it, I think. The three of them march toward us, wrapping Candice and Allie in their arms as I stand uselessly to the side.

A strange feeling grows in my chest as I watch these townspeople crowd around Candice. It takes a few moments for me to recognize it, but when I do, I take a staggering step back. It's *envy*. I'm jealous. Jealous that at the first sign of trouble, dozens of people are at Candice's side to give her support.

"Where are we going to sleep, Mom?"

"We'll figure it out, Allie."

"All my stuff is in there! My laptop! My backpack with all my notes is in the living room!"

"It's only stuff, honey." Candice puts her arm around her daughter's waist. "We'll talk to your school." The top of Candice's head only reaches her daughter's chin, and the two of them hug tightly. I wish I could do something.

"Where will we live?" Allie cries.

"We'll rent somewhere. It will all work out," Candice says, her voice flat. I want to go to her, but I can't.

"Our tenants are moving out of our rental place on Monday," one of the older ladies says. "The place isn't huge, but it's got two bedrooms and it's partially furnished."

"Oh, Margaret, that's so kind..." Candice says, extending her arm.

The rest of Candice's friends close in around her, and I realize I'm standing here, on the outside, like a lump.

I thought this was lightning striking? Ha. Yeah, right. I'm a selfish asshole and pursuing Candice will almost definitely end in disaster. What was I thinking? Maybe I can leave without anyone noticing. I can forget about the kiss, forget about the coffee date, forget about it all. I shouldn't be here. These people need each other and they need privacy. They don't need someone like me shouldering into their private pain.

I turn away, then pause when I hear one of the hotel ladies let out a disappointed noise. "Until Monday, I'd love to offer you a room at the hotel, but those damn movie people rented every-thing out." She clicks, then glances at me. "No offense, of course, Mr. Harding. We're grateful for the business."

"The room next to mine is free," I hear myself saying before I can stop myself. Shit. *Shit!* Why would I say that? I'm supposed to walk away!

Candice blinks, her long lashes heavy with tears, eyes finally focusing on me. She bites her lip, and I nearly groan.

The woman is a goddess. I thought young, flighty models were my type? I thought I wanted a woman with air between her ears to warm my bed then leave after it's over? I thought the past seventeen years of my life had been *good*?

I've been a fool. There's something between us, some spark, chemistry, whatever you want to call it. Whatever it is, I haven't felt it in a long time. Maybe ever.

And I know what it means—it means I should walk away. No, *run*. Any time I've felt something similar to this, it's ended in divorce and disaster.

There's a reason I date women who are more interested in Instagram than they are in conversation.

But Candice lets out a shaky sigh and nods her head. "Thanks, Blake. You've been so kind. And thank you for bringing me here."

She said my name, and it feels like a hook lodged itself in my gut, keeping me from walking away. I shrug. "You were in no state to drive."

"She'll take a raincheck on that coffee," the white-haired woman with the animal-print top says to me. "Won't you, Candice? And we'll get the room next door to Mr. Harding ready for you and Allie." The second woman in the pale pink pantsuit nods, her fingers running over and back along the string of pearls at her neck.

"Can I stay with Clancy?" Allie says, and I realize another blond girl has materialized by Allie's side. The two of them stare at Candice with wide eyes. "Please? It's only for a few days, right? Until Monday?"

"Sure." Her mother waves a hand, exhausted. "If Fiona and Grant agree."

"It's fine," a dark-haired woman I recognize from the café says. "Allie can stay with us as long as she likes. Grant does the school runs, so it'll be easy for him to take them both to school."

"I still have to go to school?" Allie cries, outraged, her arm thrusting toward the blackened, burning side of her house.

Backing away, I leave them all to themselves. The longer I stand here, the more I feel like I don't belong. Not that I'm better than these people, but that I'm *worse*. Compared to this type of community, my life seems so empty. I look over my shoulder and see Candice watching me. Our eyes meet for a long moment, the last hour of my life crystallizing in my mind.

It wasn't just a kiss. It rocked my world, my convictions, my future.

My phone rings, and I use the distraction to turn away, answering the unlisted number when I would normally ignore it. "Hello?"

"He lives!" A delicate female voice laughs on the other end of the line. "Mark is having an absolute hissy fit."

"Veronica," I say, pinching the bridge of my nose. "I'm on my way back."

"Take your time, handsome. I'm not leaving my trailer today. Not going to risk a catastrophe because Mercury is in retrograde. No way." She harrumphs. "Anyway, have you given any thought to my proposal?"

"It's still a no." Technically it wasn't a no when she asked, I just didn't answer. It's definitely a no now.

"We'd break the internet, Blake. Imagine the headlines! We could play it up for the movie, too. Bigger payday for us. My agent can talk to yours."

"I'm not going to pretend to fall in love with you."

"Boo. You're no fun." That delicate laugh sounds again. "I'll wear you down, honey, don't worry."

Staring up at the clear blue sky, the smell of smoke heavy in the air, I let out a breath. "I don't want to date you, Veronica."

"Well, I don't want to date *you*, you boring old blockhead. But I have this thing called a *career*, and a torrid affair with a co-star would help us both be back on the front page."

"I get enough coverage on my love life as it is," I grumble.

That's not it, though. Two hours ago, I probably would have agreed with Veronica. I would have started dating her and, fake or not, probably would have slept with her. I would have told myself I enjoyed it.

But now? Now that I know Candice exists? Now that I've felt her go soft in my arms, and seen the look in her eyes when she backed away from me, dazed and needy?

No fucking way. Nothing will ever come close to how good that felt.

Veronica snorts. "Your love life? Who, the Victoria's Secret models you parade around L.A. with for a week at a time? Please, Blake. You're not fooling anyone. I'm talking about *real* media coverage. The two of us getting together would be *huge*."

"The answer is no."

She lets out a noise that sounds like a pout, then drops her voice to a seductive drawl. "When are you coming back on set, Blake? Maybe the two of us should lock ourselves in your trailer and see how big a mess we can make."

"I'm seeing someone," I blurt, and am shocked to realize I want it to be true.

A pause. "Who?"

"You don't know her."

"Blake, you don't understand. We would be the next Brangelina. It would slingshot our careers to the stratosphere."

"My career is fine, and the last thing I want is more coverage of my relationships. I'm seeing someone, and I'm not going to sleep with you or pretend to sleep with you for the sake of your dying career. Find some other poor soul to entrap." I hang up, squeezing my phone between my fingers as I fight the urge to hurl it into the burning building.

Wonderful. Great.

I stare at the house, the back half of it engulfed in flames, seeing nothing. Then I go back to set and try to forget the taste of Candice's lips. I'm grasping at straws, trying to ignore the conviction I felt when I had Candice in my arms. Trying to stop myself from committing to this. From wanting this.

It doesn't work.

By the time we're done shooting for the day, I've made a decision. No matter what happened in my first marriage, or my second, or all the years since then, I'm starting fresh.

I'm going after Candice. Not for a night or a week or a month. Not for a quick fuck and a shot on the front page of a tabloid. I'm going after Candice for *real*.

She melted for me. She gave me something, and I took it.
I'm not giving it back.

33

FOUR

CANDICE

FIONA PLACES a mug of tea in my hands as Simone wraps a blanket around my shoulders. Jen plops herself down in an armchair with a sigh. We're in the library above the café watching dusk settle over Heart's Cove.

"How are you holding up?" Fiona asks, sipping her own cup of tea.

"I'm okay," I lie, not wanting to acknowledge the mess going on in my head. "Are you sure it's okay for Allie to stay at your place?"

"Please." Fiona waves a hand. "If we had two extra bedrooms, I'd insist on you staying there, too. The offer's still open. We can make the couch up for Allie or get her to sleep in Clancy's room."

"Wes and I have an extra room as well," Simone says. "But I think you should take Blake Harding up on his offer." She wiggles her eyebrows. "You have from now until Monday. What day is it today? Thursday?" She counts on her fingers, then glances at me with a gleam in her eyes. "Four days to see where that goes."

I groan. "I don't want to think about Blake right now." Simone opens her mouth, but I keep talking before she can interject. "What's going on with Wes, anyway? Isn't he turning forty-five next month? And if he doesn't get married, the house and inheritance get split up, right? Why don't you have a ring on your finger?"

Yes, I'm going on the attack to distract from whatever happened between Blake and me today. My house just burned down. Give me a break, okay?

Simone arches her brows. "Stop trying to deflect, Candice. We're talking about you and Hollywood heartthrob Blake Harding, not me and Wes."

"You and Wes better get busy and get married, otherwise you'll be as homeless as I am."

Simone purses her lips before straightening her shoulders, and I know from the look on her face that I'm about to get a dump truck full of sass shoveled my way.

"What did the firemen say in the end?" Jen asks, saving us all from an uncomfortable face-off. Her feet are kicked up on the coffee table, the smell of chai wafting all the way over from her seat to mine.

"They need to investigate further to find out the cause of the fire. Looks electrical at first glance. They said we were lucky, the fire only spread to the back half of the house. Our bedrooms are mostly untouched by the flames."

"I heard smoke and water is what really damages property

in a fire like that." Fiona sips her tea. "Have you gotten a look inside?"

I shake my head. "Wasn't allowed in. Hopefully in the morning, but the fire chief will call me to set it up. Fingers crossed the smoke hasn't damaged all our things. My wedding photos were in the living room." My voice cracks on the last word. If I've lost all my photos of Paul...

The creak of the staircase interrupts my thoughts. Dorothy pokes her head through the door, a foil-covered tray balanced on her arms. She gives me a sympathetic smile, then casts her eyes around the room. "I've missed coming up here." She lifts the tray up a couple of inches. "Sandwiches, although I'd test them for poison. Agnes made them."

I grin, shaking my head. I'm not even sure why Agnes, the bookstore owner, and Dorothy are feuding. All I know is it will probably never end.

"You used to have your book club up here when Mrs. Byron was alive, right?" Simone takes the tray from Dorothy's hands as the older woman drifts toward the bookcases lining one wall. Mrs. Byron was Wesley's mother, who passed away before Simone started dating Wes.

A soft smile tugs at Dorothy's lips. "We only called it a book club to the uninitiated." She glances over her shoulder. "There wasn't much reading going on up here when we all got together. We used to smuggle the empty wine bottles to the recycling bin in batches so the men wouldn't catch on."

I laugh. "What are we doing drinking tea, then?"

In response, Dorothy—the sweet, elderly, slightly eccentric hotel owner—pulls a full bottle of whiskey out of her purse.

Simone whoops as Fiona groans. Jen, ever the pragmatist, just gets up to grab some glasses for everyone. The door opens again and Margaret pokes her head through the opening. Fiona waves her in, and we all take our seats—and our drinks.

Conversation drifts from the fire to more normal things, and my muscles slowly unwind. Clancy is trying out for the school track and field team, and with her latest growth spurt, Fiona's hopeful she'll qualify for a few of the running events. I smile. Clancy only moved to Heart's Cove just shy of two years ago. Grant and Fiona had barely started seeing each other, and Grant was surprised to know Clancy even existed. Now the three of them are a tight family unit, and it warms my heart to know that she's thriving at school.

"Allie didn't mention track," I say. "But no doubt she'll be following in Clancy's footsteps."

Fiona smiles and leans over to squeeze my hand, and conversation drifts away from us. Simone has had a few new clients sign on for her online marketing agency, and business is good. Jen is happy baking and catering full-time at the café, but she grumbles about our other chef, Fallon, and his tendency to eyeball measurements that she'd rather weigh down to the gram.

Margaret and Dorothy tell us that the movie staff have booked out most of the hotel but are only using half the rooms. After the movie wraps, the hotel is booking up quickly with summer—and Heart's Cove's famous Fringe Festival—on the way. Year after year, Heart's Cove is becoming a more popular tourist destination, especially in the summertime. It's gotten a reputation as a great place with lots of outdoor activities as well as a haven for artists.

The hotel, in particular, is a hub for all things that call to artists and eccentrics. That's where my yoga studio is housed. It's also where, once a month, Grant models for a nude life-drawing class, to Clancy's abject horror. Fiona attends religiously, and I don't blame her.

"I never thought the hotel would be fully booked," Margaret says. "When my husband died and Dorothy came to me with this crackpot idea, I thought it'd be something to keep me busy in my old age. I didn't think we'd actually make *money*."

"You deserve it," I tell her with a smile.

Margaret's lips curl in response, but there's a sadness in her eyes.

"We've prepared the cabana next to Mr. Harding's for you," Dorothy says to me as she sips her coffee mug full of whiskey. "I've got the keys here, so we can head straight there whenever you're tired of these old bags." She jerks her head to the other women.

A chorus of protests rings out, and Dorothy just laughs.

When the noise dies down, I shake my head. "I think I might stay at Simone and Wes's, if the offer's still on the table."

"Don't be ridiculous," Margaret says. "Blake Harding is a handsome man, and I could tell by the look on his face that he wanted to do more than offer you a room next door."

I gape at Margaret. She's the last person I'd expect to be encouraging a tawdry romance between me and some celebrity. "Why is everyone so invested in me and Blake Harding? I don't want to date him. I'm not interested! My house just burned down!"

"Honey," Margaret says, patting my hand with her manicured one, "no one said anything about dating."

I groan as more giggles sound. The wall of smutty romances that we inherited with this space suddenly makes sense.

"When was the last time you were with a man?" Surprisingly, the question comes from Jen. She's been my best friend for years, and we've never been ones to talk about intimate things. But her head is tilted, and I know by the look on her face that she won't let this question go. Once she pulls herself out of her own head and focuses on something, she's like a dog with a bone.

Still, I try to wave the question away with a flick of my hand. "I went on a date with Rudy last year. We kissed. It didn't work out. Now every time he comes into Four Cups I feel vaguely uncomfortable."

"What is this, middle school?" Simone snorts. "We're not talking about kissing and holding hands, Candice. We're talking about sex. Doing the *nasty* nasty."

My cheeks flush. I shrug and try to make my voice sound normal. It comes out squeaky. "It's been a while, but it doesn't matter. That part of my life is over. I've accepted that."

I expect gentle ribbing and teasing laughter, but all I get is silence.

"Sweetie," Fiona starts, leaning her elbows on her thighs, "that part of your life isn't over. We know your husband passed away, but it doesn't mean you're not a woman, you're not human. It doesn't have to be Blake, and it doesn't have to be right now, but you're still allowed to have sex and you're definitely allowed to enjoy it."

My face heats. I shake my head. "When Paul died—even before that, when he got sick—I accepted it. It's no big deal."

A few worried glances are exchanged. Margaret runs her fingers over her pearl necklace before taking my hand in hers. "Candice, darling, you know that's not true, right? I'm not one to tell you how to grieve, but you know your life isn't over, don't you?"

Jen leans forward, her eyes sharp. "How long has it been since you had sex, Candice?"

My throat closes up as embarrassment threatens to swallow me whole. How did we get on this subject again? We were talking about the kids running track a minute ago!

I look at the faces staring back at me, words stuck somewhere in my chest. They all think my marriage with Paul was idyllic. In a lot of ways it was...and a lot of other ways, it wasn't. But how can I even *think* that? I'm betraying his memory. He was *wonderful*. He was!

I put a hand to my cheek and shake my head.

"You don't have to answer that," Fiona says softly. "Jen, don't push her."

Jen ignores her. "Candice." Her voice is harder than I've heard it. I lift my eyes to meet hers and immediately regret it. She sits back, brows arching. "It's been a lot longer than three years, hasn't it?"

Paul died just about three years ago, and Jen knows it. I close my eyes.

"Candice." The edge is still evident in Jen's voice, but I look up to see her eyes soft.

Oh, what the hell. We're all adults here. We know that life

sometimes doesn't work out the way we hope. I take a deep breath. "Nine. Nearly ten."

Silence settles over the room.

Simone clears her throat. "Nine what? Nine *years*?"

I put my mug of whiskey between my thighs and cover my face with my hands. Gently, someone—Dorothy—pulls my arm away from my face, fills my mug with more alcohol, and places it in my hand. "Drink," she orders. "Drink it all, honey."

For some insane reason, I do what she says, throwing the whole thing back in one gulp. I'm probably hoping it'll help the embarrassment, but all it does is burn my throat on the way down. I stare at the shocked faces of my friends and let out a long sigh. "Now do you understand why I can't do anything with Blake? How can I possibly end a nine-year dry spell with a movie star?"

"Why" —Fiona clears her throat— "why so long?"

I let out a long sigh. This is too personal. I haven't told anyone about this. But here, in this room, surrounded by women who have been nothing but supportive to me, I feel like I might be able to shed this weight that's rested on my shoulders for an eternity. I hold out my mug and Dorothy dutifully replenishes it. Sipping lukewarm whiskey, I steel myself before speaking.

"Paul and I...slowed down...after Allie was born. I felt like a stranger in my own skin, like I'd gone from inhabiting my own body to this postpartum deflated balloon. I didn't want sex."

When my friends try to protest, I just shake my head. They haven't had kids. They don't get it.

Taking a deep breath, I keep going. In a way, it feels good to say these things out loud, to admit all the things that seemed so shameful and embarrassing for so long. "When she was a toddler, we still tried, but it just became too hard to have sex. We were both so *tired*. I thought he might have lost interest in me because my body…"

"Your body is amazing, Candice," Simone says. "You're, what, five foot one and a hundred pounds soaking wet? You do yoga every day, for goodness sake. You're stronger than most men. Deflated balloon, my ass."

I shrug. "I discovered yoga later. I think I was trying to… make him more interested. Maybe I was trying to just appreciate my body for what it could do. Accept the way it had changed. Allie grew up and it got easier with her, but Paul and I just didn't… I guess we didn't try. Then he got sick. We both knew it was a possibility, you know. He'd had leukemia when he was a child, and his lungs were damaged. It had always been a problem. When he was diagnosed with heart disease it wasn't a surprise. It just kept coming, one thing after another. We were in and out of the hospital so much and sex just wasn't a priority. We still kissed and cuddled and we were intimate in other ways, but that part of our marriage just…drifted away. I thought I didn't need it. My libido was so low I just assumed it'd never come back." Until today. I look at the faces staring back at me and shake my head. "Stop looking at me with so much fucking sympathy."

Instead of stopping, everyone's brows just collectively rise, concern—or pity?—written on every face.

"You've still…taken care of yourself, though, right?" That question comes from Fiona, her brows tugged together.

My face flushes red. Or, redder, because I'm already

burning to the tips of my ears. I shake my head. "Not really. I didn't want that. I didn't feel the need. I'm telling you, that part of my life is done. I don't... It's gone now."

"I'm buying you a box full of vibrators for your birthday," Simone announces.

The tension inside me snaps, and I let out a surprised chuckle. "I wouldn't even know where to start."

"Start with the 'on' button," Simone deadpans, and another laugh falls out of me.

"Maybe I *should* get a vibrator."

Simone freezes. "You don't have one? Candice, honey." She shakes her head, then thrusts her finger in the air. "A whole box full! That's what you're getting from me."

My laughter bubbles up, dispelling the horrifying embarrassment that had just been overwhelming me a moment ago.

"Screw the vibrators!" Dorothy exclaims. "How about Blake Harding? Bet his hands could get the job done."

I snort, then laugh, and snort again. Then giggles fill the air, and pretty soon everyone is laughing. I lean my head against Margaret's shoulder as she wraps her arm around me. Fiona, on the other side of me, puts her hand on my thigh.

When everyone quiets down, Jen lets out a long sigh as she stares at me from her armchair. "You should take the room at the hotel, Candice."

This surprises me. I'd expect it from Simone, from Dorothy, from Fiona. But Jen? I wouldn't think she'd prioritize sex over comfort.

I stare at her and gently shake my head. "Blake Harding has a new woman on his arm every week. I've seen the stories about him," I say. "He's not the type of man I want to get involved with."

"So? Doesn't that make it better? No chance of catching feelings." Simone shrugs and sips her drink. "He'll be using you, and you'll use him right back."

"This is ridiculous. We're all assuming that Blake Harding is interested in me. He's a Hollywood movie star!"

"I saw the kiss, Candice," Fiona says, brows arching high. "I know for a fact he was interested. He chased you all the way to the café afterward!"

"I'm not ready to date anyone. It's too soon."

"Treat it as an experiment," Dorothy says, flicking her long silver mane over her shoulder. "He's a handsome man in his prime, he's obviously interested in you, and you are in need of his...services."

I catch Simone biting her lip to stop her laughter. She shrugs at me. "She's right. It doesn't have to be some deep connection. It's just sex."

"This is ridiculous." I throw back another mouthful of whiskey and slam my mug down on the coffee table. "This is crazy. This isn't happening. My house didn't burn down, and I didn't kiss Blake Harding this morning."

"Stay at the hotel until Monday, then move into our rental," Margaret says. "You're welcome to stay there rent-free until your insurance pays out your claim. Then we can talk about you staying in the place long-term, or you can move out to rent somewhere else." Margaret pats my leg, her pink pantsuit still somehow unruffled. "That gives you four days to explore whatever is happening between you and Mr. Gorgeous."

"I can't believe you're encouraging this, Margaret. I thought you of all people would be reasonable."

"Nine years is too long for a woman in her prime," she says with a gentle smile. "Now, Dor, give her the room keys and let's go home and go to bed."

Dorothy hunts through her purse and hands me a silver key with a big wooden keychain with the number two carved into it. "Good luck." She winks, then follows her twin out the door.

As soon as it closes behind them, Simone lets out a little giggle. "I love this town, and I love those women. I mean, Margaret? Really? She wears a Chanel tweed skirt suit in the height of summer, and then she turns around and encourages you to have freaky movie star sex. Amazing."

"I don't think she mentioned anything about freaky movie star sex," I hedge.

Simone ignores me. "We better hear every sordid detail, okay, Candice?"

"You worry about your own man and the fact that he should be taking you to the courthouse tomorrow so you don't lose your home," I snap, then groan as I take in Simone's wide eyes. I lie back on the couch. "Sorry. That was uncalled for. Totally rude."

Simone lets out a sigh. "It's fine, Candice. You've had a hard day."

"Maybe I do need to get laid."

"Damn straight," Fiona huffs. "I mean, ten years?"

"Nine."

"I had to resort to sleeping with my ex-husband, but that was still better than going nine years without any nookie!"

Simone shakes her head and pours herself more whiskey. She winks at me, clearly not cut up about me being rude.

I love these women.

I extend my mug toward her. "Top me up. If I'm going to get hot and heavy with Blake Harding, I need some liquid courage."

"Atta girl," Fiona says with a laugh.

Jen just smiles at me and lifts her cup in a silent salute.

I throw the drink back and sink into the couch, surrounded by my three best friends but thinking of the man who shook me to my core this morning.

The truth is, the thought of sleeping with Blake excites me. A lot. It scares me, obviously, and vaguely, it makes me feel like I'm betraying Paul's memory, but it definitely excites me too.

If I know for sure there are no feelings involved, maybe I can do this. I can end the dry spell of the century and see if that part of me still works. After all, Blake will be gone in a couple of weeks, and he's not exactly known for getting attached.

I'll sleep with him, scratch the itch, then walk away. Even if it ends up being a huge mistake, it'll be over faster than I can blink.

Easy...right?

FIVE

SIMONE

HAVING CALLED Wes after drinking far too much alcohol to drive, I smile as a message arrives on my phone to tell me he's here. After many goodbye hugs with the rest of the ladies, I stumble down the steps (when did they get so steep?) and make my way outside.

Wes is leaning against his beat-up truck, faded jeans hanging low on his hips, white T-shirt stretched tight across his mile-wide pecs. Yum. I collide with his chest and wait for his arms to encircle me, enclosing me in his warmth and strength and smell.

"Thanks for coming to get me."

"No problem, my beautiful little drunk."

I scowl up at him. "I'm not little."

Wes laughs, his eyes twinkling as he drops his lips to mine. He taps my ass with a broad palm and nudges me toward the truck. "Get in. I'm going to take advantage of you tonight and

I'm going to enjoy it." He opens the door for me, one hand on the door, the other braced on the side of the truck, his body a warm wall at my back.

As I start to enter the cab, I pause and spin around, my eyes searching his. Emerald green stares back at me, humor dancing in his irises. He arches a brow as if to say, *Yes?*

"Why haven't you asked me to marry you?" It just falls out of my mouth. Oops.

Wes goes utterly still, his eyes turning intent as they search mine, then drop to my lips. His lids drop for a long moment, and ice chills my veins. I shouldn't have said that. I *really* shouldn't have said that. Wes would have asked me to marry him by now if he wanted to marry me.

When he turns forty-five, the trust that contains his inheritance gets chopped up into little pieces and parceled out to various family members and charities. The beautiful, wooded property that I've called home for nearly a year will go to his uncle.

That is, unless Wes gets married. His parents wanted him to find someone to share his life with, so they wrote it as a condition to his inheritance.

Thing is, we've been together nearly a year. *Together* together. After all the drama and the "will-we-won't-we" that defined our early relationship, we took things to the next level. He's the man for me, no question. I know he loves that house, and from a purely practical point of view, we should get married. His forty-fifth birthday is in less than a month!

"We should talk about this in the morning," Wes says softly. "When we're both clear-headed."

"I'm not that drunk, Wes." I pull away from him and cross my arms, then uncross them to cover my face with my hands. A delayed wave of embarrassment crashes into me.

Oh *God*. I really just went and said that. I couldn't just leave things be and enjoy this relationship for what it was. I had to go and talk about marriage to a man who made it clear he didn't even want the inheritance.

But that was last year, when Wes thought he didn't deserve a good life. It was before the two of us were...*us*. The beautiful, healthy relationship full of love and laughter and sex. The type of relationship I thought only existed in fairy tales.

The type of relationship that makes me think of marriage when I'd always thought I'd never marry again.

Just last month, Wes surprised me with a candlelit dinner on the oceanfront porch of our home. He said it was the first day of spring, and he wanted to mark the occasion. He told me when I walked into his life, it felt like the end of a long winter. I was his springtime.

A man said that to me and then *didn't propose*. I mean, excuse me? What?

Another black wave of shame crashes into me as the seconds tick by, slow as molasses. I squeeze my eyes shut behind the wall of my hands, sucking in a hard breath as I try to pull myself together.

I had way too much whiskey. I should have known. Me plus alcohol equals an emotional, outspoken mess. I've known this since college, but have I learned? No. Evidently not.

A gentle hand wraps around my wrist and pulls it from my face. Then the same happens to my other hand. Wes ducks his head to look at me, his face carefully blank. "Do you want to get married, Simone?"

"Well...it makes sense, doesn't it? The trust, the house...?"

Wes's face hardens. He drops his eyes to the ground, his hands still clutching my wrists. He nods. "It makes sense, but Simone, I'm not getting married for money or logistics. And I'm not asking you to get married for those reasons, either. Not after everything you've told me about your first marriage. If and when we get married, it'll be because we love each other and because we're ready for that step."

Somehow, in my whiskey-addled brain, his words pierce through some shield I erected long ago. My eyes widen as I stare at him, realization dawning. "You've been waiting for me to ask you," I whisper.

His jaw is a brutal line. "I won't trap you the way your ex-husband did. I won't use money to build you a gilded cage. I won't ask you to do that for me."

My bottom lip trembles. "But Wes..."

"I won't."

My throat is so tight I have to force the words out in a harsh whisper. "What if I *want* to marry you?"

He freezes, his grip on my wrists tightening for a moment, then loosening completely as I lift my hands to cup his face. His green eyes are wild, searching my face as if he expects to see some sort of deception.

I brush my fingers over his cheekbones and through the hair at his temples, my heart thundering in my chest.

Wes's eyes close, his lashes fanning over his cheeks as his forehead drops to rest against mine. "You want that?"

"I've been waiting for you to ask me, Wes," I whisper, tears barely contained as my bottom lip trembles. "I love you so much it feels like I'm about to burst. I want to be able to call you my husband. We're too old for the boyfriend/girlfriend thing."

A soft chuckle, his eyes still closed. "My grandfather used to call them his lady-friends."

"I'm too young to be your lady-friend."

Wes's hands slide over my hips as his lips tug into a smile. I trace his dimples with the tips of my fingers as he opens his eyes, silver lining his gaze. He turns his head and nips at my fingers, then grins when I yelp.

Silence stretches between us, taut with anticipation as our eyes meet. His gaze softens, arms tightening around my hips. "Be my wife," he rasps. "Please, Simone. Marry me tomorrow." He stares at me, his lips tilting. "I'd say marry me right now, but the courthouse is closed."

I laugh, tears already streaming down my face, and nod. "Of course I'll marry you, you big dummy. I can't believe you would've given up your inheritance to stop me feeling trapped."

"I'd give up the world for you, Simone."

Love feels like a warm blanket draped over every inch of my body. Wes's lips are warm and soft as he kisses me, claims me, shows me once more just how much I mean to him. I melt into his embrace, only freezing when I hear someone clear their throat behind us.

"Does this mean I'll be making two wedding cakes?" Jen crosses her arms and glances at me, then at Fiona, and finally lifts her eyes up to the sky. "I need more warning for this stuff, ladies. *Way* more warning. I'm not a magician."

"Could've fooled me," Fiona says, her eyes on me even though she's talking to Jen. "Four Cups' success is mostly due to your croissants and your weekly special creations."

"Those were Simone's idea," Jen grumbles.

"Yeah, but you're the one who comes up with them," Fiona shoots back. My best friend crosses the distance between us and yanks me out of Wes's grasp. She hugs me close and whispers in my ear, "Congratulations, babe. About time."

She releases me, only for the rest of the crew to haul me into their arms. Even Wes isn't immune, smothered by female attention and affection as congratulations are exchanged.

Candice wipes the stress and sadness from her face long enough to give me a genuine smile. "You two are perfect for each other. I'm so happy for you, Simone. I've watched you blossom over the past two years. This town wouldn't be the same without you."

"At least give me a day for the cake," Jen huffs. "Get married Saturday morning. Reception at Four Cups afterward."

"Deal." I glance up at Wes. "Deal?"

"Saturday it is," he says. "Now come on, gorgeous." Wes slides his fingers though mine and tugs me toward his truck. "I need to get away from all this drunk female energy."

Laughing dissent rings out, and I giggle as he lifts me in his arms and places me in the passenger seat. I wave at my friends through the window, then watch Wes's tall, powerful body circle around the front of the truck before sliding into the seat beside me.

He gives me a wink, a smile, and leans over to give me a

quick kiss that's wet and hot and promises a thousand delicious things.

"Love you," he says against my lips.

"Love you back."

He grins, a smile so clear and bright it burns a track of happiness through my heart, then Wes turns the key in the ignition.

I lean against the headrest and let a smile tug at my lips. Then I turn to look at his beautiful, masculine profile. "Are you still planning on taking advantage of me?"

Wes just responds with a glance and a grin that say it all. I bite my lip and try not squirm, then I head home with my hunky babe of a soon-to-be husband.

SIX

BLAKE

A NOISE outside my hotel room door draws my attention away from my laptop screen.

"Who's there?" My mother's eagle-eyed stare misses nothing, even through a video call. "Is someone at your door? Is it a woman? Who is she? Tell her to come in, I want to meet her. I hope it's not one of your twenty-six-year-old playthings, Blake, honey, because you deserve someone your own age who can stand up to you. Why you insist on dating young, airheaded bimbos is beyond me. Your father and I agree, by the way. You should be dating someone your own age. Isn't that right, Merv?"

A muffled, "That's right," sounds from the next room.

My mother nods, arching her brows at me, waiting for a response—a response she isn't going to get. There are times when you should not engage with your mother's line of questioning, and now is one of those times.

"It's no one, Mom. Just someone checking in to the room next door."

"I thought you said they booked out the cabanas next to yours for privacy." My mother frowns as she moves in close to the laptop. Her forehead fills the screen as if she's leaning in, trying to inspect my background for clues. "Why is someone checking in next door? You should tell the hotel not to let anyone in. They agreed to keep the rooms empty for you, didn't they?"

"I told them they could move someone in, Mom."

"Why would you do that?" Her face fills the screen again as she sits back, crossing her arms. "You know how much focus you need when you're filming. You shouldn't let people push you around. They can find another room for that guest. It's probably just someone trying to get close to you. One of those bimbos, most likely. Don't you dare sleep with her, Blake Andrew Harding. You should be focusing on your acting, not on these clingy women who are barely out of diapers."

I love my mother. I do. But sometimes she forgets that I'm a grown man with a life of my own. She also seems to think that everyone under forty years old is barely old enough to function on their own and definitely too young for me to date. Taking a deep breath, I draw on the deep well of patience that always seems to run dry when my mother starts talking about my love life.

"I offered up the room," I tell her. "A woman in town just lost her home in a fire. She has nowhere to stay, so it would be truly selfish of me not to let them use the cabana next door. She's a single mother."

"So it *is* a woman," my mother breathes. "Merv! Blake met a woman. A single mother." Her eyes return to me. "What's her name, honey? A house fire, too, that poor woman. What are you waiting for? Get her in here! I want to see her face. I could send her a care package. Did she lose everything in the fire? How horrible."

"Mom," I snap, then take a deep breath. "It's not like that. We're not together. She's the caterer on set. I can't go asking her to meet my parents."

No matter how much I want to see where this goes with Candice, I am *not* ready for that.

"A businesswoman," she says with an appreciative nod. "That's good. Yes!" she calls out off-screen so loud I have to take my earbuds out. "She owns a catering business. Single mother who runs her own business!" Her eyes return to me. "She's not one of those teen moms, is she?" I shake my head, to my mother's great relief. "No. That's good. Okay."

I never actually told my mother that Candice owns the business, but that's neither here nor there. My mother makes her own reality and only hears what she wants to hear. I'm not telling my mother anything else about Candice. Not one word.

An expectant silence stretches. Then she leans in and says, "Name, honey. What's her name?"

"Candice," I answer before I can stop myself. Shit. How the hell does my mother do that? Extract information like she's a special agent in the CIA?

"Candice," Mom says slowly, tapping her chin. "Interesting. I've never met a Candice before."

"I have to go," I say through clenched teeth.

"Of course, honey. Say hi to Candice for us! Looking forward to meeting her. Love you!"

"Love you too, Mom." I hang up the call before the inquisition can continue, then close my laptop screen with a soft click. A long sigh slips through my lips as I massage my temples.

My mother is not, under any circumstances, meeting Candice. Not for a long, long time.

I listen to the silence for a moment. After the initial noise of her checking in, I haven't heard a thing. The hotel is set up in two sections. The main building is a traditional hotel, with four floors filled with rooms off one long hallway. The other part of the hotel, the one I'm in, consists of half a dozen cabana-style rooms. My room, along with two others, looks out on a small rectangular pool. The other three cabanas are nestled in a wooded patch of land, mostly hidden from view. It affords quite a bit of privacy and more luxury than I'd expect from this small town. Didn't stop Veronica Taylor from kicking up a fuss and forcing her team to scramble to find a suitably luxurious mansion for her to stay in while we film, but I'm glad she did. She gets carted from her rental mansion to the trailers on set, and I only have to see her when we film. Works for me.

Pushing my chair back as I stand, I brush the thought of Veronica from my mind. She's the last person I want to think about right now. If I have to spend the rest of my time on this project dodging her advances, it'll be a miserable last two weeks. It'll probably show in the final product, too, and we'll get terrible reviews about our lack of onscreen chemistry.

A knock on the door pulls me from my thoughts. Combing

my fingers through my hair, I open the door to find Candice standing on the other side. My brows jump. "Oh. Hi."

She gives me a shy, sexy smile that sends a line of heat straight to my cock. "Hi. Sorry to bother you. I heard your voice and..." A flush sweeps over her cheekbones. "Sorry. I just wanted to say thank you for offering the room. I hadn't realized until I actually got here how much I needed a bit of privacy. Everyone has been so wonderful today, but sometimes this town can be a bit...overbearing. It's nice to have a bit of peace and quiet, if only for a couple of nights." She huffs a laugh, a hot little blush creeping over her cheeks. "I'm rambling."

"It's fine." I realize I'm smiling when her eyes meet mine, light sparking in them. The yellow lights around the pool glint off the gold in her hair. It's brown near the roots, tied back in a ponytail that turns blond at the ends. With a thin cardigan and figure-hugging jeans, Candice looks nothing like the airheaded bimbos my mother so hates. I curl my fingers into my palm to stop myself reaching for her ponytail, to stop myself wrapping that hair around my fist and feeling those silky strands between my fingers. I'd pull her tight to my body and repeat what we did earlier, kiss her breathless until she melts into me.

I want to feel that again. Feel her body give in, get soft for me. Feel her let go of whatever she holds so tight.

She licks her lips as if she can read my mind.

Fucking *hell*. My body goes hard. Everything turns hot, and I find myself leaning toward her, shoulder on the doorjamb, the air between us electric.

No, this isn't like other women. This is palpable—a real,

physical thing between us. It's not just sexual attraction, it's bigger.

"Well," she says, her chest heaving with a shallow breath, "I better get to bed."

"How about that coffee?" I blurt. "Well, it might be a bit late for coffee. I have tea, I think." I jab my thumb over my shoulder toward the mini fridge, kettle, and coffee maker in the corner of the room.

Candice opens her mouth, then pauses, and my mind produces a thousand images of other things she could be doing with that mouth.

Some sort of internal battle wages inside her, and she finally nods. "Okay. Let me put something more comfortable on and I'll meet you by the pool in five."

"I'll get the drinks ready." As I close the door, my heart jumps. I'm smiling again. I'm smiling at the thought of drinking a cup of tea with this woman.

And at the thought of doing a lot more than drinking tea.

Then I shake off my stupor and grab some mugs.

SEVEN

CANDICE

ANY OTHER DAY, I probably would have agonized over what to wear for a poolside tea date with a hot Hollywood actor. Today, though? After half my house was engulfed by flames, my daughter decided she'd rather stay with her friend than with me, I drank whiskey, of all things, and I happened to feel sexual attraction toward a man for the first time in far too many years?

After I admitted my celibacy, *out loud,* to a gaggle of women I call friends?

Today, I don't care. My brain is fried. Operation Have Sex With Blake (Freaking) Harding will need to wait, because all I can manage is a hot drink by the pool.

I choose sweatpants and a comfy knit sweater, then I throw a towel over my arm. I'm going to drink tea with my feet in the pool, because I know Dorothy and Margaret keep it warm year-round. I'm going to enjoy Blake's voice, his smile, and maybe even his laugh, and then I'm going to go to bed and hopefully wake up to a world that makes sense.

I'm going to let my thoughts simmer, and decide what to do about the whole ending-a-nine-year-dry-spell-with-Blake-freaking-Harding thing later. Much later. When I'm totally sober and not so frazzled.

Blake is already sitting next to the pool when I exit my room. He's got a grey hoodie on over jeans that hug all the right places. His long legs stretch over one of the pool chaise lounges as he twists around to look at me, nodding to the chair next to his. "Hope you like peppermint tea. It was either that or Earl Grey, and I thought I'd play it safe for nighttime."

"Good choice." I wrap my fingers around the mug and inhale, letting the minty-smelling steam clear some of the cobwebs from my mind.

In the silence, Blake speaks. "My mother wants to meet you."

I spit out my mouthful of tea as Blake laughs, his shoulders shaking as his eyes sparkle with mischief. He arches a brow, and all I can say is *wow*. Maybe Margaret's whole "we're not talking about dating" thing has some merit. This man is ridiculously attractive when he smiles. Well, he's attractive all the time, but the warmth of his smile turns my insides to goo. Would it be so bad to get physical with him?

But— "Your mother?"

He leans back in the chair, staring up at the stars. His toes wiggle as if he's trying to get comfortable. Clasping his arms behind his head, Blake looks like some kind of powerful fighter in repose. His biceps flex on either side of his head, and I wonder what it would feel like to have those arms around me.

To have them around me *again*, I mean. Maybe without cameras and lights and an entire film crew watching.

"I'm joking. She heard you checking in and quizzed me."

"Did you tell her…"

"That we kissed?" He glances at me, his gaze penetrating. "No. All she knows is a woman who does the catering on set just moved into the room next to mine, but she likes to make up fairy tales about me meeting the woman of my dreams and riding off into the sunset with her."

"I'm detecting a slight hint of sarcasm in your tone."

Blake chuckles. "Riding off into the sunset isn't in the cards for me. Or at least, it hasn't been so far, but you never know." His eyes land on me, and fire rips through my veins.

Um, what does *that* mean?

I nod. "That makes two of us," I answer lamely. I sip my tea, listening to the pool filter gurgling for a few moments. Our chairs are a foot apart, but I can sense every inch of his body. I've never felt so alive, so on edge.

He shifts his weight, leaning to the side to grab his mug. I can almost *feel* the muscles of his obliques shifting under his shirt, his arms uncurling, his body bending and stretching. He moves with liquid grace, totally in control, every movement purposeful and steady.

He would be dynamite in bed.

I squeeze my eyes shut. Too much whiskey. Damn Dorothy! She did that on purpose. Then they all ganged up on me and put ideas in my head. Now I can't stop thinking of sex. Of the way his hands felt over my hips, or how his mouth was hot and wet and tasted so damn good. Or how the whole world fell away, and I'm not even sure how long the director was calling for us to cut.

"Is it weird?" I ask, doing my best not to stare at the gorgeous man sitting next to me.

"Huh?"

"Kissing people on screen. Sex scenes."

He pauses, considering. "It's pretty clinical. There are people and cameras all around. It can get really awkward, but most of us are professionals. Just part of the job."

I nod, ice water sluicing through my veins. *Just part of the job.* Is that what today was for him? God, I'm such an idiot. I'm falling over myself, thinking our kiss was something electric, and to him it was just another day at the office.

"I shouldn't have kissed you today," he says quietly. I turn to stare, finding his eyes on me. He blinks and shifts his gaze to my shoulder, my body. "That's not how it's done. I shouldn't have kissed you or touched you without your permission and without any warning. I'm sorry if I made you uncomfortable."

"You didn't." Did I say that too fast to sound casual?

His head jerks, his eyes searching mine. "No?" I shake my head. "But you ran away so quickly," he says. "You looked..." He trails off, and I wonder what word was on the tip of his tongue. By the softness of his voice and the heat of his gaze, it doesn't sound like I looked bad. At least, that's what I'm telling myself to keep the humiliation at bay.

I tear my gaze away from his, standing up onto stiff legs. I shove my sweatpants legs up to my knees and plonk myself down on the edge of the pool, back to Blake, feet in the water, and I take a big gulp of tea.

"How's the water?"

"Nice," I answer, voice rusty. This isn't helping me feel less frazzled. Why did I agree to drink tea with a movie star?

I hear the rustling of clothes and the creak of the chair. He's standing up. Blake Harding is standing up behind me, asking me about the temperature of pool water. I can't deal with this. My poor brain is overloading.

I should go to bed. I should really, really just get up and go to bed. Tomorrow, I'll tell Margaret and Simone and Jen and all the rest of them that I can't do it. My days of hot, nasty sex are over. Have I ever had hot, nasty sex? Even once?

That's not a question I want to answer.

All I know is I can't do this, especially not with someone like Blake. To think that he would want me is ridiculous. He *apologized* for kissing me. That's not exactly a ringing endorsement. I imagined the sparks. Fiona imagined them, too. It's not—

Blake Harding, Hollywood heartthrob and certified silver fox, slips into the pool beside me wearing nothing but a pair of tight, black boxer briefs, leaving absolutely nothing to the imagination. Oh my sweet Lord. Holy fucking moly. Is this real life? Is this really happening?

The arms of his muscles look carved from stone as he lowers himself inch by inch, water lapping higher and higher on his abs. A sprinkling of dark chest hair covers his chest, and I curl my fingers into the edge of the pool to stop myself from reaching over to touch it.

He is all man. All glorious, muscular man.

And I like it. A lot. Too much. Way, *way* too much.

Dropping into the pool with the water coming up to his neck, Blake turns around to look at me. "You should come in."

"I don't have a swimsuit."

"Neither do I." A mischievous glimmer in his eyes.

"Blake Harding. Are you trying to get me to strip down to my underwear? Was one kiss not enough for you?"

"Never." His body slices through the water as he walks toward me, and I barely have enough time to set my mug down before Blake has his hand around my wrist and is yanking me into the water.

I yelp, falling in on top of him, the two of us going under before Blake catches me around the waist and lifts me up above the surface. I gasp, spluttering, only realizing a moment later that my arms and legs are wrapped around his body, chest pressed against his, with something very hard pressed up against my stomach.

Whoa. Oh my—*whoa.*

"You strike me as the type of woman that needs to be shown how to relax," he says, his voice low, lids dropping as his eyes trace the outline of my lips.

I lick the chlorinated water off my bottom lip and watch his eyes heat. "That's very presumptuous of you." My heart is kicking against my ribs, my body screaming for me to *do this, do it now!*

It's been so long. So damn long since I've been in a man's arms. So long since my pulse quickened like this, since I felt so hot my skin was about to burst.

"Kissing you didn't feel like another day at the office," Blake says in a low, growly voice.

Everything inside me tightens. My stomach is nothing more than a twisted ball of ache. My clothes float around me, drenched, and I'm so, so keenly aware that Blake only has underwear on. My hands are on his shoulders, smooth and wet and hard.

The girls were right. I need this. I need to feel like a woman. I need to give in to these urges, these desires. Waking up the part of me that I thought was dead isn't a betrayal, it's a necessity. Paul was a wonderful husband, father, and partner, but our marriage was far from perfect. Doing this has nothing to do with him.

Blake and the rest of the film crew will be gone in two weeks. Two weeks is nothing! If this ends in disaster, I can just avoid him and be glad when he leaves. Two weeks of awkwardness would be worth it if it meant feeling like I deserve pleasure, if only for a night.

"What are you thinking right now?" Blake asks, his voice a low rasp that sends heat spearing through my core.

I bite my lip. "I was thinking about this."

"This?"

"Having my arms around you in a pool. How far from my typical reality it is. How much I'm enjoying it."

A wolfish smile full of sinful promises. His eyes grow dark, molten. Oh, my.

Blake's head angles toward mine, his arms tightening around my waist. With him standing on the bottom of the pool, he holds me up above the water. I squeeze my thighs around his hips as my breath hitches. I'm going to kiss Blake Harding again. This time, in private. In a pool. With nothing but a carpet of stars above and no thoughts of the consequences.

And I'm going to love it. After we kiss, I'm going to reach between us and feel that hard steel between his legs. I'm not going to worry about being rusty, or old, or out of practice. I'm going to do everything I can to make him shove it inside me, fill me with his hot hardness. I'll beg if I need to. I'll beg him to put his cock inside me and fuck me blind.

"Blake?" a female voice calls out behind me.

We both freeze, mouths an inch apart.

I pull away from him, dropping my legs as I disengage my arms from his neck. The water suddenly feels freezing. I look back to see Veronica Taylor tilting her head, a manicured hand on her hip as her eyes dart from me to Blake, back to me again.

She's short, like me, with long brown hair. I can see how I could stand in for her, body-shape-wise...but that's where the resemblance stops. She oozes wealth. Her eyes are almond-shaped, green, and rimmed with thick, black lashes. Her mouth is full, skin Botoxed and filled to look as youthful and radiant as possible.

And she's arching a brow at me, eyes hard.

"I, uh, fell in," I say lamely. She doesn't move, so I keep babbling. "Blake jumped in to save me. He thought I couldn't swim."

Veronica's eyes flick to the pile of clothes on Blake's chair. "He had time to strip down to his underwear?" Her eyebrow arches higher, voice drenched in skepticism.

Blake coughs, and it sounds a lot like he's trying to cover up a laugh.

"Um. Yeah." In one long stroke, I'm at the edge of the pool. I pull myself out, looking at the growing pool of water dripping from my clothes. My sweatpants are so heavy with water that they hang low on my hips, showing off the little pink bow at the front of my panties. I turn toward Blake and his eyes drop to the ribbon. His eyes glaze, then sharpen, then shift away from me.

"What are you doing here, Veronica?" Blake wades to the edge of the pool but doesn't get out.

Veronica watches me as I remove my sweater.

I hold it up in front of me, momentarily ignoring my audience as I lament how long it'll take for this knit to dry. I wring it out into the pool. Hopefully the chlorine won't wreck it.

"I thought we could run some lines," Veronica finally says as she turns fully to Blake, dismissing me. "Make sure we nail the meet-cute tomorrow."

I clear my throat as I grab the towel on my chair, shuffling toward my room. I'm not sure what *running lines* means to Veronica, but it certainly doesn't sound like it has to do with acting. Ignoring the pang in my chest, I wrap the towel around myself and walk to my cabana door. My socks squelch, and I pause. How should I do this? Do I strip with two ridiculously attractive movie stars watching me or risk getting water all over my room?

It only takes me a second to decide.

My sweatpants fall from beneath my towel with a wet *thunk*. Bending over, I pick them up and wring them out, this time doing it into a bush by my door, then lay them flat over the chair in front of my cabana. Then I do the same to my socks and cardigan, making sure to keep my towel tight around my waist. I can wring my tank top out in the shower inside.

Glancing over my shoulder, I give the two beautiful people behind me what I hope is a casual nod. "Well, goodnight. Thanks for the tea," I say to Blake. "And the rescue."

His eyes glimmer. "Any time, Candice."

"Okay, then." I walk in my door and close it behind me, letting out a long sigh.

Stupid, stupid, stupid. I almost hooked up with Blake in the pool! Well, I'm not sure I would have actually done it *in* the pool, because a yeast infection is the last thing I need right now. But my motor was running and I was *ready.*

He's probably going to take Veronica into his room and sleep with her right next door. They probably do this most nights. She's his co-star! Of course they have a thing going on. That's how Hollywood stars meet their lovers, isn't it?

Blake probably sleeps with all his co-stars. The tabloids are plastered with pictures of him cuddled up to various models and actresses and pop stars; I'm sure it's only a fraction of the women he actually sleeps with. He's a player, which seemed like a great thing when I was with the girls rationalizing having sex with him. It doesn't seem so great when his player status is shoved in my face.

Ignoring the stab of jealousy that spears through my heart, I square my shoulders and take the rest of my clothes off before running a hot shower. It's only when I've stood under the hot stream of water for a few minutes that my muscles unwind and I'm able to think clearly.

The jealousy clears, and I let out a long breath. A man like Blake is *perfect* for what I need. I don't want someone who will get involved with me. I don't want love. I don't want a relationship.

I just want sex, and from the look of it, Blake is more than happy to provide.

He's not relationship material, and I'm not looking.

Even if he's screwing Veronica senseless next door doesn't mean he can't screw *me* senseless when I'm ready for him.

I'll wrap my heart in barbed wire and keep it safe. This is just sex. That's all it can be, and that's okay.

EIGHT

BLAKE

MY KNUCKLES RAP on the cabana door, a cardboard tray holding two coffees balanced in my other hand. I listen for a few moments, then knock again.

It's eight o'clock, and Candice wasn't at the café. Maybe she's not awake yet?

"Blake?"

I turn to see Candice padding toward me, floral yoga pants hugging her shapely legs, matching sports bra leaving very little to the imagination, feet clad in black flip-flops, hair undone and flowing around her shoulders. Damn.

I lift the tray. "I brought coffees. Our evening got interrupted yesterday, so I thought..."

Candice looks surprised, then a smile lights up her whole face. "You do know I get those coffees for free, right? I'm one of the owners of that café."

"I support small businesses." Grabbing one of the coffees, I extend it to her. "Medium latte, one sugar. They said it was your usual."

"I'm never going to hear the end of this," Candice grumbles as she accepts the coffee, her lips tilting up. "The whole town will think we're sleeping together."

"Well, I wouldn't want to disappoint them." I arch a brow.

Laughing, Candice smacks my arm. She moves to touch the sweatpants and cardigan laid out on the chairs next to her door but leaves them there. Probably still damp. She takes a sip of her coffee and sighs, happy.

My heart squeezes at the sight of it, and I have the sudden urge to make her sigh like that again. I want to be the one who gives that to her. Who makes her feel content. Who makes her melt.

Being around this woman sets my head spinning. One minute, I see her in those tight yoga clothes and I want to bend her over the bed and fuck her blind. The next, she smiles at me and I'd do anything to make it happen again.

This isn't normal. It's not how things usually go.

Am I really ready to do this again? To commit to something like this?

"Do you do yoga?" I ask, nodding to her outfit and shamelessly letting my eyes sweep over her petite body again. Just above the waist of her yoga pants, across her stomach, there are a few white stretch marks that make my mouth water. I've never been attracted to stretch marks before, but damn. I want to trace them with my fingers, then my tongue. See where they lead when they disappear beneath those spandex tights.

"I teach it, actually." Candice points her coffee cup toward the back of the hotel, and I tear my eyes away from her body. "I have a studio space back there. My original space flooded."

"Seems to be a lot of property damage in this town."

Candice laughs, and another spark of happiness ignites in my chest. I like making her laugh. A lot. More than I should.

Maybe my mother is right—not that I'd ever admit that to her. I've been dating models that are waif-thin and twenty years younger than me. It's easy to keep them at arm's length. The last time I met a woman who made me think of anything except myself was my second wife, and that ended just as badly as my first marriage.

But Candice...she's strong. Physically strong, as far as I can tell by the lean, shapely muscles of her shoulders, arms, and the slight shadow of her abs. But mentally strong, too. Her house caught fire yesterday, and she's still able to function today. To *laugh* today.

I gesture to the pool chairs and arch a brow, a silent invitation to sit with me. "Unless you're worried you'll need another rescue?"

Candice's answering grin is a little self-deprecating and a lot adorable. She plops herself down on a chair and kicks her legs out, staring up at the cloudless blue sky. "She didn't buy a word of my explanation, did she?"

"Who, Veronica?"

"Mm."

"I don't think so, no." I sit sideways across the other lounge chair, knees toward Candice. "But it was entertaining to see the expression on her face."

I love the way Candice blushes. How she flicks her eyes

away, then back to me. How her gaze grows warmer as her smile spreads. Then, her smile fades again. "I'm sorry if I interrupted..." Candice drifts off and takes a sip of her coffee.

"Interrupted what?"

"You know. The two of you. *Reading your lines*, or whatever the kids are calling it these days."

I snort. "You weren't the one doing the interrupting, Candice." It comes out as a growl, and Candice's eyes lift to mine. Hazel eyes with flecks of green in them. Beautiful. I tilt my head. "Will you let me take you out to dinner?"

"Okay," she says instantly, then jerks, as if she hadn't meant to speak.

I grin, arching a brow. God, I love it when she blushes. "Good. Tonight?"

She takes a deep breath. "Blake, I feel like I need to be honest with you about some stuff. You know, lay it all out."

I pause, watching her face shut down as the warmth drains away. "I'm not sure I like the sound of that."

She bites her lip. "Look, you're hot."

"Okay, I do like the sound of that."

Candice laughs, then shakes her head as if she's mad at herself for doing so. She opens her mouth to speak again, but—

"Yoo-hoo, Candice! Oh!" An elderly woman with a pixie cut rounds the corner. She's wearing a pink T-shirt with glittery writing proclaiming her a "Heart's Cove Hottie," a neon-pink purse slung over her shoulder. Below her dark jeans, her shoes are a matching baby pink with a big rhinestone-encrusted bow on the toe. It's...a look. It's definitely a look. The woman's eyes widen when she sees me, then flick to Candice and start to sparkle. She smirks. "Hi, sweetheart."

"Mom," Candice says in a strangled voice. She sits up, looks at me, looks at her mother, then stands on stiff legs. "What are you doing here?"

"Dorothy told me about the fire. Sweetheart, come here." She spreads her arms and wraps Candice in a hug. When they pull away, Candice's mother spins to me. "And who do we have *here*?" Her eyebrows wiggle as she exchanges a glance with Candice, who starts rubbing her temples.

I hide my grin. I know how she feels. "Blake," I say, extending a hand.

"Well, Blake, aren't you a handsome devil? Isn't he handsome, Candice? And look at those *arms*." She grabs my bicep and fondles it for a moment. "Call me Lottie, Blake. Well, call me anything you like, but most people call me Lottie."

"*Mom*."

"Oh, calm down, Candy Cane. I'm seventy-six years old, but I'm not blind."

"Candy Cane?" I ask, fighting my grin and failing.

"How about we go say hi to Dorothy?" Candice says, almost frantic as she ushers her mother away from the pool. Away from me.

A squeal sounds from just behind her cabana, followed by childish giggles, and two little torpedoes fly past us and cannonball into the water.

"Toby! Katie! What did I say about running near the pool?" A woman appears on the path, hauling a bag on each shoulder, her face lined with worry. She has the same hazel eyes as

Candice, the same color hair, but hers is wavy where Candice's is straight. Taller than both other women, the new arrival drops her bags and lets out a long sigh before wrapping her arms around Candice.

"Hey, Trina," Candice says, her voice muffled in the other woman's shoulder.

"We got on the first flight. Are you okay?"

"I'll be better when Mom stops flirting with Blake Harding."

"Blake H—" Trina's eyes finally land on me.

I give her a little wave. "Hi."

Trina stares at me with narrowed eyes, then looks at her sister. "Why is Blake Harding at the Heart's Cove Hotel pool?" She holds up a hand. "Wait. Don't tell me. I don't want to know. I have too many things on my mind right now, and I can't handle some movie star short-circuiting my brain. Toby! Don't push your sister's head under water!"

Candice turns to me, mouth agape, then turns to her mother. "So, Dorothy? I'm sure she wants to see you."

"Yes, yes, sweetheart, of course. But it's not every day I get to meet a real-life movie star!" Lottie hooks her arm through mine and drags me onto the lounge chair next to her. "Tell me, Blake, what are your intentions with my daughter?"

"I, uh..."

Lottie cackles. "I'm kidding. Although"—she looks at Candice—"I wouldn't kick *him* out of bed for eating crackers. Even if it isn't true love, it would be one hell of a story, Candy Cane."

"Mom," Candice pleads, a little helpless.

Her rescue comes in the form of one of the movie PAs, a young, blond-haired guy who hasn't yet been chewed up and spit out by the film industry, arriving to take me to set. I extricate myself from Lottie's hold, grab my coffee, and move toward Candice.

Leaning in to give her a kiss on the cheek, I whisper, "You still owe me dinner, Candy Cane," and chuckle when her expression grows more panicked. I lift my paper cup toward her mother, who gives me a shit-eating grin, then ride to the movie set, smiling the whole way.

NINE
CANDICE

I'M GOING to kill my mother. Kill her dead, then wait for the earth to open up and swallow me whole. Complete disappearance—that's the only solution.

Not only did I immediately break my resolution to keep Blake at arm's length when I agreed to go to dinner with him, but I also introduced him to the craziness that is my family. My mother *touched* him. She basically propositioned him on my behalf!

The last thing I need is for my mother to play matchmaker.

I never thought I'd turn into a murderer, but I'm not seeing any other options.

But my mother bustles into my cabana and grabs clothes off the chair, saying something about doing my laundry. She tells me she's already organized a short-term rental house in town, and she intends to stay until I'm back on my feet.

"You stay in this room as long as you want to, though,

Candy Cane. That Blake fellow was looking at you like he couldn't get enough."

"I think he was laughing at me."

"Oh, honey." My mom chucks my cheek. "Trina! We have to get the suitcases over to the rental."

"The kids are swimming, Mom. I can't just leave them. Why don't you go visit with Marge and Dor?"

"Oh, fine." My mother sweeps all my laundry into a bag and sets it down by the door. "I'll be back in ten minutes."

I watch her walk away, letting out a long sigh.

Trina grins. "You know ten minutes means two hours, right?"

"And thank goodness for that."

Trina laughs. "Where's Allie?" She sits back in the lounge chair I vacated earlier and takes a sip of my coffee.

"School. She called me this morning before she left. She's sleeping at a friend's place while I get our accommodation figured out. Having the time of her life, as far as I can tell."

"Kids. They're more resilient than we give them credit for." Something in my sister's voice makes me pause. I glance at her as I lie back in Blake's lounge chair.

"Where's Kevin?"

Trina grimaces. "We're separated."

I freeze. "What? Since when?"

"Mom! Look what I can do." Toby dives under water and sticks his legs up above the surface. A moment later, his head pops up. "Did you see?"

"Very good, Toby!" Trina calls back with a tight smile. She turns to me. "Three months. I've been living with Mom."

"Wow." I arch my brows. "Are you doing okay?"

A wry smile. "What, about living with Mom, or about the separation?"

"Both."

"Mom is fine. Makes me want to tear my hair out, but she's great with the kids and she's always in my corner. Last time Kevin tried to weasel his way back into my life, she growled at him and threatened him with a kitchen knife." Trina snorts, then her face grows sad. "The separation makes me feel like a failure."

"Oh, Katrina." I reach over and squeeze my sister's hand. She passes the coffee back over to me and I take a sip, leaning back to watch the kids play for a moment.

"Have you spoken to Iliana lately?" Trina asks. Our youngest sister has always been a free spirit. She stopped by Heart's Cove a year and a half ago on her way to Paris—or was it Amsterdam?—on another one of her world tours.

"Not for a few weeks. She sent me a postcard from the Taj Mahal." I take another sip of coffee. It's cold. "Sometimes I wonder if she had it right all along. Just go where the wind takes you and don't worry about men or kids or roots. Sounds a lot less painful than what we've got going on. Marriages ending, deaths, fires. Wouldn't it be better to be able to pack a bag and take off?"

Trina shrugs. "Wouldn't be for me." She nods to her kids. "They make me happier than all my trips combined. Plus, if you were traveling, you wouldn't be sharing a morning coffee with Blake Harding." My sister's eyes gleam. "What's going on there?"

"Oh, nothing," I lie. "I don't know. I think maybe he's a bit attracted to me, but from what I've read about him, he's attracted to anyone and everyone."

"I say go for it," Trina says with a nod. "You deserve a little tryst."

"So everyone keeps telling me. I had no idea I throw off such a strong 'repressed forty-something-year-old woman' vibe."

Trina laughs.

"Girls, time to go!" Mom calls from the main hotel building. How she manages to make her voice carry like that must be some motherly skill that was never imparted on me.

Trina coaxes Toby and Katie out of the water with lots of protests and promises to return. How kids enjoy swimming in the chill of April weather is beyond me. My sister gets them dried off and dressed, and the four of us join my mother in the parking lot, where a rental car awaits. I tell them I'll meet them at the café once they're settled, since I need to shower and change and talk to the fire chief about their findings at my house.

Amazingly, I haven't thought about Blake's promise to take me to dinner at all until I'm on my own again. Is dinner allowed when I'm planning on using him purely for sex? Should I refuse the date and just invite him to my room tonight?

The thought of getting naked with him fills me with fear. No one has seen me naked in years. *No one.* But last night, in the pool, it was *very* obvious how much his body responded to mine. And the heat in his eyes was unmistakable when he spotted me in my yoga clothes.

It makes me feel...sexy. Is it wrong to enjoy that feeling? To want more of it?

As I shower, I find myself letting my hand drift between my legs at the thought of Blake's hard length pressed against my stomach. The feel of his lips on mine. The breadth of his shoulders as he wrapped his arms around me.

Pleasure mounts as my legs start to tremble. I haven't touched myself in a long time. It feels *good*. Really good...until it doesn't. Until it feels wrong. Until I pull my hand away and lean my head against the cool tile, trying to dispel the images in my mind.

Everyone keeps telling me it's normal and healthy and human...so why does it feel so wrong? Why does pleasure feel like a betrayal?

I finish my shower with my teeth gritted. Even on my own, I can't get past this wall. It's when I'm toweling off that I realize the truth: the only time I've set aside my guilt and sense of betrayal has been in Blake's arms. Both the kiss and the pool rocked me out of the dark pit where I've buried myself alongside my grief, when nothing else has even penetrated the surface.

That's when I know I want to sleep with him.

Sex, physicality, pleasure—if he can give me those things, I'll take them, if only to remind myself of all I've been missing.

But my heart still belongs to Paul. It has to.

THE FIRE CHIEF is a black-haired man in his early fifties with an impressive mustache. I've met him a few times at school events over the years—his two boys are around Allie's age. Chief Michael Allen meets me and Simone, who insisted on coming with me for moral support, at the charred husk that used to be my home, handing both of us a hardhat and high-vis vest to put on before we make our way inside.

"We were able to get the fire under control quickly, which is fortunate. A good portion of your house was unaffected by the flames or water, but there will be some smoke damage." He walks me through the intact front door.

Simone puts her arm around my waist and squeezes. Her lips are pinched in a thin line. We poke our heads into the relatively undamaged living room, and Simone helps me grab a few photo albums from the shelves. We take frames off the walls and stuff them into a reusable grocery bag. Simone hauls it over her shoulder and gives me a stern look when I try to carry it myself. "You just take care of you, Candice. I'll carry the bag."

I want to cry and I'm not sure why. My friends are so good to me. There's too much going on.

Is it completely pathetic that I wish Blake were here with me? Why in the *world* am I thinking of Blake right now? He's supposed to be kept in a small box in my brain reserved for sex. Nothing else.

We walk farther into the house and make it to the kitchen, and my heart squeezes. Black soot and demolished remains of cabinets stare back at me. There used to be walls with photos on them there. Now I can see straight through to the blue sky outside.

We walk out to the back patio and turn to look at the black, soot-covered shell of the building. On the second floor, I can see the edge of the small fourth bedroom, the old nursery that turned into Allie's first bedroom. She'd asked Paul to paint whales all over the walls because she was obsessed with them, devouring every book she could find, sleeping with half a dozen stuffed animal whales. She even painted some of them, and I think that's what started her love of drawing and doodling and art.

When she became a moody teenager, she asked to move to the spare bedroom since it had a bigger closet. I never painted over the whales, partly because I just never got around to it, and partly because I loved thinking about Paul and Allie cuddled up on that old La-Z-Boy recliner, reading books about marine mammals.

Chief Allen draws my attention to a room off the kitchen on the first floor, the exterior walls completely demolished. "Preliminary findings indicate that the fire started in the utility room." The space is mostly ash. The damage is heart wrenching. I can't let Allie see this. Not right now.

"Ms. Viceroy, did you have your dryer running when the fire started?"

I frown. "No. And I clean the lint trap every time I use it. I know it's a fire hazard."

He nods. "Air conditioner?"

I gape at the chief. "Yes," I whisper. "We'd turned it on in the early hours of the morning because it was too hot. It was the first time we had it on this season."

Chief Allen pinches his lips. "That's probably where it started. Looks electrical, and if you hadn't had your A.C. serviced in over a year, it's likely something shorted and sparked. There could have been flammable material in there, could have blown in from outside. Could have been tiny particles of lint floating in the air from the dryer since it was in the same room. Impossible to know."

"It could have started in the night when we were in there," I whisper, horror flooding my veins. "We could have been sleeping. Allie..." My voice catches.

Simone squeezes my hand.

Chief Allen puts a heavy hand on my shoulder. "You weren't. That's the important thing. You have insurance?"

I nod, mute. That's one thing Paul taught me. Everything big—life, health, car, home—was covered. He'd been sick his whole life, and he wanted to make sure we were safe. We always took out the best policies, because he'd learned young that disaster can strike when you least expect it. I kept the same policies after he passed, mostly out of laziness and unwillingness to switch, but partially because I knew he was right.

I send a silent thank you to my husband. He was a good man. Responsible. Loyal.

The rest of the tour is short. The stairs were damaged, and it's too dangerous to see the second story. Chief Allen escorts Simone and me out of the house, gives me his card, and tells me to call him if I need anything. His voice is gruff, his eyes intent on me. I expect him to walk away, but he...lingers. "The insurance company should be able to release the funds to you fairly quickly. If they don't, keep calling them. Tell them you're a single mother with nowhere to stay, and raise hell if they try to delay. If they're being difficult, call me. I'll be happy to be your attack dog. I don't want to see you and your daughter homeless."

I glance at the chief, at his wide, protective stance, at the intensity of his gaze. He moves his hand as if to reach for me, then drops it. "You'll be all right, Candice." My name comes out as a rasp when he says it. "Call me if you need anything."

"Okay," I answer, wrapping his words around me like armor.

"Everything will be okay," the gruff man says, his voice softening. "I see this all the time. You were lucky the damage was localized. You should thank your neighbors for being vigilant and calling the fire department at the first sign of smoke."

I nod. "I'll give them free coffee for life. And you too. Free coffee any time you want it. Pastries, too. Whatever you want."

"That doesn't sound like a smart business model," Simone says from the corner of her mouth. Her eyes shine with humor I don't understand as she meets my gaze.

A slight smile from the chief. "Might take you up on that, Candice." He waits until Simone is behind the wheel and I'm safely in the passenger seat of my car before giving me a wave and walking away.

Simone grips the steering wheel, watching him until he disappears into his own vehicle. Then she turns to me. "That man wants to sleep with you."

"What?" I whirl toward her.

"'Call me if you need *anything*, Candice,'" she says, lowering her voice to a deep register. "'Maybe a late-night massage with my big, strong, fireman hands?'"

"You're imagining things." I wave my hand, face heating. "He was being professional."

"Uh-huh. Professional, my ass." She turns the key in the ignition. "If I hadn't been there, he probably would have asked if you wanted a tour of the firehouse. Maybe a ride on the pole, if you know what I mean."

"Stop it." I'm blushing, trying to keep my head angled away from Simone so she doesn't see.

She sees, obviously, nudging my arm before putting the car in gear. "Look at you. Men lining up around the block to take you out. About time they realized what a babe you are."

"You live in a fantasy land, Simone."

"Maybe you should join me. It's more fun on this side of reality." A slash of a grin as we drive toward the café where my mother, my sister, and her kids are probably going to be more interested in interrogating me about Blake Harding than they are about the fire or the sorry state of my life.

I stiffen in my seat. "Don't you dare tell my mother that Chief Allen wants to sleep with me."

Simone giggles.

"I'm serious!"

TEN
CANDICE

WE ARRIVE at the café to a whirlwind of activity. Behind the counter, the barista, Sven, is doing his thing. Almost all the tables are full, and two customers stand at our display of books perusing the bestsellers. A baby in a stroller screams bloody murder in the corner. Fiona sits at one of the tables near the back of the space with Grant across from her, three plates laid out in front of her with elaborate, delicious-looking slices of cake on them. Jen wrings her hands as she worries her bottom lip, brows arched.

Cake tasting.

"Honestly, Jen, don't look so worried. You could have made us a box cake and we'd be happy," Fiona says as I approach.

I flinch. Wrong thing to say. *Wrong* thing to say.

"A *box cake?*" Jen repeats, outraged. Her palm splays over her chest, worry transforming to insult. "You think I'd feed your wedding guests a *box cake?*"

Fiona sees Simone and me approaching, and stares at us with a wild look in her eyes, silently asking for support. "I'm just saying, I'd be happy with anything."

"I think you misunderstand the type of baker I am, Fiona."

"Jen—"

"I should take these cakes away for that comment alone. If you can't tell the difference between these and"—she sucks in a hard breath, releasing it on a whisper—"a *box cake*, then you don't deserve my bakes."

"Please don't take them away," Grant says after swallowing a bite of what looks like chocolate cake with some sort of whipped caramel filling. "I like this one." He points his fork to the cake. "Although I haven't tried the others."

Jen harrumphs, and Fiona plucks her fork from the table.

Simone sidles up to Jen and throws her arm around the baker's shoulders, tugging her close. "You know we love you, right, Jen?"

"Is this your opening salvo, Simone? You're about to remind me I promised to 'whip up' a wedding cake for you and Wes for tomorrow?"

"Well, since you mentioned it..." Simone glances at me, grins. "Otherwise I'll get a box cake from the store and throw it together tonight."

Jen reels back, lifting her hands. "Fine. *Fine.* Don't call me, don't text me, don't talk to me. I'm busy for the next twenty-four hours." She retreats to the kitchen, where Fallon is standing idle, watching the action through the opening in the wall. He grins at me, chuckling softly before returning to the multitude of dishes he's creating.

Fiona lets out a sigh. "I was trying to be nice."

"She knows that," I say. "She's just a perfectionist, and wedding cakes aren't her specialty."

Grant, now having tasted all three cakes, points to a white cake with pink filling on the far edge of the table. "What's that one?"

"Vanilla cake with Swiss meringue frosting and raspberry curd filling." Fiona sinks her fork into the tender cake. "You like it?"

"I want to marry it," Grant says, then glances up at his fiancée. "No offense."

Fiona cracks a smile, shakes her head, and takes a bite. Her eyes roll back with a moan. "Holy crap. Me too."

"Are you two going to share, or are we supposed to just stand here watching you make love to this cake?" Simone crosses her arms, a smile teasing her lips.

"Grab a fork," Grant says. "Be quick, though, because I'm about to shove the rest of this in my mouth out of pure greed, then go back there and face Jen's wrath for the rest of the cake."

Simone laughs, leaves my side, and reappears with two forks. The four of us demolish the three pieces of cake in mere seconds, and I shake my head at my friend's skill. Jen is a maestro.

"Chocolate with whipped caramel filling," Grant says as he places his fork down.

"What? No way. That rose and orange cake was divine." Fiona points to the middle plate. "But the vanilla-raspberry combination might be my favorite."

"Chocolate wins any day," he counters. "No contest."

"Go half and half," Simone says, piling the plates. "Or one tier of each."

"Jen's head might explode if we suggest that," Grant points out, and I laugh. This is true.

The café door opens, and the hurricane that is my family blows through the door. Toby and Katie sprint to the display cabinet of pastries, their little hands splayed over it as Trina yells at them not to touch the glass.

My mother, her hair stylishly spiked and her clothes changed from the pink, glittery Heart's Cove T-shirt to an equally outrageous purple-and-pink, tie-dye sheath dress, walks straight to me and wraps her arms around me. "How was the house?"

"Chief Allen thinks the fire started in the utility room, probably with the air conditioner." I glance at my friends. "Get your A.C. checked before you turn it on for the first time. Apparently it's quite common."

"And your stuff?" Mom asks, squeezing my arm. "Your clothes, photos, furniture?"

"Downstairs is pretty trashed. The smoke got to nearly everything, so I'm pretty sure I'll have to get rid of all the soft furniture even if it looks okay. Haven't seen upstairs; the staircase was too damaged to be safe."

My mother blows out a breath and shakes her head. Then she turns to my friends and nudges me with a surprisingly sharp shoulder. Introductions are made, and despite my protests to leave Jen alone, Mom ends up toddling to the kitchen to say hello.

Trina comes over next, kids happy and quiet with pastries

shoved in their mouths, and I pull a chair over for my sister to sit with my friends. The kids choose a table a small distance away and Trina glances at them, then nods and takes her seat next to Fiona. Even though my life is upside down and my mother drives me crazy, I'm glad they're all here. Not everyone's family would drop everything to come help as soon as they heard about a house fire. I can feel the stress in my body unwinding, hope blooming in my chest.

Things will be okay. I'll get the insurance payment, I'll hire a contractor to rebuild my house, I'll move on. My photos are safe, Allie and I are unhurt, and the rest of it is just stuff. Stuff can be replaced.

Whatever is happening with Blake is happening. Or not. I don't know.

As if I wished him into existence, the café door opens again and Blake strides through, his eyes immediately finding mine.

Everything inside me tightens.

Well, I guess it *is* happening.

Would he still have this effect on me if I slept with him? Maybe it's just anticipation. Excitement. It's the fact that I haven't had sex in damn near a decade, and he happens to be stupidly attractive. Not to mention the fact that the only time I've felt even close to normal has been in his arms, but I'm not thinking about what that means right now.

Lifting a hand up to push back a strand of dark hair, Blake's eyes crinkle as he smiles at me. A female sigh sounds out from somewhere in the café.

"Hey, you," he says, eating the distance between us with long, powerful steps.

"Hi," I breathe.

He drops a bag beside my feet. "I talked to the wardrobe department on set and was able to get Caitlyn to part with a few things. I figured you'd need new clothes and necessities."

The table full of family and friends to my right is totally, utterly quiet. Watching.

I glance at the big duffel bag Blake deposited beside my feet, then lift my gaze to meet his. "You did this...for me?"

"I hope you don't mind." He rubs the back of his neck, looking adorably unsure of himself. I've never seen him like this. "I just thought, you know, the fire and everything..."

"Thank you." The words come out breathy. I reach for his arm and squeeze, my heart jumping in my chest. "Thank you so much, Blake."

"There's stuff for your daughter in there, too, although I'm not sure if she'll like it. I talked to Caitlyn—our costume designer—and tried to describe the two of you. She knows what teenagers like more than I do, obviously. It might not fit, but you know, it's something, and—"

"Blake," I say, taking a step toward him. "*Thank you.*"

He finally stops talking, his eyes caught on mine. His throat bobs as he swallows, nodding once. "Cool. Well, I'd better..." he points his thumb over his shoulder.

"Okay," I say.

Blake Harding, Hollywood movie star and sexiest man I've ever seen, leans toward me and brushes his lips across my cheek. My body comes to attention, tightening and tensing from head to toe. My nipples peak, brushing ever so slightly against his chest, which sends a signal between my legs that it's time to party. His hand slides over my waist, the warmth of it sinking into my skin through my shirt. He smells so damn good. I close my eyes for the briefest moment, lost in the warmth and strength and smell of him.

And it happens again.

The spot of pain deep in my chest vanishes. I forget about the past, about the future, about the fire. For a moment, a breath, I just...exist.

Then he pulls away, and I realize I'm leaning into him. My stomach is taut, my breasts feel heavy and full, and my skin is suddenly stretched tight over my body.

Desire. That's what I'm feeling. Intense, red-hot sexual desire that burns away everything else from my psyche. All the pain. All the grief. All the guilt. As soon as he touches me, it's just...gone.

Blake's eyes blaze as he looks at me one more time, his full lips—lips I've kissed, by the way—tilt into a smile. "I'll see you later."

"Okay," I whisper, unable to make my vocal cords make actual noise.

Then he walks away.

I stand there, watching him leave, until he's in his car and out of sight. Then I turn to the table of gaping faces and shake my head. "I can't sleep with that man," I announce.

"Excuse me, *what?*" My sister glares at me. "You absolutely can."

I shake my head. "It's too much. Too intense. I actually *like* him."

"Oh, honey," Fiona says. She squeezes my hand. "You're supposed to like the people you sleep with."

Grant clears his throat. "I think I've missed something crucial here. Was that Blake Harding? And you're going to sleep with him?"

Everyone says, "Yes," while I say, "No."

I groan. They laugh.

"I'll tell you later," Fiona says with a grin. "I would have told you last night, but...whiskey."

"What the hell goes on in that library upstairs?" Grant frowns.

"Don't you worry about that." Dorothy comes breezing toward us and pats Grant's shoulder. "None of your business, Mr. Greene." She winks, then steals toward the kitchen, toward my mother. A few seconds later, I hear a loud greeting and I pray Jen doesn't rip anyone's head off.

I take my seat again as Trina nudges me with her shoulder. "You okay?"

"No." I groan. "The entire town has a front-row seat for this weird...thing...going on between me and Blake. Even if it didn't terrify me to be interested in a man—even if it didn't feel like a betrayal to Paul—I still wouldn't want everyone watching me flirt awkwardly with a man who's way more attractive than me."

"Okay. First of all, you're hot. I say that as your sister, so you know I'd tell you if you weren't."

I roll my eyes as half a chuckle falls from my lips.

"Second of all, you're a driven entrepreneur who helps run not one but *two* businesses, you're loved by everyone in this community, you're fit, you're healthy, and you're a wonderful mother. That man"—she points to the door—"knows it. He sees you and sees everything he wants in a woman."

"He dates supermodels. I don't know why he keeps talking to me. Even if he did see all that, he's not the type of man who dates. He's the type of man who screws."

"So? Doesn't that suit you just fine?"

I chew my lip. She's got me there.

Trina rubs her temples. "You're infuriating, Candice. Stop overthinking it! Just *enjoy* life, for once. You've been carrying everyone around on your shoulders for years. Paul passed while you were holding your life and business together on your own. Allie emerged from her grief and now she *laughs*, Candice. She laughs all the time when I talk to her on the phone. *You* did that. You helped her through. Stop beating yourself up for wanting something for yourself, for once."

"I like her," Simone says, nodding to my sister.

"Why is everyone so invested in my love life?" I huff.

"Because we care about you." Simone leans across the table toward me. "Candice, just see where this goes with Blake. Screw the bejeezus out of him and then move on, if that makes you feel any better. You do yoga, right?" I nod. "So you know all about living in the moment. Being present. Being aware of your body. When was the last time you felt that way with another person?"

My heart thumps. She's right. They're all right. I need to get over this fear. If Blake is interested in me, I should see where it goes. If all I can give him is a fling, then that ought to work for him, too, judging by his track record. This can just be about sex and flirting and fun.

Two weeks. That's all. I can do two weeks. And if it's only sex, then it's not a betrayal—it's just a need.

"I'll do it. I'll have sex with him," I announce.

All the ladies at the table cheer.

Grant frowns. "Is this how women talk to each other? Is this what goes on when we're not around?" Bewildered, he stares at Fiona. "Did you and the girls decree you'd have sex with me before it happened?"

Fiona bites her lip.

"Don't answer that!" Simone shouts. She turns to Grant. "If we tell you, we'll have to kill you."

I giggle as Grant gapes. He shakes his head and pushes his chair back, mumbling something about getting more cake.

Laughing with the girls, I lean my shoulder against Trina's and come to a decision. I'll do it tonight. No dinner date, no beating around the bush. I'll sleep with Blake tonight.

ELEVEN
JEN

THE CAKES ARE COOLED and leveled, the frosting and fillings are ready, and my cake stand is prepped to receive the final product. Soft music plays over the café speakers, the front of the restaurant long since closed and locked. I'm alone with my bakes. My happy place.

The first layer goes on. I went with a chocolate cake for Simone and Wes, with a hazelnut crème filling studded with finely chopped hazelnuts. Simone sometimes brings in Ferrero Rochers to work and always gets a happy look on her face when she bites in, so chocolate and hazelnut was an obvious choice.

The second layer goes on smoothly, another layer of filling, then the top layer. I crumb coat the cake—the thin layer of frosting that makes it easier to do the final, clean layer of frosting to finish—and step back.

This cake is going to be delicious. It's very "Wes and Simone" and definitely worthy of a wedding. I have elegant decorations planned including gold foil, chocolate, and hazelnut.

After putting the crumb-coated bottom layer in the fridge to set, the second and third tiers are assembled in the same order, and I pop them in the fridge before reaching for the largest bottom tier, now ready for the final layer of frosting.

This is what I'm good at. I complained earlier today because I was stressed and worried about making not one but two wedding cakes for my closest friends, but the truth is, I'm happy to do this. The other owners of Four Cups are my best friends, but I sometimes feel a bit...apart. They think I'm quirky and anal about baking. They think I'm neurotic. But mostly I'm just an introvert who's been adopted by three large personalities, and I'm not quite sure exactly where I fit in.

I want them to love these cakes. It's hard for me to show how much I appreciate their friendship, but I'm hoping these cakes will be enough.

Taking the bottom tier from the fridge, I touch the side of it and feel the hardened layer of the crumb coat, nodding. It's ready. I walk to the stainless steel countertop on the far end of the kitchen where my tools are laid out, holding the cake stand up while my gaze runs over the assembled piping bags, offset spatulas, bowls of frosting, and support dowels that will be shoved in the cake to hold the top tiers.

While my eyes are on my tools, the bottom of the cake stand catches on the edge of the counter. I stumble, trying to right the cake but overcorrecting. It comes tipping toward my chest, so I tilt it away, then watch in horror as the whole bottom tier of

Simone's wedding cake goes toppling off the cake stand and crashes into my workspace.

I freeze. Oh, no. No, no, no.

Half the cake is smooshed up against the stainless steel. Filing oozes out between the layers. The crumb coat cracks and crumbles.

Ruined.

It's *ruined*.

I stare in shock for a beat, two, then my breath catches. It takes me a moment to realize I'm sobbing. I take a step back, the cake stand clattering to the floor, and press my hand to my heart.

I ruined Simone's wedding cake. It's smashed on my counter because I was too worried about my tools and I wasn't watching where I was going. Oh, no. No, this can't be happening.

My cheeks are wet. I'm crying, and I know it's stupid. It's just a cake, but it's *not* just a cake! It's the only thing I can give back to Simone, who's been funny and supportive and always in my corner for nearly two years. She's the one who convinced me that Guillaume, my boss at my old job, was a jerk who didn't deserve me. She told me I didn't need him to advance my career. She told me to experiment with pastries, and even implemented a spot in the display cabinet for my weekly special creations.

The first thing I made was a simple muffin, but I put an apple pie filling in the center of them and sprinkled a streusel topping on it. Apple pie muffins. They were such a hit, they became part of our regular rotation.

So many of my recipes have become staples of Four Cups that people come from miles around for things *I* invented. And Simone is the one who made that possible. I don't even think she knows how much she means to me.

When I made "the best cheesecake she'd ever eaten" around the holidays, Simone told me to put my recipes together in a book, and even said she could get me in touch with a photographer. She did it breezily, casually, as if she wasn't giving me the key to unlock my dreams.

Simone is the person who's given me the confidence to develop my own recipes. I made this cake for *her*. I spent hours mixing and measuring and creating this cake because she's my friend, and she loves me, and I love her.

And then I ruined it.

Wiping my cheeks with the backs of my hands, I take a step forward and whimper. Picking the cake stand up, I place it beside the collapsed bottom tier and try to right the toppled cake. Maybe I can fix this. I can cover it with icing, and it'll be fine. I can still make her a three-tiered wedding cake, I can still show her how much I care.

But when I try to push the top layer of cake back where it's supposed to go, the tender crumb falls apart in my hands. It's not going to work.

A sob racks my body, and I sink to the floor, hands covered in chocolate and hazelnut, tears flowing down my face so fast I can't stop them.

"Hey," a gentle voice says from the back door of the kitchen.

Wiping my tears on my sleeve, I turn to see Fallon Richter silhouetted in the doorway. The pinks and purples of a no doubt beautiful sunset splash across the sky beyond him, a cool breath of air sweeping through the kitchen as he enters.

"Jen," he says, putting a thermos down on the counter before sinking to his knees beside me. "Hey, come on. You're okay."

"I"—*hiccup*—"ruined Simone's cake!" A pathetic kind of wail slips through my lips and I'm so embarrassed and sad and disappointed in myself, I can't even manage to stop it.

This is so stupid. I *know* it's just a cake, and I'm not the type of person to break down like this. I'm a grown woman! I quit my stable job and started a brand-new career in my thirties to follow my passion. My pastries and creations are part of what makes the Four Cups Café what it is. I'm strong and smart and independent. I'm *good* at this.

But Simone and I have grown close, and I *ruined her cake*.

"Hey," Fallon repeats, and he wraps his arms around my waist and tugs me toward him. Stretching his legs out, he brackets my body with them and holds me close, his back leaning against the steel shelving holding large pots below the counter where my ruined cake lies in crumbles.

I sink into his broad chest, my hands still covered in cake, and cuddle up against him. He's warm and strong and his hands are making slow sweeps along my temples, through my hair. It feels good. I'll pull away in a minute, but right now I don't have the strength.

Fallon and I have reached a kind of truce over the past year. When he first started working here, I didn't like him. He was all easy grace in the kitchen, all about eyeballing and cooking by feel. I'm a baker; I like precision. He'd tease me, and I'd snap back.

But then he made me a cup of my favorite tea, and he gave me my space, and we worked well together. By that I mean we mostly ignored each other.

And...he's here. Why is he here?

"What are you doing here?" I ask, my head resting against his shoulder. My tears have slowed. I should probably get up.

"I brought you some chai. I figured you'd still be baking. Thought I might be able to help, or at least force you to take a break."

Huh. I frown. "Why?"

Fallon's hand stops moving over my back. The stubble on his jaw rasps against my forehead as he tilts his head, then a slow chuckle rumbles through his impossibly broad chest. "Because I like you, Jen."

"No, you don't." I sniffle, lifting my hands to rub my nose before seeing the cake crumbs and hazelnut filling smeared all over them. "You tell me I'm too precise and I need to loosen up. You hide my kitchen scale from me at least once a week."

"How else would I get you to notice me?"

I glance up at him, frowning. "What?"

"Jen, I've been working here for a year and a half. Up until a month ago, you'd come in three times a week and say no more than two words to me. When you started working here full-time to fulfill the catering contract, I thought I was in with a chance, but the only time you actually *saw* me was when you were annoyed with me. What choice did I have?"

My heart thunders. I'm too old for my heart to thunder. I'm

sitting on the floor covered in ruined cake, my face probably blotchy and red from crying. I'm going to be fifty years old in a few years, for crying out loud. I shouldn't be feeling like this. But... "You...like me?"

Fallon's dark eyes turn soft. His arm slides down to tighten around my back, pulling me close to his chest. His other hand slides over my jaw, fingers splaying over my cheek and neck as his thumb sweeps over my bottom lip. "I like you, Jen."

Without preamble, without waiting for me to pull away and run, Fallon dips his head and kisses me. I freeze for a moment, and then instinct takes over. With a whimper, I melt into his touch, and I kiss him back. He teases my lips open and deepens the kiss, holding me tight to his big body as his mouth works magic over mine. He tastes... He tastes amazing. Slightly minty and warm. A low growl rumbles through him, making every-thing inside me tighten. His hand moves from my cheek to the nape of my neck, holding me against him as he kisses me harder.

His tongue—wow, his tongue feels good.

My heart races as I move my hands to cling to his shirt, pulling him close. Fallon *likes* me. *Fallon* likes *me*. I moan, earning a satisfied smile from Fallon as his lips move to kiss my lips, my cheek, my jaw. I shape his shoulders with my hands, eyes closed as he nips my ear, kisses my neck, wraps his body around mine in a way I never knew I wanted.

The last time I slept with a man was over a year ago. I went on a date after meeting a man online. His hands were clammy and his body was that of someone who sits at a computer all day. Kissing him felt slightly awkward and sent my brain into an overthinking frenzy.

Not Fallon.

Kissing Fallon turns my brain *off*. It just shuts down. No thought enters my head except wanting more. My body turns hotter, my stomach tightens, and I lean into him until my entire side is plastered against his chest. His legs bend at the knee and press in on either side of my body, so every inch of me is surrounded by him.

"Fallon," I whisper.

"Jen." He kisses my jaw and swipes his tongue up the thudding pulse on my neck. I gasp, only for my lips to be caught in his.

A broad palm drops from my nape to my breast, shaping my curves, teasing my nipple. He groans again, a needy sound that sends my mind spiraling.

I open my eyes and see a smear of chocolate over the side of his face and neck. Chocolate cake. From Simone's cake. I'm sitting on the floor of the kitchen at Four Cups. Oh God—

I pull away, eyes wide, and Fallon's lips try to follow mine.

He stops and leans back against the shelving at his back, a satisfied smile tugging his lips. "Don't even try to tell me you didn't enjoy that, Jen. I'm not going to let you push me away."

"I—" The words just die. I swallow. "The cake."

Eyes lazy, his lips tug. "I don't give a shit about the cake."

"But I do."

His gaze softens, a hand lifting to my face as he brushes his thumb over my skin. "Okay. Let's fix it. After that, we can pick up where we left off."

I'm blushing so hard I think my skin might burn off, but somehow manage to shake my head. "I can't fix it. It's ruined."

"Show me."

We stand and I turn to face the mass of cake on the counter. Fallon stands behind me, both hands braced on either side of me so I can feel every inch of his body at my back. Um...wow. I blink slowly, letting my brain adjust to the feel of him so close.

Maybe...maybe I like him, too. Have I been avoiding him because I'm attracted to him?

I mean, obviously he looks like *that*. All brown-skinned and melty-eyed with thick, dark stubble. Big arms and a chest that Simone said reminded her of a blacksmith. Of course he's attractive. Way, *way* attractive.

I lean into him slightly, and Fallon brushes his jaw against my temple. His lips dip down to kiss my cheekbone, and the very feminine heart of me swoons.

Swallowing thickly, I gesture to the brown mass on the countertop. "See? Ruined. I could make more tiers, but I won't have time to finish before the reception tomorrow. All I have are two small tiers in the fridge, and that's not enough to feed everyone."

Fallon hums. "Cake pops."

"What?" I tilt my head to look at him, and Fallon uses that opportunity to lay a kiss on my lips. I'm too stunned to push him away. Okay, and also, I like it.

He grins. He knows. "We make cake pops with this." He dips his finger into the filling and tastes it. "Hazelnut? We could make them look like Ferrero Rochers."

I gape at him. That's... Huh. That's a good idea. "And with this many cake pops, everyone could have a taste," I breathe.

He grins. "See? I'm not just a pretty face."

I roll my eyes, only to feel him chuckling at my back. His hands move from the counter to my waist, tugging my back against his front. I melt into him, not even fighting it. It feels too good. Then I look at the cake and let out a breath. "I'll look up a recipe."

"No need," he says, and I stiffen. "I know how to make these. I'll get started on them while you work on the tiered cake. They'll need a little while to set, so we can decorate them with chocolate and hazelnuts together once you're done. You know how to temper chocolate?"

I roll my eyes. "Did you seriously just ask me if I know how to temper chocolate?"

Fallon chuckles again, as if I'm joking. "There's my girl." He grins, and my stomach does a funny kind of flip at the words *my girl*.

We work in silence for an hour or so. I ice the two remaining tiers while Fallon takes the ruined cake and mixes it with some extra frosting, shapes it into balls, and inserts sticks into them. He hums to himself as he sets them in the refrigerator, then comes to lean against the counter next to me as I apply the last little bit of gold foil to the cake.

"You're so damn good at this, Jen, it's crazy."

"Good at what?"

"Baking. I thought you were good at pastries, but you can even make beautiful wedding cakes decorated to perfection. It's sexy, is what it is."

I straighten up, tweezers with gold foil dangling from them in one hand, and frown. "You think it's sexy that I'm good at baking?"

No one has ever called me sexy before. When I was young, I was dorky. Then I was a nerd. Then I blinked and I was in my thirties, working a job I didn't like while my life passed me by. So I went from a plain old computer science nerd to a nerdy pastry chef, and I became the weird, obsessive, anal baker. I've never been sexy.

"I think it's hot how much you care about your food. I've never met anyone so passionate about something, who becomes so single-minded about it. Someone who is creative and technical at the same time. So yeah, I think it's sexy. Who wouldn't?"

"Um. A lot of people."

He laughs, as if he thinks I was joking.

I blink, then turn back to the cake. A final touch of gold foil and I step back.

The cake looks clean, sophisticated, and a bit whimsical. I let out a breath, and for the first time in days—weeks, maybe—I feel my lips curl into a smile.

Fallon slides his arm across my back and tugs me into a tight hug. "See? Nothing is ruined. You're a master at this, Jen."

I tilt my head up to see the edges of his dark-brown eyes crinkle.

He smiles and touches his nose to mine. "You want to see if the chai is still warm?"

I nod, my throat too thick to speak. Fallon's lips brush mine, and a shiver of something warm passes through me.

Something changed tonight. Something big.

TWELVE
CANDICE

"UM, MOM?" Allie straightens up beside my bed at the cabana, a pale blue, silky, lacy teddy dangling from her fingers. "Why is this in the duffel bag of clothes from the movie set?"

Hmm. Good question.

"Give me that." I snatch it from her hands and shove it back in the bag. "Must have been a mistake. Did you get everything you needed?"

"Clancy has better clothes than this." Her eyes brighten. "Wait. Does this mean we can go shopping for all new stuff?"

"We'll see how our own clothes survived first. The insurance company should have someone out early next week to assess the damage, then we'll know how much of a payout we're entitled to. No shopping until then, apart from necessities."

My daughter nods, taking the black printed tee and white long-sleeved Henley she chose from the duffel and shoving them in her purse. I have a feeling she took them not because she liked them, but because she wanted mementos from The Duffel Bag Blake Harding Gave Us.

Her phone beeps, and she takes a quick glance at it. "Clancy's waiting. I gotta go."

"Give me a kiss."

That earns me an eye roll, but Allie gives me a kiss on the cheek and a quick one-arm hug. "Later!"

"Bye, honey. Be good. I'll see you at the café tomorrow morning?"

"Can't. Me and Clancy are going for a training run in the morning. Sprints. Tryouts start next week."

I tilt my head and let a smile tug at my lips. "Good for you. Where are you practicing? You need me to pick you up afterward?"

"No, Mom," Allie huffs, as if me picking her up from somewhere is the most outrageous idea to ever have been uttered aloud. "I'll be fine."

"Okay, well, when you're done, come to the café. You can help us decorate for Simone's reception tomorrow afternoon."

Her eyes brighten. "Yeah?"

I nod. "Yeah."

"Sure." Then, as if she caught herself being too enthusiastic about doing something as lame as decorating for her mother's friend's wedding, my teenage daughter shrugs. "Whatever." With a wave, Allie exits my room and slams the door. She doesn't mean to slam the door; I'm pretty sure she just doesn't notice where her body is and what's she's doing with it. I'm hoping she'll grow out of it.

I stare at the closed door and let out a breath. My daughter's nearly seventeen, and soon she'll be gone. She'll be a senior in high school come September—when the heck did that happen?

I feel like I should be spending more time with her, making sure she's okay with everything, but she seems remarkably unaffected by the fire. If anything, she's happy to be spending time with Clancy. I do a slow turn of the room as a sigh slips from my lips, feeling weird and empty and unsettled.

Then my eyes snag on a bit of pale blue silk edged with cream lace sticking out of the duffel bag.

I shouldn't.

I really shouldn't.

It was obviously a mistake. I mean, why would the costume department give me lingerie?

Somehow I end up beside the duffel bag, my fingers running over the delicate material. It feels nice and soft between my fingers, and I wonder how it would feel over my body. I bite my lip, and... Oh, what the hell. It only takes a few moments to tug off my own clothes and slip the teddy on. The lace cups my breasts, silky fabric falling tight to my torso before flaring out over my hips. It lands a bit higher than mid-thigh, definitely in the sexy zone.

I stare at myself in the mirror, running my hands over my hips. I look ridiculous. Right? I turn to look at the back, seeing how far the teddy plunges, showing off my spine all the way down to my lower back. The blue is edged with cream all around, and the color sets off my skin. I turn around again and tilt my head, biting my lip.

It doesn't look bad. It looks...kinda good.

A knock on the door makes me jump. Probably Simone. She

said she'd swing by with some nice candles for me, since—according to her—all the world's ills can be fixed with scented candles. The irony of her dropping candles off after my house just burned down doesn't seem to have penetrated, but I didn't have the heart to say no. And she *does* have good taste in candles.

I finger the edge of the lace on my thigh as I glance at the thick white hotel robe, and shake my head. Simone will tell me if this looks ridiculous. She's blunt enough to let me know if I look silly. So, without giving me time to hesitate, I grab the handle and fling the door open.

But it's not Simone standing on my stoop.

It's Blake.

Blake Harding.

Blake Harding, Hollywood heartthrob and certified silver fox.

My lips drop open as I freeze, deer in headlights. Oh no.

His mouth parts as if he's about to speak, then his eyes bug as he takes me in. A strangled sort of sound comes from his throat before he clears it, his hand moving to the doorjamb as if he needs help keeping himself steady. "Candice." It comes out as a rasp, sliding over my skin like the silk on my body.

"Um..."

He blinks, his eyes still on my legs, the teddy, my breasts. His gaze feels like a physical touch, and he's not laughing. The look in his eyes is dark, hungry, and it makes something warm slide through my veins.

I guess I don't look ridiculous.

My heart hammers, thumping so hard I can barely hear myself think. All I know is Blake licks his lips, then lifts his gaze to meet mine. The look in his eyes makes my knees go weak. Then he moves. It's subtle, barely noticeable, but it shifts the air between us in a big way. It's like everything inside him goes tense. Every muscle. Every tendon. Every inch of him turns rock hard.

"I found it in the duffel bag," I blurt.

"I'll have to thank Caitlyn tomorrow," he says, a low growl riding on his words. The sound sends shivers down my spine, sexy shivers, hot shivers, shivers that land in the space between my legs. Shivers I haven't felt in a long time.

Then I remember what I promised myself this morning. Tonight is the night. Blake is the man. Just sex; no commitments. Physical itch-scratching only.

"I wanted to see if you'd had dinner," Blake finally grinds out, his eyes returning to mine after another long perusal of my body.

"Oh. I ate earlier," I say. "Sorry."

"Nothing to be sorry about, babe."

Babe. Why does that make my stomach flutter? I've never liked pet names. I'm not a pet name kind of gal, unless it's Dorothy or Margaret calling me sweetheart. I tolerate Candy Cane from my mother, but only because it's not worth the effort to make her stop.

But I like the way *babe* rolls off Blake's tongue.

Okay, time to do this. I want to sleep with him, and he looks like he wants to sleep with me. I'm wearing a lacy, silky teddy. My daughter is staying with a friend. Blake is leaving after the movie finishes filming, and he's a no-strings-attached kind of guy.

This is my chance.

"Do you want to come in?" I ask before I can talk myself out of it. My voice is low, barely more than a whisper.

Blake closes his eyes for a brief moment. He lets out a low groan. "More than anything."

Everything inside me clenches. His eyes are dark, dark chocolate, heated to the core. He takes one step, and I back up. Another step forward as I back up, my hand rising up to fiddle with the end of my hair. He kicks the door closed behind him, his eyes still on me.

I take another step back, but Blake's hand shoots out to grab my wrist. He yanks me forward so hard I crash into his chest. I gasp, arms pinned against him, eyes wide as I stare up at the hungry expression on his face. His hands encircle me, sliding over the silky fabric to rest on top of my ass. I thought the silk felt good against my skin, but it feels even better with his hands over it.

"You wear this kind of thing to bed every night?" A low, growly question.

I bite my lip. "Do you want the sexy answer or the truth?"

He chuckles, his hands bunching the silk to tug it up until his palms hit my bare skin. I suck in a breath as his hands glide down to my thighs then back up again, fingertips nudging the gusset of my panties.

My core is molten. So hot it burns.

Holy moly. This is happening fast.

"I want the truth," he says, nose nudging mine as his hands

do another slow sweep. My blood turns to honey. It's fast, but it's *heaven*.

"I wear old T-shirts to bed. I've never worn anything like this before." My voice comes out breathy, my weight pressed fully into his body.

"Why'd you put it on today?"

"I wanted to know what it felt like against my skin."

Something softens and heats in his gaze as a sexy smirk tugs at his lips. "And what's the verdict?"

"It feels good," I whisper.

"I agree." He dips his head to my neck and lays a soft kiss there.

My heart is beating so fast I'm worried for my health. I close my eyes, spreading my palms so they lay flat against his chest. I take a shuddering breath as he kisses my neck again, higher, right below my ear.

It feels good. Better than good. The warmth of his arms, every solid muscular inch of him, the feel of his hands against my ass and his lips against my pulse. As if he can sense my attention on his hands, they do another slow sweep, sending another wave of heat between my legs.

I open my eyes and catch a glimpse of my wedding ring, gleaming in the low light of the room on my right hand. This is happening. For the first time since Paul, it's happening. I stiffen.

Blake feels it and pulls away. Not far enough for there to be space between us, but just enough so he can look in my eyes. "What's wrong?"

"I..." I close my eyes and shake my head. "Nothing. Let's do this." I lick my lips and wait, eyes closed, heart thundering.

Seconds slide by. One, two, three.

Nothing happens.

I wait some more.

Then Blake speaks. "Candice, I'm not saying I'm hot shit, but women aren't usually trembling like rabbits and saying things like 'Let's do this' as if they're getting a tooth extracted when they're in my arms."

I open my eyes and glance at him, embarrassment threatening to sweep over me, but all I see is warmth in his gaze. His hands stop moving and he lifts them slightly, letting the silky fabric of my teddy fall back over my curves.

"It's just..." I take a deep breath. I can either tell him the truth or come up with some lie that will probably make me sound like a crazy person or an idiot. But the truth is so completely humiliating. I mean, how many people haven't had sex in a decade? It's not like I haven't had the chance. I was *married*.

His arms tighten around me. "I'm not liking the look on your face, Candice."

I blink and stare up at him. His lush mouth, his warm, chocolatey eyes. He can't be hot *and* nice. That's just not fair. I won't be able to have sex with him and let him go if he's truly this perfect.

Someone who sleeps with a new woman every week isn't perfect. He can't be.

So why does it feel like he's really, really great, and why does it feel like I'm seeing the real him?

"I haven't had sex in nine years," I whisper. "My husband died three years ago, and before that he was sick, and before that we were in a slump, I guess. I don't know. I just saw my ring, and I remembered everything, and this will be the first time, and…" I trail off, not knowing what to say.

I feel embarrassed. Guilty. Ashamed.

Blake swallows. His throat—muscular, male, *hot* throat—bobs right in front of me and I stare at it, half entranced, half avoiding his gaze. Then he pulls away from me, and a jagged sort of pain rips through my chest.

I should have lied.

How utterly *humiliating* to admit that to a man like Blake Harding. What was I thinking? I should have come up with some excuse as to why I was nervous. Anything, *anything* but the awful, embarrassing truth.

I opened the door to Blake Harding and invited him in wearing lacy lingerie, then admitted I'm basically a born-again virgin. Oh. My. God. I stare at his throat some more because I can't bear to meet his eyes. His arms disengage from my back and I curl my shoulders in, moving my gaze to the floor.

Tears threaten to spill over my cheeks. I do my very, very best to stop them, but I know my lip is wobbling.

"Candice." His voice is soft, low. He takes a gentle finger and uses it to tilt my chin up.

I stare at his throat again. It's a nice throat. It's a sexy throat. It's better than seeing the pity in his eyes.

"Look at me."

I close my eyes for a moment, then open them and meet his gaze. The knot in my chest loosens. There's no pity. Only warmth.

His finger moves from my chin as he slides his palm over my neck, thumb resting on my jaw. "You want me to stop?"

I suck in a breath, not sure what he's saying. "What?"

"Is this too much for you? Do you want me to stop? We can sit by the pool, talk, have a drink. We can watch a movie."

I blink once, twice. "You want to watch a movie?"

His lips tilt into a sexy grin. "I don't particularly want to watch a movie, no."

Oh. My heart skips as everything inside me tightens. I bite my lip. "Me neither." It comes out as a whisper.

Blake's eyes turn warmer. He watches me for a moment, then dips his head toward mine and kisses me. I know it's coming, but I'm still not ready. His kiss rocks my damn world. It's the way his arms tighten around me, how his hand skates up my spine and tangles into the hair at the base of my neck, how the calluses on his palm snag against the silky fabric of my teddy. It's the way a low groan escapes from the back of his throat when he parts his lips to sweep his tongue into my mouth.

Kissing Blake is all-consuming, and I'm burning up. My hesitation evaporates in an instant. He tugs my hair to tilt my head, deepening the kiss, while his other hand slides under the open back of my teddy to wrap around my waist, fingers sliding higher to tease the underside of my breast. I'm wrapped up in him, hooking my arms around his shoulders as my body melts.

When I soften, he lets out a low groan, as if he can sense exactly what's happening inside me. As if it's exactly what he wanted me to do.

That's something I've never experienced before, and it feels incredible.

I'm going to have sex with Blake, and it's going to be life-changing. I move my hands to his waist, tugging his shirt up to feel the heat of his skin against my palms. He smiles against my mouth and nips at my bottom lip before kissing me again, harder, hotter.

My palms flatten against his back, nails finding the groove of his spine. He responds by pulling my teddy up with one hand—the other still banded across my back and oh-so-gently teasing the edge of my breast—and sweeps his hand down the crease of my exposed ass, all the way down between my legs.

I nearly come, just from that touch. From the brush of his fingertips against the gusset of my underwear, from the blaze of his heat against my front—

Then someone knocks on the door.

I freeze, eyes wide, and try to pull away.

Blake's arms tighten, the hand on my panties pulling me closer. His voice is a growl. "Leave it." His head dips toward me and pauses when another knock sounds.

I shake my head. "I can't."

He lets out a sigh, then loosens his hold.

I nab the fluffy white robe and throw it on while I close the distance to the door. I'm flushed and flustered, tying the belt on the robe as I open the door.

"Oh!" Simone says, eyes flicking from me, to my robe, to the space behind me where I'm sure Blake is standing. I steal a glance back to catch him readjusting his shirt and jeans, and immediately blush. Simone grins. "Sorry to interrupt." She extends a bag. "Candles."

"Thank you." I clear my throat. "We were just..." There's a pause while I try to think of a suitable excuse and come up short, then decide on a change of subject. "Are you ready for tomorrow?"

Simone's impish smile melts into a tender one. She nods. "Yeah." Her eyes shift to Blake. "You should come. Four Cups, tomorrow, four o'clock."

"What's happening?" His voice sends delicious shivers down my spine as the heat of his body warms my back. Mm.

"I'm getting married," Simone replies with a smile. "Well, I better go. Bye!" She winks, then turns without waiting for an answer and hustles away from my room.

I'm never going to hear the end of it.

"Candles?" Blake asks, his hands sliding over my hips.

I glance over my shoulder. "They make everything better."

"Oh." He grins. "Of course."

I close the door and turn, looking up at his gorgeous face, ready to pick up where we left off...

And another knock sounds on the door. "Candice!" Dorothy's voice comes through the door. "Candice! Come quick. Allie went to your house with Clancy. The stairs collapsed."

I whip the door open just as Dorothy's hand moves to knock again. "What?"

"I was on the phone with Lottie. She was walking by the house when she heard the noise. The girls were inside."

Shit. Shit shit, *shit, shit, shit!*

"I need to get changed. I'll be right out." I close the door and yelp when I see Blake in my room. Right. He's still here. Um. "Sorry, Blake, I need to—"

"It's fine. Get ready, I'll meet you outside in five." He slides his hand over my neck and places a soft kiss on my lips.

"Uh..." I frown, but before I can ask why he's meeting me outside in five, he's gone.

I throw on the first clothes I find—a pair of jeans and a sweatshirt, the teddy still on underneath—and slide my feet into sneakers without socks while I rush out the door.

Blake is there, wearing the clothes he had on before plus a cool leather bomber jacket. He nods and extends his hands. "Keys."

"Blake," I huff.

He arches a brow.

"Ugh. Men!" I give him my keys and stomp ahead of him, missing the grin that tugs his lips.

NO ONE'S HURT. Clancy and Allie decided to go check out the house for themselves instead of going home, and tried to go up the steps. Thankfully, they had enough sense to jump off when the creaks and groans of the charred wood became too loud, and the whole staircase collapsed in front of them.

My mother happened to be out for her evening walk, chatting on the phone with Dorothy when it happened. She heard the noise, ran in, and was still in the process of giving the girls a stern tongue-lashing when I arrived to take over. Trina arrives with Toby and Katie, who are wearing fuzzy pajamas. My sister watches the action with a worried look on her face.

In soot-stained clothes, with suitably chastised expressions on their faces, Allie and Clancy apologize to me for the thousandth time as I herd them toward the car. My mother follows, Dorothy beside her, having jumped in the car with me and Blake to get over here. The neighbors on all sides have poked their heads out of their houses to see what's going on, and the Heart's Cove game of telephone is starting. I hear whispers of Blake's name, and I know news of his presence will spread far and wide within minutes.

"I told you it was unsafe, Allie. I told you not to go in there." I throw her a withering Mom Glare.

"I just wanted to see my room." She ducks her head, then glances at Blake, who's closing the gate on the temporary fencing around our house. "Why is he even here?"

"Uh..."

A fire engine comes screaming down the street, saving me from having to answer uncomfortable questions from my sixteen-going-on-twenty-six-year-old daughter.

Chief Allen jumps out of the cab, striding toward me. He slides his hand over my shoulder. "Are you okay?" His eyes search mine, lips pinched, worry tugging his brows together, and I start thinking maybe Simone was right about him wanting to get in my pants.

I gulp. "I'm good. My daughter and her friend just decided to go exploring." I throw Allie another scowl, which bounces right off her. She's too busy staring at the chief's hand on my shoulder.

"All locked up," Blake says to me, eyes, coincidentally, also on the fire chief's hand. His jaw clenches.

Uh-oh.

Chief Allen straightens up, dropping his palm from my shoulder. "You are?"

"Blake Harding." He walks up beside me, close enough for my shoulder to hit his chest, then slides his hand over the back of my neck.

What. The. Hell?

Paul was never the possessive type, and I know I haven't been intimate with a man in nearly a decade, but even I know this is some sort of territorial male display. Instead of hurling Blake off me and giving him my best Feminist Woman Glare, I just...freeze.

His hand squeezes my nape as he tugs me closer and I... I like it? Am I enjoying this right now? What's this warm feeling spreading through my stomach? *Why do I like this?*

Chief Allen bristles. His eyes drill into Blake's, who holds the fireman's gaze. The air is getting thick. I'm frozen in between two big male bodies and I don't really think either of them have a claim on me, but somehow I've ended up here. I need to defuse this.

"Well, *this* is certainly a development," my mother says in a stage whisper to a laughing Trina. Dorothy is taking a picture with her phone. Why the *hell* is Dorothy taking a picture of this?

"For Eli," she explains, bringing her phone closer to her face and pecking at the screen with her index finger.

I roll my eyes, but Chief Allen looks away from Blake to glance at my mother, then at Dorothy. The tension drains. Lottie and Dor to the rescue.

My mother hustles over to us and pats Blake on the cheek—she pats Blake on the cheek!—then pulls his hand away from my nape. "No need for that, honey. Come on. You drive Candice home, and I'll take Allie and Clancy back to Fiona's place."

"No way," I say, snapping out of my stupor. "I'm going with Allie and Clancy. I'm explaining to Grant and Fiona exactly what happened, and we're coming up with a punishment for you two together. We had a good few months without you two causing trouble. This is unacceptable. You could have been seriously hurt."

"Candice." My mother arches her brows and looks pointedly at Blake. "You should go to the hotel. I can take the girls home." Her eyes drop to my hips, where a bit of cream lace and blue satin pokes through from beneath my sweater.

I shove the silk into my jeans. "I'm taking Allie and Clancy to Fiona's place. I'll drop Blake off at the hotel on the way there. Mom, you go home with Trina and the kids." I turn to Chief Allen. "I'm sorry to disturb your evening, Chief Allen—"

"Michael."

I'm blushing. Why am I blushing? I am a grown woman, and there's no need for me to blush right now. "Michael." I nod. "I'll get a padlock for that fence tomorrow so we don't get any other silly teenagers thinking they can go exploring." A glare at my daughter, who ducks her head. There. At least *that* glare worked.

Everyone disperses, I drive Blake to the hotel in a silent car, then take the girls to Fiona's. By the time their punishments are meted out, they've showered, changed, been chastised yet again, and I've had a large glass of wine with Fiona, I'm exhausted.

I don't knock on Blake's door when I get back to the hotel, and he doesn't knock on mine.

FIONA, Grant, and I agreed that Allie and Clancy are grounded for several thousand years. The girls both work part-time at Four Cups, have both moved up from bussers and waitress tasks to trainee baristas, but they've officially been relegated to dishwashing duty. For the foreseeable future.

Those girls have a taste for trouble. We were due. I'm just thankful no one got hurt.

In the morning, I buy a big chain and padlock at the hardware store and lock the temporary fencing up. It would be relatively easy to climb, but I'm hoping the insurance money comes through quickly and I can hire a contractor to secure the house next week.

As it is, it's a beautiful Saturday morning in April in Northern California, and I have a wedding reception to prepare. A padlock will have to do.

Once the chain and lock are secured, I make my way to

Four Cups and help Fiona and Jen with the preparations. We've shut the kitchen and done takeout coffees only for the morning, and by the time I arrive, Fiona already has all our small tables pushed off to one side. There's a DJ booth in the corner by the front window, just beside the cash register counter and display cabinet, and an open space for dancing.

Allie and Clancy are in the kitchen doing dishes. I see their surly faces through the opening in the wall and nod, satisfied. They would have wanted to decorate the space for Simone's reception, but they'll be scrubbing pots for another two hours.

I'd say it'll teach them, but I know it won't.

"Help me with the chairs, will you?" Fiona jerks her head toward the stacked seats. For the next two hours, we're busy sweeping, mopping, setting up tables and tablecloths, arranging chairs and tables in small clusters. The café is small, but along with the patio space reserved on the sidewalk, we're able to get enough standing room for most of our friends and family.

Decorations start going up. Soft, white, gauzy material gets draped across the display counter and over the windows. Agnes stops by with flowers from her garden, which we place in small bouquets around the place. Fairy lights are hung up on every wall and draped across the ceiling.

I steal into the kitchen to grab a glass of water and spy Jen taking a look at her creation. A delicate, elegant two-tiered cake sits on a white cake stand, with a huge display holding hundreds of cake pops that look like Ferrero Rochers. I gape. "Jen."

She looks up, biting her lip. "You think it's okay?"

"Do I think it's okay?" I laugh. "It looks incredible. You did this in one day?"

"Fallon helped." She blushes.

I tilt my head. "He did?" That's strange. The two of them don't exactly get along.

Before she can answer, the back door opens and Fallon enters holding a case of wine in each hand. He jerks his bearded chin to me. "Candice." His eyes warm. "Jen."

Huh.

"Mom, how many more dishes do we have to do?" Allie arches her brows at me and gives me her best impression of puppy-dog eyes. "I want to decorate."

"Maybe you should have thought of that last night."

Allie and Clancy exchange a glance, their shoulders rounding. I almost—*almost*—take pity on them, then I remember the two of them could have broken their necks if they'd been on the stairs when they collapsed. So I leave them to the dishes.

By noon, we close up the café to the public, do the finishing touches of decorations, and finally steal away to get ready. Since all my nice clothes are in my bedroom, inaccessible and possibly smoke-damaged, I end up making my way to my mother's and Trina's rental house.

Trina is the epitome of chic. She's classy, thin, taller than me by five inches, and a total knockout. She's always had style. It's in her blood. If I'm lucky, she'll have some sort of sheath dress that will look okay on my stumpy legs.

My sister greets me with a hug, her robe on, makeup half done, hair in a towel. The kids are running around while my mother tries to feed them lunch.

"Chaos, as usual," Trina says on an eye roll. "Come on. I have an outfit planned for you."

"How can you have an outfit planned when you didn't even know you'd be attending a wedding?"

"I'm an overpacker." She grins, then points to the two massive suitcases by the bed. My sister sits me down by a vanity and thrusts makeup toward me. She does my hair, gives me pointers on my makeup, then tuts at my plain, unpadded bra and taps her chin. "That's not going to work with the dress I'm putting you in."

"All I have are sports bras." I check my watch. "I could go and buy a bra, but that'd be cutting it close."

"Here. I've never worn this." She rustles through her suitcase and pulls out a...shapewear-bustier-corset...thing. Whatever it is, it's definitely not from the section of the department store where I buy my underwear. "I bought it to wear under a gown for a gallery opening. I thought the event was supposed to be a surprise from Kevin, so I planned a surprise of my own with the lingerie. I saw the confirmation email on his laptop one day, but it turns out he wanted to take his mistress instead."

"Oh, Trina." My throat closes.

Trina lets out a bitter huff. "Maybe I should have let Mom stick him with the steak knife the day he came by." She shakes her head. "Anyway, this has ties in the back. It should fit you. Like I said, brand new, I never even got the chance to try it on. It's yours now."

Stealing into the bathroom, I pull on the bustier, tugging it over my hips and up to my torso. I glance at myself in the mirror and snort. I feel ridiculous. It's white with sheer, lacy panels on the side, solid black boning swooping up my stomach and spreading out to cup my breasts. I tug on the matching underwear—almost a thong, lacy, white, with a ruched back—just as Trina knocks on the door.

"You'll have to wear stockings." She cracks the door open and throws over a packet of unopened black thigh-highs.

I dutifully pull them on, then look at myself in the mirror and start laughing. For the second day in a row I'm wearing lingerie, and I feel just as ridiculous as I did last night. But I spin around and kind of like the way the bustier nips in at the waist, and how my legs look shapely with the garter holding up the stockings. The petite, yoga-sculpted, athletic body I've become accustomed to looks very...feminine. No deflated balloon in sight, apart from the slight sag of skin below my belly button. But the bustier hides it.

Shaking my head, I turn to the gown my sister picked out for me, which hangs on the shower rail, and pull it on. Hitting me just above the knee, the dress is a beautiful deep purple color. It hugs my hips and waist, flaring ever so slightly at mid-thigh. The top is a square-cut neckline with cap sleeves, giving the whole look a sort of sophisticated sexiness.

It's so typically Katrina Viceroy. Classy, sexy, sophisticated, and chic. It's not something I'd even try on in a store, let alone buy, but I stare at myself in the mirror and look at my reflection from all angles.

I feel good. And I mean *really* good. Maybe I should wear lingerie more often.

Trina whistles when I step out, thrusting black platform heels with a thin ankle strap and a peep toe at me.

I snort. "I'm too old for platform shoes, Trina."

"Shut up and put the shoes on." She waves her hand as a kid starts screaming, then my sister is gone.

I put the shoes on.

WES AND SIMONE come back from the courthouse with Grant and Fiona, their witnesses, at four o'clock sharp. Simone has her hand in Wes's and the biggest smile I've ever seen. She's wearing an ivory dress, chiffon, with a nipped waist and a flowy, floor-length skirt. Her red hair is still wild, but pulled back from her face. She looks incredible. Fiona has on an emerald-green chiffon dress with a similar vibe, but it hits her mid-calf.

They enter to cheers and hoots.

Simone laughs, leaning against Wes, as someone puts a glass of champagne in her hand. She wiggles her finger, where a simple gold wedding band gleams. "Took us a while, but we got there," she says, stars in her eyes as she looks up at Wes.

Wes puts his hand around Simone's shoulders, handing her drink off to a nearby Grant, and "Let's Stay Together" by Al Green starts playing. I meet Fiona's gaze and start laughing. This song is so perfect for them. Smiling, hands clasped at my heart, I let out a long sigh. It's good to see Simone this happy.

Across the room, I see Wes's uncle Sean and Sean's fiancée Alina. Sean has his arm around the much younger woman, and the two of them are smiling. After all the drama last year, they've grown closer to everyone. Still not exactly part of the family, but closer. It's good to see them here. They must have made the trip out last-minute especially for Wes and Simone.

Everyone else is here, watching the happy couple with soft

smiles on their faces. Dorothy with Eli, Margaret with a glass of champagne, Agnes and Mr. Cheswick, Fiona, Jen, me, the kids...even Sven and his girlfriend. Frank, the building inspector who condemned our original café building, is pillaging the snack table. I make a note to thank him; without the original flood, Four Cups wouldn't exist the way it does now. Wes and Simone probably wouldn't be together. I wouldn't have started this chapter of my life.

My eyes drift to the window, then away, then back again, and I know I'm looking for Blake. I tear my gaze away and clap when the song ends, then get swept up in dancing and drinking and laughing. Allie and Clancy are done with dishwashing duty, dressed in their best, looking positively angelic.

"They're meant for each other, aren't they?"

I turn to see Rudy, Agnes's grandson and the man I went on a date with last year. He nods at Wes and Simone.

I smile at him. "Never seen a better match."

We fall into easy conversation, and I realize there's no awkwardness between us—but there's no spark, either. I'm glad I never took things further than a date and a short kiss with him.

Agnes slides up to Dorothy, who has her arm intertwined in Eli's—an elderly gentleman who moved to Heart's Cove last year after retiring from his job with Uncle Sean—and shoves a finger in Dorothy's face. "This is a happy occasion, so I'm not going to make a scene, but I saw you wandering near my raspberry bushes yesterday."

"Who, me?" Dorothy puts a hand to her chest, innocence personified.

Agnes whirls on Eli. "Do you know she's a serial urinator?"

"Oh, Agnes. Don't be vulgar." Dorothy huffs, eyes sparkling.

Agnes growls, flicking her two fingers between her eyes and Dorothy's. Eli drops his face to Dorothy's neck to hide his smile, and I have a feeling he's heard, in great detail, about the saga between the two women. He's still here, which makes me happy for Dorothy.

As night falls, the fairy lights in the café come on and the party gets louder. Dorothy and my mom are dancing up a storm, both dressed as if they were trying to outdo each other with outrageousness. Dorothy's in head-to-toe leopard print, and my mother has on a swirly blue-and-teal pantsuit with a neon-blue lace camisole, complete with blue streak in her hair. How she had time to dye a streak into her hair between lunchtime and now, I have no idea.

I find myself carting food and drink back and forth from the kitchen to the party, if only to stop myself glancing toward the door every five minutes.

Blake's not going to come. Why would he? Why do I care?

A movie star doesn't go to small-town impromptu weddings. A movie star doesn't care about my friends getting married. A movie star doesn't care about *me*, and that's the way it should stay. If—big *if*—anything happens between us, it'll be physical only.

Then, as if he could hear my doubts, his body fills the door and my breath catches.

"Blake!" Simone shouts, arms thrust in the air as champagne goes flying from her glass. She reaches for him, tugging him inside the fray. She turns to the room. "Make way! Make way, Hollywood hottie coming through! Where's Candice?"

I close my eyes for a beat as everyone turns to stare at me. Kill me now.

She spots me in the parting crowd, brightening, and the smile that had been on Blake's face freezes. He does a slow sweep down my body and back up again, sending heat rushing through my veins. I stand, unable to move an inch, as his gaze sweeps over me like a touch—a touch I felt just last night.

His legs erase the distance between us in two long steps. He stops inches away from me, gazing down at me, his eyes moving over my face, my hair, my body. When he finally meets my gaze again, he lets out a breath. "You're beautiful."

My heart seizes. I nod to his suit—obviously tailored to his exact measurements—and touch the lapel. "Not bad yourself, Mr. Harding."

"Dance with me."

It's not a question; it's a demand, and it sends a spear of desire piercing right through my stomach. I nod.

Blake takes my hand and leads me to the postage-stamp-sized dance floor, right beside where my mom and Dorothy are tearing it up, and wraps his arms around my waist. I have no choice but to put my hands on his shoulders, and because I can't resist, I slide them over to wrap around his neck.

My mom gives me a wink, and Dorothy gives a not-subtle-at-all thumbs-up. I spy Agnes in the corner rolling her eyes at Dorothy, and can't quite hide my grin.

We sway, my body pressed up again Blake's, and I find

myself lifting my gaze to meet his. His lids are low, eyes on me, gaze full of heat and promises.

"Sorry I'm late," he says, tightening his hold on my waist. "I tried to get away as soon as I could."

I shrug, as if I hadn't been lamenting his absence for hours. "It's fine. I know you're in town for work."

He nods, his hands sliding ever so slightly lower. If he feels the bustier under my dress, he doesn't say anything. His fingers tease over the top of my hips, sliding over and back as his head dips to my neck. "If I'd known you'd look like this, I would have made up any excuse to get here sooner," he says in my ear, his voice like velvet.

I give a little shiver, and judging by the way his palms press against my body, he feels it. Closing my eyes, I lean against him, letting myself enjoy these few moments.

His hands slide across my waist, then back, lower, lower...

And freeze.

His body goes still, and his finger follows the line of a garter strap that attaches my bustier to my stockings. His breath comes out in a whoosh, eyes lowering to meet mine. "Are you wearing stockings?" It comes out as a growl, his eyes fully molten.

My breath catches, and all I can do is nod.

"How soon can we leave?"

"Blake..."

"I'm serious, Candice." He bands his arm around my waist and pulls me close. I gasp when I feel the hardness of him against my stomach.

Um, *wow*. A heavy fog settles over me, so much so that I don't see my mother until she shoves her face right beside mine.

"Hi, lovebirds. Should we be planning another wedding?" She grins, winking at me, and the space between me and Blake immediately increases. He clears his throat and I shuffle to spin around in front of him, hoping his erection is disappearing as quickly as my lustful fog.

"Mom." I widen my eyes at her.

"Oh hush, Candice. I haven't been able to have fun like this in years. Years! You and Paul got married so soon, then Trina married that asshole, and I just had to put up with it! Iliana took off and I've never even met any of her boyfriends. Now I finally get to have fun, and I intend to enjoy it. Blake is sexy as can be, and he's going after my eldest daughter. So, if I want to call you lovebirds when you're cuddled up on the dance floor, I will. So there."

I squeeze my eyes shut, but feel Blake's body shaking with what surprisingly sounds like a chuckle.

Then another person walks up to our huddle, and I only just manage to hide my panic when I see it's Chief Michael Allen.

"Candice." He nods to me, then my mother. "Mrs. Viceroy."

"Lottie, please," Mom says, swatting the chief's muscular arm.

I do another eye squeeze, but when I open them again, everyone is still in exactly the same position. Damn. I smile at the fire chief and notice his eyes are an indigo blue with a ridge of really deep navy near the iris. Nice eyes. Warm eyes. Eyes that I could stare at for a long time. Why am I only noticing this now? Has he always been this handsome, or has some switch flicked inside my brain and all of a sudden I can see it?

Blake's heat at my back somehow grows warmer. I bite my lip, drawing the chief's gaze to my mouth. Oops.

Chief Allen opens his mouth and I know he's going to ask me to dance. He's going to say it as a challenge to Blake, and it's going to be so painfully awkward for me.

How did this happen?

For a long, long time, I've been off men's radars. Sure, when I was married the odd flirtation would happen, but I'd usually shut it down pretty quickly. Then after Paul died, I was given what I assume is the wide berth given to widows.

There's no wide berth here. In fact, the space separating me from the two men sandwiching me is very, very small.

"We're out of ice!" someone calls out from the kitchen. "Ice machine's broken." Fallon comes into view, his eyes meeting mine, then jumping to Blake, then Michael. A slight grin tilts his lips.

"I'll get some," I call out on a breath. "The hotel has an ice machine. I'll bring back a cooler full." I squeeze out from between the two mountains of testosterone, but before I can make my escape I hear Blake's voice.

"I'll help."

I open my mouth to protest, then reconsider, choosing instead to nod and shuffle toward the exit. The cool air hits me hard and I pull in a breath, immediately running my hands over my arms. A warm weight settles over my shoulders as Blake slides his suit jacket over me, his smell and heat ensconcing me completely.

I can't help it. I let out a little sigh and a smile. It feels too good not to.

Blake's lips curl, his head jerking down the street toward the hotel. His arm brushes mine as we walk, my heart jumping in my chest. We walk in silence toward the hotel, then snake through the lobby, the courtyard, and around the back of the building where the outdoor ice machine resides.

I put my hands on my hips. "I forgot to bring a cooler."

When I glance at Blake, his eyes aren't on the ice machine. They're on me, and they're sinful. He slides his hand over my waist and without a word, dips his head to kiss me. It's wet, it's hot, it's full of tongue, and it knocks me out of this galaxy.

I slide my hands around his neck and barely notice when his suit jacket falls from my shoulders. His hands start a rough exploration of my body, one curving up my back to wrap around the nape of my neck, the other diving down to slide over my ass.

A shiver courses through me at his touch, his brand. His hand squeezes on my neck as he pulls away, eyes on mine. "I gotta be honest with you, Candice, I'm finding myself not caring about the ice right now."

My stomach does a curl, thighs squeezing together, then I say something I really didn't mean to say. "Maybe no one will notice if we don't come back right away."

A wolfish grin tugs at Blake's lips, then I'm thrown over his shoulder. I yelp, shocked more than anything, as I dangle over his shoulder and feel his strong arm banded over my thighs. His thumb slides up between my legs, teasing the edge of my thigh-high stockings as a rumble courses thought his chest.

Then we're walking toward the cabanas, and I know things are about to get serious.

MY BRAIN DOESN'T CATCH up with me until Blake's door is unlocked and I'm tossed down on the bed. I bounce once as Blake's body comes down over mine, his legs shoved between my thighs, his arms pressed down on the bed by my head.

I'm being manhandled, and to my absolute shock, I like it. A lot.

Then Blake (freaking) Harding kisses me again, and my brain short-circuits. His big, hard body presses down on me, covering me completely, and all I can do is wrap myself around him. My hands go roaming across his back, his neck, tangling into his silky, tousled hair.

His hands work magic. Up my sides, over my breasts, back down over my slight curves. He tugs my dress up and lets out a low groan at the feel of my undergarments. His hand slides over the garters, the edge of the stockings, the side of my panties.

Shoving my dress up higher, he disengages the kiss and curls his back to look down. "Fuck." The word is torn out of him, and when his eyes meet mine again, they're not molten, they're black. "Candice, I want you."

The breath is ripped right from my lungs. Just...gone.

Blake's mouth crashes into mine, his kiss devouring. I part my lips on instinct and moan when he thrusts his tongue inside, frenzied, as if he needs to taste me to live. I tug his hair, tear at his clothes, lift my knees to wrap my legs around his waist.

For once, my mind is quiet. There are no thoughts about my departed husband, about this being a betrayal, about how long it's been, about anything but the feel and weight of Blake's body against mine. His hand stroking the outside of my thigh while his other arm cups the back of my head. His fingers moving as he shifts his weight away from me just enough to slide his hand between my legs. His palm grinding down on the perfect spot.

Pleasure gushes through me. I gasp into Blake's mouth, earning a smile from him. His lips move against mine before he kisses me again, mouth still curved in a grin. His palm moves again, and even over my panties, the sensation is almost too much.

But I want it.

Eyes closed, I let my head fall back on the bed and release a sigh. Blake tugs my panties aside and groans when he feels my arousal. "So wet," he rasps, lips by my ear. His tongue flicks out to lick my neck, then his lips, his teeth are on me, as if he can't get enough of tasting me.

His fingers slide, twirl, press, and I feel it coming. Faster than I've ever felt it, faster than I can think. I open my eyes and find Blake watching me, his nose close to mine, breath mixing, deep brown eyes all I can see. My breath catches as his fingers do another twirl, touching exactly the right places as if he's had a map of my body to study for decades.

With one hand cupped around my neck and his other hand between my legs, he brushes his lips against mine. "Let go, babe." A soft kiss that sends shivers through my veins. "Give it to me."

As he speaks the words, his long, talented fingers slide right inside me while his thumb strokes me just right. So fucking right it's perfect.

So I give it to him. I give it all. I come apart at his touch, arching my back as I moan his name, my body electric. My legs fall apart and I whimper when I feel Blake's fingers slide out of me.

But not for long.

He fiddles with his belt, his fly, and then I feel something else between my legs. Eyes hooded, Blake glances down between us. A strangled groan sounds from the back of his throat as he lifts his eyes to me again. "Tell me you want this, Candice. Please, fuck. Tell me you want this."

"I want this." It comes out on a breath before I can think, before I can stop myself.

Then he thrusts inside me in one long, powerful stroke, and my world falls apart at the seams. A cry escapes my lips as my nails dig into his shirt, body arching into him, hips bucking. His hands wrap around my hips and tug me where he wants me, rough, needy, beautiful. He drives into me again, deeper, his fingers pressing into my hips before they slide to my knees and lift my legs up over his shoulders. His hands slide over my stockings, tracing the garter, yanking my panties farther aside.

Then his body is curving over mine and it turns fast and hard and feral, and my second orgasm slams into me so hard I see stars.

Another stroke, two, and Blake is grunting, panting, his eyes dazed. He collapses on top of me, letting my legs fall to the side as I wrap my arms around his shoulders, staring at the ceiling and seeing nothing.

It takes a long time for us to move. Long, beautiful minutes spent doing nothing but listening to Blake's breath, to my own heartbeat, feeling the unfamiliar yet incredible feeling of him softening inside me. With slow, careful movements, Blake shifts his weight onto his elbow and pulls out of me as I whimper, empty once again. His lips curl into a smile, a broad hand coming to cover my cheek as his fingers trace the hairline at my temple.

"Well," I whisper.

"Well," he replies.

"That happened." I bite my lip to hide my smile, but Blake's eyes are dancing.

"It sure as hell did."

My heartbeat is still erratic. I let out a breath and stare at the ceiling, boneless in bed, dress bunched up around my waist. Blake shifts, his hand brushing the neckline of my dress in a feather-light touch that makes goosebumps rise over my skin. Then his hand moves down the side of my breast all the way to my leg. He spreads his palm over my thigh and brushes the space between my legs in the same gentle touch. I buck, but my legs fall apart a bit wider of their own volition.

"Do you always wear these types of undergarments?" Blake asks in a rough, raspy voice, his eyes on his own hand, on my legs, the space between them. I find I like him watching.

"No," I answer honestly.

"Lucky me," he says almost to himself. His hand cups the space between my legs, eyes returning to mine.

I whimper when his fingers slide through the slickness there. "It's sensitive," I say on a breath.

His eyes darken, touch soft. His fingers tease my opening, sliding in slowly, torturously. "Give me one more, Candice," he growls. "You deserve another one."

I'm not sure I have another orgasm in me, but my body still melts into the bed. His fingers are so soft, so beautiful as they move between my legs. His mouth moves to my neck, my chest, and he groans when he tugs the neckline of my dress down to see the top of my bustier. With gentle, sure movements, he pushes the bra cup down and brings his lips to my breast.

Turns out I do, in fact, have another orgasm in me.

WE RETURN to the party with a bunch of plastic bags full of ice. My makeup took a lot of effort to fix, and I mostly gave up on my hair. Blake has a satisfied look on his face that makes me want to blush.

The instant we walk back inside, Simone's eyes dart to me, then to Blake, and back to me again. She grins and hustles toward Fiona.

Wonderful.

The fire chief is nowhere to be seen, thank goodness.

We bring the ice to the kitchen, where Fallon and Jen are standing close to each other. Very close. They jump apart when we enter.

"We were just getting the cake ready," Jen explains, even though I didn't ask.

"Okay," I answer.

"Just needed a few finishing touches," she goes on.

"Uh-huh." I glance at Fallon, who has a hungry look on his face, and it doesn't look like he's thinking of cake. I dump the ice into the ice machine. Even if it's broken, it's still cold and it's big enough to hold all our bags. Blake does the same, and we head back out to the party.

From there, my night passes in a daze. I stay at the party for another hour or two, laughing and dancing with all the people that are closest to me, all the people I love. My daughter is on her best behavior, and I almost, *almost* let her convince me to take her off dishwashing duty.

I blame Blake for this new relaxed feeling.

My eyes drift to his, and I find him watching me from across the room more than once. He's often surrounded by people, including my mother and Dorothy and Margaret, who I'm sure are regaling him with a variety of embarrassing stories.

In short, I'm happy. It's a beautiful party, Simone and Wes are in love, and everyone I care about is in the same place and in a good mood. The cake is delicious, impromptu speeches are tear-jerking, and there's a lightness to my spirit that I haven't felt in a long, long time.

Maybe I can blame Blake for that, too.

Toward the end of the evening, I see that Allie and Clancy are safe with Fiona and Grant, who leave after the cake, and I let my mother and Dorothy convince me that I don't need to worry about clean-up.

"A house fire excuses you from party clean-up duties," Dorothy says sagely.

"You go. Have fun." My mother wiggles her eyebrows, an implication I decide to ignore.

And that's how I find myself walking back to my cabana with Blake by my side. When we got the ice, he retrieved his suit jacket from the ground and now he places it back over my shoulders. It's still warm and snuggly and it smells like him, so I find myself smiling up at him while he tugs it closed at my neck with a hand, and still smiling when he drops his lips to touch mine.

"You're sleeping in my bed tonight," he informs me.

I cock a brow. "Am I, now?"

His arm curls around my shoulders and we start walking again, my question totally ignored, and my scowl not even noticed.

So I sleep in his bed.

Well, we do things other than sleep first, but I do fall asleep eventually.

FIFTEEN
BLAKE

CANDICE FITS PERFECTLY AGAINST ME. I wake up with my arm around her waist, my leg notched between her thighs, our naked bodies pressed together. She smells sweet and floral and right.

This is what I want. That conviction is the single bright, clear thought that burns through my mind. This, right here, is what I want.

I tighten my hold on her waist, pulling her deeper into my arms. She lets out a soft feminine noise, still asleep, and wiggles her butt against me. I bite back a groan.

We went wild last night. I haven't had sex like that in years. Decades. Maybe ever. Candice was as hungry as I was, the chemistry between us explosive. When we got home from the party, she tore my clothes off and dropped to her knees in front of me. I could only stand it for a few seconds before I had my hands hooked under her armpits and I was tossing her on the bed, climbing after her to splay her legs open like my own personal dessert.

And I like dessert.

Now, she's soft and sweet and sleepy against me, and I feel calm for the first time in a long, long time.

Candice makes a noise and turns her head, blinking sleepily at me. "Hey."

I snake one arm under her body, curving it up to tease her breasts. Small breasts that fit perfectly in the palm of my hand. She sighs when I swipe my thumb over her nipple, those gorgeous lips falling open.

"Morning," I reply.

"Blake—" A shiver as my other hand slides down her stomach and through her curls, all the way down to the sweet honey between her thighs.

I'm hard already. I haven't *not* been hard since I felt that garter belt over her dress last night. This morning, with her body pliant, I find myself burying my face in Candice's neck while she arches back toward me. I guide myself inside her. Moments after waking up, she's wet for me, ready, wanting it as much as I do.

"God, you feel good," I groan as she pushes back into me, both of us still spooning and sleepy. Her arm curls back to tangle into my hair, giving me better access to tease and roll her nipple between my fingers. I love the noises she makes, the way she shivers and trembles and bucks against me. The way she's wet for me, always. The way she comes for me, soft and sweet and mine.

Just like the first kiss, she *melts*. She gives herself to me, fitting her body against mine like we were made for each other. And every time she hands me that piece of her, I cradle it close and cherish it. It's mine now.

It doesn't take us long, and once it's over, I hold her against my body and don't pull out. "I could stay here forever," I tell her, face buried in her neck.

I get a soft whimper in response, then feel Candice stiffen.

Palm still on her breast, hand still between her legs, I give her nipple a teasing pinch. "Why'd you go still on me?" I ask.

"We haven't used protection. We've had sex, like, a million times and we haven't used protection."

"I got the snip when I was thirty-eight," I tell her.

"There are reasons to use protection other than pregnancy, you know."

"I get tested twice a year, and you're the only woman I haven't used protection with since I divorced my second wife seventeen years ago. I figured since it's been nine years for you, we were probably okay."

I probably shouldn't be this blasé about it. It's not like me. But I can't bring myself to care.

She turns her head to look at me, not moving her lower body. She's worried about protection but she still wants me inside her. I grin.

"What are you grinning about?"

"You."

"What about me?"

"You're funny."

"I am *not* funny."

"You are."

"You're crazy." She huffs, turning her head again.

I pinch her nipple again and feel her clench around me, down there, so I do it again, and she clenches again. "You keep doing that and I'll be hard again in an instant," I growl, banding my arms around her tight and thrusting inside her gently, teasing.

"You're insatiable," she says, but there's no bite to her words. The stiffness in her eases, then reappears. "But I guess everyone and their dog already knows that."

I frown. "What's that supposed to mean?"

"Blake," she says on a dry snort. "You must know the reputation you have with women, so don't try to tell me that I'm the only woman you do this with. I'm not an idiot."

I flinch. How would she react if I told her that yes, she's the only woman I do this with? The only woman I've invited to stay in my bed till sunrise in a long, long time.

But I swallow the words, knowing she won't believe them. "What does my reputation have to do with us?" I'm still holding her close, still inside her, still feeling every inch of her back plastered to my front. And I don't like hearing her talking about my fucking reputation in the tabloids.

"Are you seriously asking me what your reputation as the world's premier playboy has to do with us sleeping together?"

"What else would I be asking about?"

"Blake."

"Candice."

She shifts away from me and the connection between us disengages, but I don't let her get far. I tug her closer so she's on her back, my body lying on top of her, my weight on my elbow by her head. Her gaze slides to the side until I turn her head with my palm. Grudgingly, she meets my gaze, and I speak. "My reputation with women has nothing to do with what just happened between us, Candice." I study her eyes, wanting her to understand. Needing her to understand.

She's not some distraction. She wouldn't be in my bed waking up beside me if she was one of the women I get photographed with. I thought she could feel it, the connection between us. I wouldn't even call it a spark, because it's a fucking inferno. From the moment I kissed her on set, I haven't been able to get her out of my mind.

I'm not insatiable, not usually. I just can't get enough of *her*.

But she thinks she's just like the others?

Something enters her gaze, and it looks a lot like panic. She swallows and closes her eyes. "I need to get up."

"Candice." My voice is a low growl.

"Look, Blake, this was"—amazing, earth-shattering, mind-bending—"nice, but I know where we stand and I'm okay with it. Actually, I'm great with it. It works for me. I don't have the emotional bandwidth to have anything more than...this...with a man."

"Anything more than what?" Anger nips at my words. Even I can hear the growl, the temper, and I don't try to hide it.

To her credit, Candice doesn't react. She just blinks. "Nothing more than sex, Blake. Good sex. Great sex." She snorts. "Not that I would know, but hey. It's been fun." Her voice is different. Higher-pitched, faster, as if she's pushing the words out despite herself.

"Fun?" I repeat slowly. "Last night was 'fun?' This morning? Fun?"

Candice's eyes finally snap back to me. "It wasn't fun for you?"

It was a hell of a lot more than just fucking fun. Last night made me feel like I've been wasting my whole fucking life, like I've spent the past seventeen years—the past thirty years since Mickey!—stumbling blindly, not knowing what I was missing.

Fun doesn't exactly cover it.

She doesn't wait for me to answer. "I need to get up. I'm supposed to be at the café this morning and I have a yoga class to teach at ten o'clock." She nudges my shoulder. "Let me up."

Her body isn't soft. She isn't melting into me. She's stiff as a board and pushing me away.

I almost laugh. Isn't this what I deserve? A taste of my own medicine?

I've spent as long as I can remember keeping women at arm's length, and the first time I meet someone I actually like, she tells me I'm nothing more than a bit of fun. Emotional bandwidth? What's that supposed to mean?

I slide off her and watch her swing her legs over the side of the bed, hustling to the bathroom and re-emerging with a robe on. I'm still in bed, naked, with nothing but a sheet over me. Her eyes drift over my body and something like hunger enters her gaze. She blinks, and it's gone.

"I'll, um, see you around."

Then she picks up her dress, her sexy-as-hell lingerie, her shoes, bundles them up under her arm, and heads for the door.

If she thinks that's it between us, she's sorely fucking mistaken.

"Candice, wait."

"I'll talk to you later."

"Talk to me now." I haven't spent this long on my own to let a woman like her slip through my fingers. Gritting my teeth, determined, I push myself off the bed and throw on a pair of briefs just as Candice opens the door—

And freezes, because my mother and father are standing on the threshold.

SIXTEEN
CANDICE

THE BLOND-HAIRED LADY with inch-long white roots slicked back in an elegant French twist on the threshold gives me a bright smile. "You must be Candice."

"Uh, yes?" It comes out as a question.

"Well, don't just stand there, honey," she says over my shoulder. "Introduce us!"

Blake makes a strangled noise. "Mom? Dad?"

Holy freaking moly. Oh no. Oh no, no, no. His mom and dad are here? Blake Harding's parents are in town? I'm meeting a movie star's parents right after I had a night of debauched sex with him while I'm wearing nothing but post-coital hair and a bathrobe?

And...wait.

They know my name?

I mean, I know they heard me over the video call, and Blake

made that joke about them meeting me, but... Dear God, was he being *serious*?

"I'm Gina," his mother says. "And this is Merv."

Blake's dad sticks out his hand. I have to give him an awkward left-handed shake because my right hand has shoes and a dress and stockings and lingerie in it, on full display.

Merv clears his throat. "Let's grab a coffee while we wait for the kids to get dressed, Gina."

Kids. We're "the kids." Lovely.

Gina doesn't seem to hear Merv, because she bustles right past me into the room and starts picking Blake's clothes up off the floor. Clothes which, by the way, are on the floor because I tore them off his body in a sexual frenzy last night, right before I dropped to my knees and took him in my mouth. And *liked* it.

Oh my goodness. She's doing exactly the same thing my mother did.

"Mom, go get a coffee." Blake's voice is gruff. "We'll be right out to meet you."

"We will?" I whirl, eyes wild.

"Candice owns the Four Cups Café down the street. Why don't you go check it out?" He takes the pile of clothes from his mother's arms and tosses it on the bed, to her great dissatis-faction.

She harrumphs when his hands land on her shoulders and guide her to the door. "You have laundry to do, Blake. You expect me to just go drink a coffee while your room looks like this?"

"I'm a grown man, Mom."

"You're my baby. And your room smells like sex. Open a damn window!"

Oh. My. God.

My face is on fire. It's so hot, the skin will burn right off. I've never felt so embarrassed in my life, and my mother is Lottie Viceroy, so you know I've spent a lot of time feeling embarrassed.

Merv stares at his shoes, then spears his hand out to grab his wife around the waist and haul her out of the room. "See you in a bit, kids."

"You need to separate the lights and the darks, Blake! Otherwise the colors will bleed." His mother stares over her shoulder, then all I see is the door because Blake closes it in front of my face.

And I'm still in his room. Shit.

"Sorry about that," he says, his body close enough that I can feel its heat. I turn my head and see him just inches from me. He shakes his head with a rueful smile. "I combined lights and darks and ruined a couple white shirts when I did laundry for the first time when I was thirteen years old, and I haven't heard the end of it."

My tongue comes unstuck from the top of my mouth. "Why are your parents here?"

He runs his fingers through his hair, and I vaguely register that he looks really, really good in the morning, all undone. "They visit me sometimes. I told them they'd like this town when I spoke to them last. I didn't think they'd show up."

I nod. "Uh-huh. And why do they know my name?"

His hand moves to rub the back of his neck as he stares at the floor next to my feet.

"Blake?"

His eyes climb up to meet mine, and I note that he's blushing. Blake Harding, certified silver fox, is blushing. What has the world come to? "Well, remember? I sort of told them about you."

"About me? You said they heard me check into my room. You didn't say they *knew* about me. You made a joke about your mom making up fairy tales. A *joke*, Blake, but they didn't seem surprised that I was in your room. A room that smells like sex, according to your mother." I'm blabbing. I can't stop.

Blake bites his lip, and I notice that, too, looks good on him. "My mother's like a shark scenting blood whenever I mention a woman."

"Why..." My eyes widen. He mentioned me? As in, *mentioned* mentioned me? Oh my goodness. He *was* being serious when he said his parents wanted to meet me! I shake my head and turn to the door. "I have to go."

"Candice, wait."

I don't wait. I don't walk, I *run* out and into my room, slamming the door behind me. I hear Blake protest, but I turn the lock and lean against the door, breathing heavily.

This is happening too fast. This is all wrong. It was supposed to be physical, casual, just sex. I was supposed to be ending a nine-year dry spell. Scratching an itch. I was doing something reckless and wild for *me*, for once.

But...*he told his parents about me?*

How is that even possible? He had to have told them *before* we did anything together. What?

Oh no. Oh, no way.

I squeeze my eyes shut, but all I see when I do is the way Blake looked at me this morning when I was trying to run away. How he was searching my eyes, asking me a question with his gaze that I didn't want to acknowledge, let alone answer.

He doesn't want just sex. He's not scratching an itch.

I drop my sister's dress to the floor and bury my head in my hands as shame overwhelms me. I've betrayed Paul. I've pissed all over our marriage and slept with someone else.

I know it's been three years, but what's three years? My father died when I was twenty-eight, and my mother hasn't been on so much as a date in nearly twenty years. She flirts, sure. She'll talk about men being hunks and make untoward comments all the time. But she hasn't been with anyone but Dad. Their love was everlasting. She carried on, and she's been her crazy self, but she hasn't looked for another man. Not once.

I thought that was me. I thought Paul and I had that kind of love. That kind of devastating, lifelong love. The kind of love that breaks your heart.

What kind of terrible person am I? How can I possibly move on so soon?

I *did* love Paul. I loved him a lot! The most! He was my husband and I loved him with all my heart. I *did*. I do!

Tears come so fast I don't even have the time to try to stop them. My throat gets itchy one second, and the next, tears are streaming down my cheeks. Sliding down the door, I cry on the floor as shame and embarrassment and guilt overwhelm me, because I felt it. I felt whatever is there between Blake and me. I felt it and it makes me feel like an awful person.

I'm not supposed to move on. I'm not supposed to have *feelings* for anyone else.

How can I have feelings for someone I met days ago?

Without the answer to that question, I just push myself up to my feet, get in the shower, and get ready for the day.

FOUR CUPS IS pandemonium when I arrive. Agnes stands on a chair, all four feet and nine inches of her towering over Dorothy, who's ducking behind the display cabinet, dodging the paper cups being thrown in her direction.

"You hussy!" Dorothy screams as her head pops up, long grey hair in a disheveled halo around her head. "How dare you try to steal Eli out from under me. Stick to your own romance, Agnes. What would Cheswick say? Maybe I'll call him right now."

"I was just trying to save him from a lifetime of torture with *you!*" Another cup goes flying, hitting the wall with a soft clack before falling to the ground. "And I didn't ask him out, you hag. I just told him I could order the book he wanted." *Clack.* "From the bookstore." *Clack.* "Which I own." *Clack.*

My eyes dart around the room. Fairy lights are still up from last night, but the rest of the tables have been put back to their usual places. There's a bit of confetti in the corner that got missed in the clean-up. Customers are huddled near the windows, on the opposite side of the café to the projectiles. A few phones are out, filming the altercation.

"You batted your eyelashes," Dorothy says, ducking fully behind the counter to hide behind the espresso machine.

"You peed in my raspberry bushes." *Clack.* "*Again!*"

Oh dear.

Jen and Fallon are visible in the opening between the kitchen and the front of house. They're both watching the action with unhidden laughter in their eyes. Simone is alternately trying to dodge cups while making her way to Agnes. To what end, I'm not sure. She might be thinking about carrying the elderly lady out the door.

Gina and Merv Harding stand in the hallway that leads to the bathrooms, wide-eyed.

Lovely. Just great.

I stick my fingers in my mouth and let out a loud whistle.

The room goes silent.

I turn to Agnes and point to the floor at her feet. "Off the chair."

"I—"

"*Off.*"

She grumbles, but gets off. Dorothy's expression turns smug, so I throw her a glare. It does nothing to wipe the satisfaction off her face.

"You're barred for a week. Both of you." I point to the door. "Starting now."

"Candice…" Dorothy straightens up, leaning over the counter toward me. "Let's be reasonable here."

"Reasonable? You want to be reasonable? Look at this place, Dorothy. There are a hundred cups littered all over the floor. You've scared all our customers so much they're huddled on the edge of the room. All for what? You know Eli loves you. He gets stars in his eyes every time he looks at you. He'd never go out with another woman."

"Well, I know *that*," Dorothy says with a huff. "But the fact that she even had the *audacity* to *ask*—"

"I don't care. Barred. One week." My voice is clipped.

Fiona meets my gaze from across the room, eyes wide.

Agnes growls, then kicks a cup on the floor and points her index finger at me. "I never liked this place anyway. I'm taking my display of books back."

I cross my arms and meet her gaze. We have a staring contest for a beat, two, then Agnes's face changes. Something like approval flashes across her features, and she turns to Dorothy. "Well, come on, you old bag. You heard the woman."

Dorothy lets out a long sigh and heads out the door. The two women exchange a few words to each other along with polite smiles, then part ways as if they've just met up for a normal, everyday chat. Nutty. They're both completely nutty.

Fiona grabs a broom and starts sweeping up the graveyard of cups. I make my way to Gina and Merv, running a hand through my hair as I try to figure out what the hell I'm going to say to them.

Gina beats me to it. "You. Are. *Perfect!*" She lets out a little squeal, hanging off her husband's arm. "Isn't she perfect? Won't let Blake walk all over her, oh no. She'll stand up to him. Yes she will. Won't she, honey?"

"Mm-hmm," Merv says, his eyes assessing me for a moment before turning to the counter. "Our coffees ready yet or what?"

"Coming right up!" Sven says, pushing off the wall to

approach the espresso machine now that the danger has passed. He's got one of his many "Heart's Cove Hottie" pink and glittery T-shirts on, this one with the sleeves cut off to show off his colorful arm tattoos. When we hired him, he discovered a box of those shirts in the move from the old café space to this one, and now wears them like a uniform. Half the time, Allie and Clancy have them on, too. It works, somehow. Don't ask me how.

The bell over the door jingles, and Blake walks through. His face is closed off, guarded. Nothing like it was this morning, and I know it's all my fault.

"Blake! We love her," his mother announces. "Better than those bimbos you usually date."

"How do you know they're bimbos, Mom? You've never met any of them."

Wait. His parents haven't met *any* of his lovers?

Gina waves a hand. "Wouldn't take a genius to know they're bimbos. But this one"—she jerks her head to me—"she's a keeper."

"Not sure she wants to be kept," is Blake's reply, his eyes dark as they watch me.

A heavy lump lodges itself in my throat. No, I don't want to be kept. I thought I wanted to have hot sex with him, then keep him as a footnote in the story of my life. The two-week tryst I had with a movie star. The end.

Now, I'm thinking he was expecting something different.

"Candice Jane Viceroy," my mother booms from the entrance to the café. She's wearing jeans, a jean jacket, a T-shirt with an American flag on it, and cowboy boots. My mother has never even been on a farm. She lives in Seattle, yet she's wearing head-to-toe denim and cowboy boots. She plants her hands on her hips. "Did you just kick Dorothy out of Four Cups for a whole week? How dare you."

I close my eyes for a beat, then open them and let out a sigh when my mother's still standing there. "She was causing a scene, Mom."

"Mom?" Gina floats forward, a hopeful expression on her face. "Are you Candice's mother?"

My mother's eyes narrow. "Who's asking?"

"My name is Gina. I'm Blake's mother. It's a pleasure to meet you." Gina smiles. She's wearing dark-wash jeans and a white button-down, a simple gold chain at her neck. Pure elegance and simplicity next to my mother's cowboy-Americana-chic. Lord.

"Blake as in Blake Harding?" My mom's eyes dart to the only Blake in the room, a.k.a. the movie star I happened to sleep with last night, then kind of messed up with this morning.

"The one and only!" Gina laughs, a delicate sound. She waves her husband forward. "Merv and I are *so* happy to meet Candice. She and Blake are just lovely together."

"They are?" My mom's eyes dart to me, and I groan internally at the thought of the Lottie Inquisition I'll be subjected to later.

Ignoring that, I turn to Blake. "We need to talk."

His guarded face turns hard. "We talked this morning."

"Well, we need to talk again." I point to the door, letting my shoulders soften. "Please?"

Blake hesitates for a moment, then we both notice the openly curious and hopeful expressions on both our mothers' faces. Their arms are interlinked, soft smiles tugging at their lips. Merv sits at a table reading a newspaper, clearly not invested in the future happiness of his movie-star son. But then he lifts his eyes and meets my gaze, assessing. Waiting.

"Lead the way," Blake says, and I escape the probing stares, taking him outside and to the red door beside the café that leads up to our office-cum-library.

My hands shake as I unlock the door, but my mind is made up.

I need to tell Blake exactly what I expect from him, exactly what I want from him. I need to tell him that this will not go any further than just sex between us. No matter what our mothers are hoping, all we can have is a casual, two-week relationship.

It's all I can give him. It's all I *want* to give him, because my heart shattered three years ago, and it'll never be put together again.

That I know for sure.

SEVENTEEN
CANDICE

WE GET UPSTAIRS, and even the power of the library isn't able to soothe my nerves. There's a long couch on one side with armchairs facing it, the kitchenette at the back of the building, and big, bright windows with desks at the front. The entire side wall is filled with books.

I move to stand in the center of the room, between the armchairs and couch, the coffee table nudging against my calves, and I turn to Blake. "Why did you tell your parents about me? And *when* did you tell them about me?"

He stands near the door, watching for a few moments. Then lets out a sigh. "The day you moved into the hotel. I was video-calling with my mother and she noticed I was distracted."

"Okay." I take a deep breath. "You told me about that the first evening by the pool. And what, exactly, did you say about me? More specifically, what did you say about *us*?"

His jaw clenches. "I didn't say anything about us."

"So why does she think we're together?"

"Is that such a bad thing?" His eyes flash dangerously.

I rear back, shocked. Does he think it's *good* that our mothers are downstairs probably planning our wedding? "Yes, it's a bad thing!"

Blake crosses his arms, anger written on every line of his face. "So, what? You fuck me all night long but you draw the line at meeting my mother?"

My head spins at his tone, but also because, yes, that's exactly where I draw the line, but he's saying it like it's inconceivable that someone wouldn't want to meet the parents after one night. A night which, by the way, wasn't exactly planned. A night that rocked my whole world and all my notions about myself and my marriage. A night that made me question a lot of things I'd taken as truth.

Things about my future. About the rest of my life. About myself.

Planting my hands on my hips, I glare. "Blake, you don't know anything about me."

"I know your husband died. I know you think you need to be some noble widow to honor his memory, and you're ignoring the fact that you have the whole second half of your life to live."

I blink. Did he just say that? *Did he just say that?*

"*Excuse* me?"

He sighs, shoulders dropping as he lifts one of those broad hands to run his fingers through his hair. I try to ignore the way his shirt tugs against his chest and shoulders, how his bicep flexes and bulges at the movement. This would be a lot easier if he didn't look so good.

Turning away from him, I stare out the window. "Look, Blake, you're in town for two more weeks. I know what I am to you, so let's just leave it at that. No need to pretend about anything."

There's a pause before Blake speaks, and when he does, his voice is quiet, so quiet it sends shivers walking down my spine. "What, exactly, do you think you are to me?"

"Your latest piece of ass," I spit, turning back to face him.

Something like hurt flits across his face, and he drops his hands to his sides. "Candice—"

"No. Please, Blake, don't. I'm not an idiot. I know about your reputation, and I know you're the world's sexiest movie star and I'm just a single mom in a small town. I'm not delusional." I shake my head, trying to ignore how bitter those words taste in my mouth. "I'm okay with this being something purely physical. In fact, that's what I want. You know exactly how long it's been since I was intimate with a man, and I'm pretty sure you saw how much I enjoyed last night. Let's not make this more complicated than it needs to be. Please don't lie to me by telling me you care about me."

He stares at me, his gaze intense, the air thick between us. Then he takes a step toward me. Another. When he's standing on the edge of the rug next to an armchair, a muscle feathers in his cheek. "Maybe it's my turn to say that *you* don't know anything about *me*."

I grit my teeth, but I don't let that penetrate. He's acting like he *wants* his mother here. Like he doesn't mind the fact that she thinks there's an "us." Like I mean more to him than all the flings I read about in the papers.

"Blake, I'm not looking for anything—"

"Is this just sex to you?" he interrupts, his body so tense it looks made from stone.

"Yes," I lie.

His eyes darken. "Is that all you want it to be?"

"Yes." My second lie scorches across my lips.

Our gazes clash for a beat, then he lets out a short huff and dips his chin. "Fine."

Then the distance between us vanishes, and Blake's arms are around me. His eyes move from one eye to the other as he watches me for a breath, then his mouth is on mine in a devastating kiss. I don't even have time to react. His tongue thrusts into my mouth and I melt right into his arms, clinging onto his shoulders as my body gives in.

It's just sex. That's what I tell myself as my veins fill with fire at the slightest touch.

Sex is what we have. It's what we'll do. Then he'll leave.

But his arms feel so right around me, and that spot of pain deep in my chest vanishes, just as it always does whenever he's near.

And he's leaving, so I can't get used to it.

But I won't think of him leaving right now. I'll just enjoy the feeling of his arms around me, his mouth against mine, his tongue between my lips. I'll commit his taste, his smell to memory. I'll enjoy every last drop of these moments together because when it ends, I'll have to go back to my old life. Alone. The way I should be.

His hand palms my breast, rolling my nipple over my shirt and bra. I moan into his mouth without meaning to, but he doesn't break the kiss. He doesn't pull back and give me a self-satisfied grin like he did last night. Instead, he just drops his hand between us and flicks open the top button of my jeans. His fingers slide the zipper of my jeans down as his other arm bands across my back, keeping me pressed up against his hard chest.

Then his hand is in my pants, under my panties, touching me exactly how I like it. He breaks the kiss but keeps his mouth near mine, eyes open, watching me.

"Blake," I whisper, knees weak, as he tightens his hold on my waist to keep me upright.

His fingers slide inside me and I close my eyes with a moan. I want him so bad. I need him. His hands on my body are perfect, beautiful. There's no better feeling in the world, and I'm losing myself to it.

That's why it can only be sex. Because I'm losing everything I knew about myself, about how my life was supposed to go. Because he undoes me every time I soften in his arms.

"Look at me." His voice is gruff. Harsh. He slides his fingers in and out of me, the palm of his hand grinding against my bud. "Look at me, Candice."

I open my eyes and my breath catches at the intensity of his gaze, but I can't pull away. I don't want to pull away. I cling to his shoulders, my legs jelly, as his hand works magic between my legs. Strong, sure fingers. Talented fingers. Fingers I'll miss when they're gone.

He slides another one inside me and changes the angle, eyes flashing when he feels me react. I'm close, so close, and all it took was a touch of his hand. Seconds—it took seconds for him to take me to the edge.

When I close my eyes again, he makes a warning noise at the back of his throat. "Look at me when you come, Candice. I want your eyes wide open and on me."

"I don't—" My words die right on my tongue because it feels too good. I cling to his body, legs trembling, breath coming heavy against his mouth.

The truth is, I want to do what he says. I want him to watch me come, and I want him to know how much I love his hands on me. I want him to see what his touch does to me, how quickly he makes me unravel. How special it feels to have him beside me.

So I keep my eyes open, and I watch the intensity morph to something else in his gaze. He pumps his fingers inside me, then pulls them out to touch me exactly how I need it, circling me once, twice, harder—

And I come.

I fly apart so hard my whole body grows stiff, held up by the steel of his arm banded across my back. He groans low and deep, our eyes locked as I pant his name over and over again, my nails digging into the hard bulk of his shoulders.

He takes my orgasm as if it belongs to him. As if it's his right. His touch is angry and tender all at once. A promise. It tears me apart and makes me want more, more, more.

But I keep my eyes open. I hold his gaze, even when my body feels like it's falling to pieces. Even when my legs tremble and he strokes me again, extending the pleasure longer than I thought possible. I watch him watch me, not understanding the depth of his gaze, not wanting to understand what's passing between us.

Finally, unable to take it any longer, I drop my head to his shoulder. Blake slides his hand from my panties, zips me up, does my button, and cups the space between my legs over my clothes. His hand is warm, rough, possessive. When his eyes meet mine again, they're dark and hard, but his voice is soft. "Was that just sex, babe?"

My breath catches, and I wonder if I should tell him the truth. Should I tell him that I can barely hold myself upright? Should I tell him that I've never had an orgasm like the ones he's given me, not ever? Should I tell him that he makes me feel alive, but he also makes me feel like a coward and a disloyal wife?

Should I tell him that I gave up hope that I'd ever feel this kind of feeling, that I'd ever stand with this kind of deep, endless precipice at my feet, and I gave it up a lot longer than three years ago?

I want this. I want there to be an "us." I want to be able to brush away my lies and tell him that *I feel it.* I feel whatever's happening here.

Fear squeezes my heart, because if I tell him that, I'm admitting a lot of things about myself and my marriage that were never supposed to see the light of day. If I tell him that, I'm exposing the dark, dirty, rotten core of me.

Instead, I just swallow past the thickness in my throat and nod. "Yeah. Just sex."

His jaw hardens, but a humorless grin curls his lips. "Liar."

Hand still cupped between my legs, he gives me a squeeze. "You're a liar, Candice."

Then, Blake's intensity vanishes, he shakes his head once, eyes gleaming in a different way, and his lips descend toward mine for a slow, sweet, gentle kiss that has nothing at all to do with sex.

EIGHTEEN
FIONA

AS SOON AS Candice walks through the door, I know something happened upstairs, but I can't really tell what. Candice has this look on her face—kind of dazed, kind of happy, kind of confused, and a little bit mad—that makes me think something *happened* happened, if you know what I mean.

I give a table one last wipe as she pauses in the middle of the café and does a slow turn. Her eyes land on me. "Where're my mother and Blake's parents?"

Tossing the rag and cleaning spray onto the bussing station by the cashier's counter, I straighten up. "They left a few minutes ago to go look at open houses."

Candice freezes, and the weird expression on her face takes a sharp turn toward anger. "Open houses?"

I want to laugh. I know I shouldn't laugh, but after the past year in this town I've learned to go with the flow. I flick my eyes to Blake, who's frowning, albeit slightly less angrily than Candice. Then I nod. "Yeah. Lottie said there were a few properties that looked promising, and Gina got all excited. They said they'd meet you back at the hotel in a few hours."

"They said—" Candice cuts herself off, pinching the bridge of her nose. Then, with a slow breath, she puts her hands down, palms up, as if she's asking the world to slow down. "Fiona, why are they looking at properties?"

I shrug. "A keen interest in real estate?"

That's when Blake starts laughing, which, judging by the look on Candice's face, is *not* the correct reaction. He slides his arm over Candice's shoulder and tugs her close, whispering something in her ear that only makes her face go redder.

"Mom?" Allie appears in the doorway to the kitchen, frowning.

Candice straightens, putting an inch of space between her and Blake. "Yes, honey?"

"I need to go to the house. Can you give me the keys to the padlock?"

Candice snaps into Mom Mode, crossing her arms and giving Allie a flat stare. "Why's that?"

"I left my textbooks and study notes in the living room. I have a test tomorrow." Allie arches her brows. "I won't go upstairs, I promise."

"Well, there's no staircase so of course you won't go upstairs," Candice returns. "Can't you use Clancy's textbook and notes? We really shouldn't be going in there. It's not safe."

"Well..." Allie hesitates. "We're in different classes, and the school library isn't open until tomorrow."

Clancy appears beside her, and I give her my own version of the Mom Stare.

"Are you two done washing all the dishes?" I ask.

Clancy nods.

Candice and I exchange a glance, and I give her a one-shoulder shrug. She relents by lifting her arm. "Come on, then. I'll drive."

"We can go looking for our parents after you're done," Blake puts in. "If you don't mind me joining."

"Why the hell not," Candice says on a sigh, a slight tilt in her lips.

I want to ask her what happened upstairs, and why she looks so confused-yet-resigned-yet-sort-of-happy, but I don't get the chance. She nods her head to the door and she, Allie, and Blake make their way outside.

Clancy gets closer, her lip caught between her teeth. She flicks her eyes to me, then lets them slide away.

"You okay, Clancy?"

"Mm-hmm." She nods, then pauses. "Where's Dad?"

"He's at home." I still get a little happy tingle at the thought of calling that big, beautiful house home. "Why?"

"Well, I was thinking..." Clancy takes a deep breath and lifts her gaze to mine.

I arch my brows in question.

Clancy speaks then, her words coming out in a rush. "I know I haven't been the easiest to live with and I've caused all kinds of trouble these past couple of years. And you and Dad paid for me to go see my mom in New York twice already, and you encouraged me to try running, and you gave me a job here, and you've already started helping me think about college, and..."

"Clancy," I interject softly, moving toward her.

"I'm always getting in trouble, but you and Dad have been so good to me. I'm excited for track and field tryouts and I think I have a chance of making the varsity sprinting team, and I was just thinking how I never, ever, *ever* would have done something like that before, but now I am, and..."—she takes a deep breath—"and I wanted to say thank you by making dinner for you two when Allie is moved out and it's just the three of us. I looked up recipes and checked the pantry and we have everything we need except chicken."

My heart does a hard squeeze at the thought of "just the three of us" and my voice comes out raspy. "You want me to go to the grocery store when you're at school tomorrow and grab some chicken?"

Clancy nods, her eyes shining.

I spread my arms and my heart does another squeeze when Clancy doesn't hesitate, she just comes toward me and wraps her arms around me in a tight hug. I lay a soft kiss on her cheek, smoothing my hand over her blond hair.

"I've never made a whole dinner before," Clancy says quietly.

"You want me to help?"

She shakes her head. "No, I want to do it. But maybe...if it turns out bad, can we just not tell Dad, hide the evidence, and order pizza instead?"

Laughing, I give her a squeeze before pulling away. My

hands stay on her forearms as I stare in this beautiful, mature, amazing girl's face. "Absolutely not. I want your father to feel exactly how I feel right now."

"How's that?" Clancy whispers.

"Proud of the woman you're becoming," I reply, and watch as Clancy's lip wobbles.

"Love you, Fiona," she says in such a quiet whisper I almost miss it, and that's when my heart squeezes so hard I can barely breathe.

Clancy's been living with us for almost two years, and she's never said that to me. Not once. She's shown it with smiles and hugs and all the ways that she's bloomed into a mature young woman, but she's never said it.

So of course, I start crying. "I love you too, Clancy," I say between breaths.

"I'm glad you and Dad are together." She wipes her own tears off her face. "And I'm glad I stole my mom's credit card and came out here looking for him."

I huff a laugh, nodding through my tears. "Don't tell Grant I said so, but I'm glad about that too. So long as you don't steal any of our credit cards," I finish with a pointed look.

Clancy just grins and shakes her head.

I give her one last hug, feeling another piece of my heart settle in place. When I pull away, I take a deep breath. "What are we having for dinner tomorrow, anyway?"

"Chicken, rice, and black bean skillet. I'll use the cast-iron pan. We need bone-in, skin-on chicken thighs," she says, as if she's cooked a thousand dinners for us before.

My heart does another squeeze—smaller this time, but more tender—and I slide my arm around Clancy's waist. "Sounds delicious."

Giving Sven a wave behind the counter, I head out with Clancy to go home. Home to my fiancé, with my new daughter at my side.

THERE ARE people crawling all over the charred remains of my house. I stop the car and stare, not understanding. Blake, from the passenger seat, makes an annoyed sound at the back of his throat.

That's when I see Chief Michael Allen striding toward us, the front gate of the temporary fencing wide open. Scrambling out of the car, I come around the hood to meet him. Blake is by my side in an instant, and the annoyed vibes between the two men are coming in strong.

Not good.

How did this happen? Why me? A week ago, no one wanted me. Now I have to deal with two men acting like Neanderthals.

"Chief Allen," I start, ignoring Blake's annoyed presence at my side. "What's going on?"

"How many times do I have to tell you to call me Michael,"

he says, chiding. His eyes are soft on me, and I notice he's also ignoring Blake's annoyed presence at my side.

I let my lips slide into a smile. "Michael, then."

Blake is stiff as a board beside me, right before his arm juts out and wraps around my shoulders.

Um, what? I glare at him. Earlier, when we found out our mothers were looking at real estate, he brushed his lips against my ear and said, "Doesn't sound like such a bad thing." Now, he's doing another territorial male display by wrapping his arms around me.

Michael's lips press together, then he turns toward the house. "Got a few of the boys at the fire department out here today. After Allie and Clancy snuck in, I figured we could make the site secure until the insurance gets back to you to get work started."

I look behind him to see two muscular young men—firemen, I assume—lifting up a sheet of plywood in front of a window. A third man drills into the wood, securing it to the house.

My throat grows tight as my eyes widen. "You did this for me?"

"Last thing we want are squatters making their way into the home. Or kids getting hurt." He leads us forward, pointing to a chain lying on the ground next to the fence. "I had to cut your lock, but I'll replace it."

"Michael," I say softly, and Blake's arm tightens around me. I steal a glance at him to see his face set and hard, his eyes on the back of the fire chief's head.

Hmm.

I'm sensing our little episode in the library didn't exactly settle his mood. And, if I'm honest, it did nothing to settle mine. Well, okay, it did a *bit* to settle mine.

Allie appears on my other side, eyes wide. "Clancy is going to be *so* mad she missed this." She giggles, her face red, then casts her eye over the multitude of sexy, muscular firemen walking all over my property.

Oh my. My daughter is growing up far too fast.

"We just came by to pick up some of Allie's schoolwork. She said it was in the living room, so we're hoping it's undamaged," I tell Michael, even though I feel silly explaining why I'm at my own house.

He waves us forward. Blake stays quiet by my side, until the chief looks over his shoulder.

"No movie star duties for you today?" he asks, and I think there's an edge to his voice.

Blake grunts. "Day off."

"Must be nice," Michael says, and I definitely can tell there's an edge to his voice.

Time for deflection. "Allie, follow the chief inside and get your stuff. Then you're going straight to Fiona's house."

My daughter nods and walks beside the chief, her eyes darting to and fro all the men. A few of those men throw curious glances my way, so I give them a dorky little wave. That earns me a few grins.

"I can't believe they're doing this for me," I say, shaking my head.

"Wonder what they'll want in return." Blake's voice is bleak.

I turn to him, frowning. "What's that supposed to mean?"

His eyes meet mine, and the anger dissipates from his gaze.

He shakes his head. "Never mind. You want to go hunt for our mothers after we drop Allie off?"

I notice he uses the word "we" a lot, as if it's a given that we'll be spending time together. Which means my whole "this is just sex" explanation didn't exactly penetrate. Which, obviously, I knew from his reaction to it and the subsequent jelly-leg-inducing orgasm he gave me, followed by the deeply possessive touches, but still. I'm trying not to think about that right now.

I need to nip this in the bud. Well, we might be past the bud stage, but I need to nip this where we're at. Blake clearly thinks there's something between us that I'm not ready to give him. He's putting his arm around me in public, and doesn't seem at all concerned that our mothers are currently house-hunting.

Turning to him, I take a step back. He takes a step forward, so I lift my hands and put them on his chest. His eyes warm as he looks down at me, a smile tugging at his lips.

This is not the time to smile! This is the time to listen to me laying down the law.

"What's so funny?" I ask, annoyed.

"You are."

I stare at him blankly, and his smile widens. "I am not."

His brow arches, voice dropping low. "You're about to give me some big speech about keeping this casual between us, but no matter what you say, you'll still be in my bed tonight."

My mouth drops open. The au*da*city! How dare he! "I think you're misunderstanding what's going on between us."

"The only thing I'm misunderstanding is why you're fighting this so much. I know you feel it, Candice. This connection between us. Do you really want to throw it away because of your own pride?"

Yes! I want to scream. *Of course* I want to throw it away. What kind of person would it make me to jump into another relationship just three years after my husband passed away?

Sex is different. I saw my friends' faces when I told them how long it had been for me. It's acceptable, in my mind, to have sex with a man when I know he's leaving in a couple of weeks, and I know he won't look at me as anything but his latest lover in a long, long line.

The problem is, that's not how Blake is looking at me *at all*. He's looking at me like that long line of lovers ends with me, and that is *not okay*.

Not even a little bit. Not in a million years.

"My husband died not even three years ago, Blake. I'm not ready for anything serious."

"How many years, in your opinion, is an acceptable time to wait? Is there a rulebook somewhere that I can read so I know when I'll be allowed to come back to claim you?"

My jaw is just hanging open full-time now. Come back to *claim* me? Is he for real?

Also, side note—he'd come back for me?

Closing my eyes to ignore the heat burning in his gaze, I try to stay on target. "I'm not ready."

"Says who?"

"Says *me*."

"Got it!" Allie calls out from the doorway, Chief Allen behind her. She waves a textbook and a stack of papers, and I use that opportunity to step away from Blake.

Seeing my daughter, and knowing I'll have to drop her off at a friend's house yet again, I make a decision. I'd planned on waiting at least a day to check out Margaret and Dorothy's rental place, maybe do some cleaning, get the basics set up before moving my daughter in, but I need to take control of *something* in my life. I nod to Allie. "Tomorrow, you and I are moving into the twins' rental place."

She pouts. "I like staying with Clancy. Why can't I stay there?"

"Because I said so," I tell her, using the words that, before I had a child of my own, I told myself I'd never use.

Allie lets out a long sigh. "Tomorrow's Monday. I have school."

"So you'll pack up after school."

Allie's eyes narrow and dart to Blake. "Why the rush? Are you and Blake having a fight?"

"Allie, car. Now." I point to the car and watch my daughter drag her feet as she makes her way there. Then I turn to Blake. "We'll drop her off, find our parents, then I need to figure out what I need to make the move to our new place. I won't have time to see you tonight."

There, I said it.

Whatever's going on with Blake and me has to end. I won't be sleeping in the room next to his—or in his room, for that matter—and I won't be seeing him. We had sex, it was great, but that's it.

I can't get serious with him.

If I get serious, it means I have to admit to myself that I didn't love Paul in that big, earth-shattering way that widows are supposed to love their husbands. It means I can move on, but I don't want to move on. Paul was a good man. He was a decent man. He was a wonderful father.

What kind of shitty person does it make me to want to ignore that and start over with another man?

Decision made, I turn to the chief, thank him, then make my way back to the car. Blake says nothing until we've dropped Allie off at Fiona's place.

That's when things go wrong. Well, when they go *more* wrong.

We walk up to the front door. Allie rings the doorbell then walks right inside, calling out into the house, "Got my books!"

"We're in the kitchen!" comes Fiona's voice. Her head appears down the hall, flicking from Allie to me to the space behind my shoulder. "Oh, Blake! Well, come on in. You want a beer? Grant's out back."

"That's okay, Fi, we need to go find our mothers before they buy a house and never leave."

Fiona laughs, giving Allie a kiss and a hug when they cross in the hallway and coming to stand in front of me. "Would that be so bad?"

"It would be a disaster," I tell her honestly.

Fiona grins. "I don't know, Trina seems to like it. She was asking me about schools."

"Trina I can deal with. My mother?" I shake my head. "I love her dearly, but I don't want to live beside her. One Dorothy is enough in my life. She's eccentric, but she doesn't just 'pop in' to see me first thing in the morning without warning."

Fiona's eyes crinkle. "What about you, Blake?"

His arm slides across my shoulders and despite myself, I like the way it feels. I like the way he pulls me close to his warmth, the way my body fits so nicely beside his. "I wouldn't mind my mother living here. Would give me two reasons to come visit."

My eyes widen as my jaw drops. Again.

Fiona's eyes flick to me, delight dancing in her irises. Mercifully, she changes the subject. "You two want to join us for dinner tonight? Everyone's coming over."

Dinner at Fiona and Grant's house with our kids and Blake? Uh, *no fucking way*. That completely defies the "sex only" rule. I shake my head. "No, that's okay, I—"

"Sounds great," Blake cuts in. "I haven't had a home-cooked meal in months."

Before I can get angry at him, I frown. Months?

Fiona smiles. "Great! Dinner's at seven. Bring some wine." She leans in, gives me a hug, and in a daze, I follow Blake out the door.

Somehow, he ends up behind the wheel. I never even realized I gave him my keys. I stare at him from the passenger seat, tilting my head. "Has it really been months since you had a home-cooked meal?"

Blake starts the car, then turns his head to look at me. "Not since I went home for Christmas."

"None of your girlfriends cooked for you?"

He stares at me for a beat, his eyes blank. Then he lets out a soft breath and shakes his head, his voice quiet. "I haven't had a girlfriend in a long time, Candice."

I frown. That's impossible. He's a playboy. He's photographed with women all the time. I *know* he's the type of man who jumps from woman to woman to woman. He's had *hundreds* of girlfriends.

"But—"

His hand slides over my neck and he pulls me close. "Stop thinking you know everything about me, Candice." Then he presses his lips to mine and kisses me, open-mouthed, until I'm in such a daze I can't think of anything to say.

Then we go looking for our mothers.

TWENTY

BLAKE

AFTER CANDICE MAKES a phone call to Lottie, we set off
in their direction. It's a ten-minute drive through a wooded
landscape, the blue sky peeking through the green canopies.

It's beautiful here. Hard to imagine it's just a couple hours
from L.A., because it feels like a completely different world. It's
serene, quiet, and the air tastes fresh, salty, and clean.

I could live here.

The thought jags through me as I grip the steering wheel of
Candice's Ford, my teeth clenching. Then I force myself to
relax. I haven't felt this way about a place, about a woman, in a
long, *long* time.

But I feel this way about Candice.

It's so crystal clear in my mind, it surprises me that Candice
is fighting it. This is more than just attraction between us. It's a
deep sense of belonging.

I belong beside her.

It's crazy, I know. Completely insane to feel so sure about something that's only a couple of days old. But I *know*. I know that Candice gives me something special every time she melts into me. I know she throws up these walls of grief to keep me away, but there's a part of her that feels it, too. That she belongs beside me just as much as I belong beside her.

The last time I felt this way, I was nineteen. Three decades have passed, but I haven't forgotten how it felt to meet Mickey, or how much it hurt to watch her walk away. Divorce number one scarred me more than I was ever able to admit, but for the first time in my life, it feels like a distant memory. I'm able to look at it, to think of how I felt, and see the beauty in falling for someone fast and hard.

Mickey and I never would have worked out. I mean, look at what happened! She wasn't *capable* of loving me the way a wife should love her husband. Her revelation rocked my world, and not in a good way. I felt betrayed, lied to, and so fucking foolish it was humiliating.

I guess, in a way, I used the decades since then to prove to myself that I'm a real man. That women want me, and I have the power to choose whether I want them.

My second marriage was a disaster from the beginning. It never felt like this.

Stealing a glance at Candice, I gaze at her profile as she stares out the window.

She wants me. Her body speaks to mine like we were made for each other. But her mind fights it in a way I haven't encountered before. She feels the chemistry sizzling between us, but her own demons hold her down.

I want to fix that for her. I want to shake her and tell her not to waste as many years as I did wallowing in her own quagmire of guilt and shame.

She shifts in her seat. "You don't need to come to dinner if you don't want to."

"I want to."

Her gaze is heavy on me, and I don't even need to take my eyes off the road to check. I can feel it pouring into me from the other side of the car. Then she lets out a sigh and turns back to the window.

We find Lottie, my mother, and my father at a small, run-down one-bedroom bungalow nestled on a big, twelve-acre oceanfront property north of Heart's Cove. The two women are standing at the side of the house, pointing off in the direction of the ocean while my father is on his knees next to the house, staring down one of the window wells to the basement.

I park the car and glance at Candice.

She grimaces. "I don't have a good feeling about this."

I can't resist. I laugh, hooking my hand around her neck to pull her close. Her lips are soft, sweet. When I pull away, her face is flushed.

"You have to stop doing that," she tells me.

"Doing what?"

"Kissing me."

I squeeze her nape, then nod toward the house. "Let's go see what's happening."

As we exit the car, Lottie and my mother turn toward us. Lottie waves, a big smile on her face. Both of them are flushed, excited. My mother speaks first. "Honey, it's perfect!"

I exchange a glance with Candice, then look at the peeling paint and moss-covered roof. "Perfect?"

"It's a steal. This property value is going to skyrocket, considering how fast Heart's Cove is growing. And there's nearly a mile of coastline!" My mother's kitten heels sink into the grass as she makes her way to me, her arm hooked into Lottie's. Lottie's cowboy boots, I note, are doing just fine in the soft grass.

I clear my throat. "Are you buying this place?"

"No, honey, you are!"

Candice turns to stone beside me, then swivels her head toward me.

I nod slowly. "Right. I'm buying this place?"

"It's a fixer-upper for sure, but it would be a great purchase." She turns to Lottie. "I'm sure he could put up a guest house for when Merv and I visit."

"Oh, good idea!" Lottie exclaims. "Maybe in that clearing by the ocean. I bet the sunsets are incredible. I'd come by every evening until you got sick of me."

The two women laugh. Oh dear.

"Um, what?" Candice says, eyes wide. "What's going on?"

"Well, it's settled." My father walks toward us, looking determined, brushing his palms together before hooking his thumbs into his belt loops. "The house is a wash. You'd have to look at the planning conditions for building a house here, but that pile of shit is a bulldozer job." He jerks his thumb over his shoulder at the house.

"Merv, language!" my mother chides.

Dad ignores her and carries on talking. "The land is worth the price, though. I'll go get the real estate agent."

I know the look on my mother and father's faces. They've made a decision, and it'll take careful maneuvering to get them to drop this particular topic.

"Dad, don't you think I should have a look around?"

Candice gapes at me. "You're actually considering this?"

"Honey, be nice," Lottie chides. "Oh, and Gina and I are bringing dessert to Fiona's tonight, so you can grab the wine. Get a few extra bottles, and maybe some beer for Merv. Merv, what do you drink?"

"Something hoppy. IPA," my father says, eyes on the roof. He turns to me. "Roof looks bad. Definitely a bulldozer job, but we could try to talk the owners down a few grand if we say we intend to fix up the existing house. Roof needs work, and I saw some water damage on the basement walls. Good negotiation points."

"Dad," I hedge, sensing Candice's panic beside me.

"You're coming to dinner?" she squeaks.

Lottie nods. "Of course. Oh, there's the agent. Yoo-hoo, Miss Chrome!" She waves to a woman exiting the house with a young couple. "We'd like a word."

The agent waves back, then turns to the couple and excuses herself before making her way to our group.

Candice stares at her, then at Lottie, then finally at me. She grabs my bicep. "I need to talk to you."

"We'll keep the agent busy," Lottie promises on a wink. "Go that way. The view of the ocean is divine." She points down a path running along the side of the house.

Candice tugs me in that direction and as soon as we get a short distance away, still stomping along the side of the house, she glares at me. "You can't possibly be considering this."

I jerk back. "Why not?"

"You can't move here!"

I sigh, hooking my arm around her shoulders. Candice doesn't fight me, because she never fights me when I pull her close. She melts into me, putting one hand around my waist and resting the other on my abs as we come to a stop behind the house.

"Blake, you can't move here. You're supposed to leave in two weeks and never come back."

I arch a brow, grinning. "Is that so?"

"It's the only way," she says with a decisive nod. "You can't stay. If you stay, it'll complicate things."

"Are you still telling yourself there's nothing between us?"

"There isn't!" she cries, her arms still wrapped around me.

I squeeze her close and feel her soften against me in that particular perfect way that lets me know Candice feels it. Us. What we could have together.

Staring into her eyes, I see real worry, so I run my hand up and down her spine. "It's taken me a long time to learn how to deal with my parents," I tell her, "and what I've learned is that direct confrontation almost never works. Redirection is the key."

Her shoulders drop, head tilting back. "So you're not going to buy this place?"

"Not today," I tell her.

She blinks, then her eyes narrow. "What is *up* with you?

We've known each other what, a few days? Don't you think you're coming on a bit strong?"

"I've had a long time to figure out what I want in life, Candice, and I'm starting to think I've wasted a lot of it. A few days seems like long enough to me."

"You're crazy. *Loco*." She shakes her head, but there's lightness in her eyes. "How many other women have you woken up beside in the morning, then decided you wanted to uproot your whole life to be with by the afternoon?"

"I haven't woken up next to anyone in seventeen years," I tell her, then watch her eyes widen.

Her breath comes out in a whoosh right before she frowns. "What?"

"Never mind," I say softly, pulling her into my side. My gaze drifts out to the glittering ocean extending out to the horizon, framed by tall cedar trees on both sides of the huge lawn. My brows lift.

That *is* a pretty spectacular view.

Candice is stiff, but as the seconds tick by, she softens beside me. Her head comes to rest on my shoulder as we look out at the water, birds trilling in the trees as a soft breeze washes over us.

"They're not wrong about the view," Candice finally admits.

I chuckle, then gently turn her to face me. I put my hands on either side of her face, bringing my lips to touch hers.

And I feel it.

The softening. The melting. The part of her that she gives to me every time I touch her.

But I pull away and stare in her hazel eyes. "If you don't

want me and my parents to come to dinner tonight, we won't come. I'll deal with them."

Candice meets my gaze for a beat, then her shoulders drop as she shakes her head. "They're welcome. Of course they're welcome. Looks like our mothers are best friends already." Her eyes snap back to mine. "You Hardings move fast."

I grin, then pull her close for another kiss. A deeper, hotter one that I hope tells her exactly what I'm feeling—that this is right. This is what I want.

She is what I want.

When I pull away, Candice's hand is curled into my shirt, gripping me close, her body swaying as if the slightest breeze would knock her over. She shakes her head with a sigh. "You know how to kiss, that's for sure."

"I was just thinking the same about you."

Her gaze climbs to mine, the sun illuminating every perfect plane of her face.

In the stillness, I feel the deepest core of me settle. I could fall for her, make her happy...if she let me.

WELL, after dinner, I find myself in Blake's cabana with his arms wrapped around me and his mouth on mine.

So much for sleeping in my own room.

After we left the open house, Blake and I stopped to grab some wine and beer and went straight to Fiona's. We were soon joined by our parents, Simone and Wes, and Jen along with Trina and the kids. A true family dinner.

Blake was wonderful. He sat next to me on the couch and slung his arm across the back of the sofa, a bottle of beer dangling between his fingertips. He answered questions about the movie business patiently, with humor, with charm, completely down to earth.

The whole time, his heat warmed my side and part of me softened at the feel of it.

Then we had dinner.

Fiona had made two gigantic lasagnas, Simone brought over

salad, my mother came through with three pies, and Jen showed up with a box of pastries from Four Cups. Wine flowed, and I found myself forgetting about my vow to keep my distance from Blake.

The truth is, it was nice to have him next to me. He poured my wine for me, made sure I had everything I needed for dinner, kept his arm across the back of my chair while I ate. It was natural. Comfortable.

No one batted an eye. Even Allie seemed to enjoy his presence.

That messy ball of guilt writhing in the pit of my stomach just...disappeared. At one point, Allie grabbed a corner piece of lasagna and grinned at me, and I knew from the look on her face that she was remembering the fact that she and Paul used to play-fight about who got the corner pieces with all the crispy bits. It wasn't unheard of for me to look at the leftovers and see that all four corners were gone, even if less than half the dish was eaten.

But tonight, the thought didn't make me seize up. I just thought of Paul, thought of the good times, and let my thoughts drift back to the present. I glanced at Blake who turned to meet my gaze, winked, and dropped his arm from the back of my chair to rest on my shoulder. His fingers played with the ends of my hair, and something settled deep inside me.

Maybe that's why now, when I'm in his room, I don't feel the pressure of what we're about to do bearing down on me. He was accepted into the family fold so easily, and he fit at that dinner table like he ate at it every week.

So I wrap my arms around his neck and deepen the kiss, only for Blake to pull away.

He stays close, his eyes staring into mine. "Your mind was somewhere else just then."

I narrow my eyes. "How do you do that?"

"What?"

"Read my thoughts."

A sexy smirk pulls at his lips, and his arms tighten around my waist. "What were you thinking about just now?"

Oh, what the hell. "I was thinking about how you fit in so well at dinner. And how I thought of Paul during dinner but I didn't feel guilty about being beside you."

His eyes grow serious as his head tilts slightly, a hand drawing slow, delicate shapes over my lower back. "Do you feel guilty about being with me?"

"Yes," I answer immediately.

"Candice..."

I shake my head. "You can tell me I have a right to continue my life until you're blue in the face, but it won't change the fact that I married Paul with the intention of spending my life with him, or whatever time we had together. We knew there was a chance he would die young, so I guess I just made a vow to myself to enjoy the years we had. I just told myself that if he went, at least I'd have the memory of him. It was enough."

Or at least, it was supposed to be enough. This gnawing feeling in the pit of my stomach that tells me it was never enough, *he* wasn't enough, makes me feel selfish and ungrateful.

Blake doesn't answer. His hand splays over my lower back as his other palm comes to rest on my neck, his thumb brushing my jaw. "No one thinks less of you for wanting to continue your life, Candice. You're not some Sicilian widow who needs to wear black for the rest of her days."

I close my eyes, hearing his words but not accepting them. My love for Paul was true. Even without sex, our marriage was *good*. He was such a great father to Allie. Supportive, loving, strong. He faced his health issues without complaint. We laughed. We laughed so much together. He was my best friend.

I'm supposed to honor that, and instead I'm in another man's arms.

"Candice," Blake says, his voice more gentle than I've ever heard it. I open my eyes to see his face equally as soft, yet intent. "Let go."

My heart seizes. I can't. I can't let go. Letting go of this guilt means letting go of Paul. If I let this grief fade away, I'm losing him all over again. What will be left of him if I don't have grief?

But Blake's hand tilts my head up, and my vision fills with him. He's all I see. His eyes, dark brown and intense. His soft lips. His hard, warm body pressed against mine.

Then he kisses me, and it's unlike anything else I've experienced. His arms hold me close, his hand stays pressed against my neck and jaw, but his kiss is so infinitely tender. So beautifully soft. The juxtaposition of his strength holding my body up with the softness of his touch makes something unwind inside me. I close my eyes and I thaw. My lips drop open and his tongue sweeps into my mouth, every sense full of him. Every part of me touching him. Every thought melting away until the sensations in my body are all I can focus on.

Then Blake takes me to bed. He lays me down softly,

covering my body with his. The weight of him mollifies something else inside me, and I find myself running my hands over his back, into his hair, kissing him back deeper and wetter and hotter than before.

He undresses me with deliberate carefulness, laying soft kisses on every inch of exposed skin, focusing his attention to my stomach, my navel, up to my breasts, my hardened nipples. He touches the stretch marks that streak across my stomach like tiger's stripes, letting his tongue drift over them in his fingers' wake. Lifting up to his knees, he reaches behind his head to tear his T-shirt off, then lays his body against mine. Chest to chest. Skin to skin.

Blake's mouth on mine, his hands tangled in my hair, I let out a soft moan.

Then with the same care, he removes our bottoms and comes back to me. Even as his length is hard and pinned between our bodies, Blake spends time kissing my neck, running his hand from my shoulder to my breast, down my side, all the way to my thigh. He pulls my knee up so I'm wrapping myself around him, the warmth of him permeating every pore.

Finally, propping himself up on his elbows, Blake reaches between us and positions himself between my legs.

I half expect him to drive himself home, to fuck me the way he did yesterday. I crave it. I want to feel so full of him that I can't think of anything else. I want to forget about my life, about my past, about my lonely future.

Instead, Blake brackets my face with his hands and lays a soft kiss on my lips. Inch by slow inch, he slides inside me, his eyes open and on me.

I drop my lips at the beautiful intrusion, the ecstasy, the perfect feel of him. "Blake," I whisper as his hips drive forward, my knees bent, allowing him to bury himself to the hilt. The last hard part of me dissolves, and I soften in his arms.

"There she is," he growls, staying exactly where he is, his lips brushing mine with every word, his body pressing mine into the bed. "There's my woman."

"Your—"

He cuts me off by dragging himself out of me and thrusting back in. Still tender, still slow, but oh-so-intense. I arch my back and wrap my arms around him, pulling my knees up, bucking my hips because all I want is more. More of this. More of him.

Torturing me, he doesn't speed up. He rounds his back to take my breast in his mouth, sucking deep as he drives into me, but we don't devolve into the kind of feral lovemaking of last night.

This is different. Intense. Beautiful.

Rocking inside me, spending time at my breasts, my neck, my lips, Blake makes love to me. I tangle my fingers in his hair, taking everything he gives.

And I let go.

I WAKE up with a hard body pressed at my back, my legs tangled in Blake's, his hand curved up over my body, cupping my breast. The alarm clock tells me I have a yoga class to teach in fifteen minutes. Shit.

Slowly, trying not to wake him, I disengage his hand from my chest.

He tightens, his lips finding my ear. "Morning, beautiful."

"I have to get up."

"No." He hooks his leg around my hips, pulling me close.

I let out a chuckle. "I have a yoga class to teach in a quarter of an hour. I need to shower, brush my teeth, and get dressed for it."

A soft kiss drops on my shoulder as Blake's leg falls off me.

I swing my legs off the bed then turn around to look at him.

Blake Harding is beautiful in the morning. Eyes sleepy, hair mussed, he hooks an arm behind his head and watches me through hooded lids. A soft smile plays at his lips, his arm reaching out to smooth over my hip. "How long does your class run?"

"An hour."

He glances at the clock. "I have time for an hour before I have to be on set."

My brows jump. "You do yoga?"

"Today, I do."

Warmth spreads through my chest at the thought of Blake pulling himself out of bed to practice yoga with me. Paul never once did a class with me. Not once. He was supportive, he was great, but he never tried.

Wait. Why am I comparing them? That's wrong. I shouldn't do that.

As my smile fades, Blake's hand tightens on my hip, as if he knows exactly what I'm feeling.

I meet his gaze and force my lips to curl up. "Wear comfortable clothing. Shorts and a tee will be fine."

He nods, his eyes drifting from my face to my bare back,

down to the legs hanging off the side of the bed. "Have I ever told you you're gorgeous?"

That warmth in my chest intensifies. I huff a laugh and shake my head, grabbing a bathrobe from the back of a nearby chair. "You've already slept with me, Blake. There's no need to smooth-talk me."

"It's not smooth-talking if it's true."

Oh. I bite my lip, which draws his gaze, then let it fall from my teeth. His eyes flick back to mine, more heated than they were a minute ago.

"I have to go get ready," I announce. "I'll be back here in ten minutes and we can walk over together."

"Yes ma'am." He grins when I shoot him a glare, then flips the covers off and gives me a view of his hard, beautiful body that makes me stumble over my feet.

Then he laughs at me, which makes me scowl harder.

"Ten minutes," I say, then stomp out of the room.

TWENTY-TWO
CANDICE

BLAKE DOES PRETTY WELL at yoga, but does draw a few looks and giggles from my other students. I guess that's to be expected when you have a movie star doing yoga on a Monday morning at the Heart's Cove Hotel. After class, he comes and drops a kiss on my lips—in front of everyone—then leaves for a day of filming.

I wander out to the lobby, where Margaret and Dorothy give me keys to their rental property and make plans to meet me there after I've gotten out of my yoga gear.

Unsurprisingly, my mother, Trina, and the kids meet me at the rental along with Margaret and Dorothy. My mom makes a few looks with wiggly eyebrows about dinner last night, which I brush off, then the seven of us walk through the rental.

It's a small two-bedroom, one-bathroom single-story home on a quiet street. It hasn't been renovated since the eighties, but the furniture is sturdy and everything is in working condition.

"Thank you, ladies," I tell the twins. They wave off my gratitude and show me how to work the finicky lock on the gate to the backyard, then leave me in the house with my mother, sister, and niece and nephew. The kids end up finding a ball that came from who-knows-where, and the three of us sit on an old patio set watching them play.

I glance at the house and let out a breath.

It's sinking in that my home burned down, that Allie and I will live here for at least a few months, and my weekend of sex and bliss with Blake is coming to an end.

"I'm flying back home to get the kids back to school," Trina says in the silence, "but we're coming back once the school year is done."

I stare at her. "Yeah? Fiona mentioned you were asking about schools in the area."

"We're both moving here," my mother announces.

I spin around to stare at her. "What about the house?" Mom still lives in my childhood home.

She waves a hand. "What's left for me in Seattle? Nothing. With you and Trina here, I'll be close to you and the grandkids. I can downsize."

Logically, I know my mother is getting older and she has no need for a four-bedroom house in the suburbs. It makes sense for her to move here. She knows Dorothy well, she fits in with the eclectic population of Heart's Cove, and if Trina moves here, she'll want to be close to us.

But selling our childhood home feels like yet another loss I'm not prepared for. I let out a sigh, and my mother reaches over to squeeze my hand. "Change can be good, Candice."

Her eyes hold mine until I blink and turn away, knowing exactly what she's referring to: Blake. Everyone has been supportive. My friends, the twins, my family—everyone wants me to pursue this romance.

It's me that's the problem. This messy, black guilt writhing inside me that won't let me move on. That won't let me even *want* to move on.

I just give my mother a tight smile. "I'm going to call the insurance company again, then go buy some cleaning supplies and basics. I want to have this place cleaned before Allie moves in tonight."

"I'll help," my mother says, and I know she won't hear any different.

So, we get to work.

I SUCCEED in not thinking about Blake all day while I'm cleaning and shopping for everything I need. My mother surprises me by bringing boxes of cleaning supplies, kitchen utensils, pots, pans, tea towels, sheets, towels...a thousand and one things I need. Some of them, like the sheets and towels, brand new, some of them obviously used.

"Spent the past couple of days putting this together. Everyone chipped in. Once it's unpacked, I'll make a trip to the grocery store to stock your fridge."

I stare at the boxes of gifts, the evidence of the community support in this town, and I burst into tears.

My mother wraps her arms around me and holds me close,

patting my back and cooing in my ear. "Let it out, honey. Let it out."

That makes my sobs come harder, because it reminds me of what Blake told me last night. When I finally pull myself together and straighten up, my mother wipes her thumbs over my cheeks and gives me a soft smile. "I'm glad I'll be living close to you, Candy Cane. I've missed enough of your and Allie's life already."

And in that moment, I'm glad she's decided to move, too.

THAT EVENING, I pack up the last of my few things in the hotel room into the duffel bag from the movie set and haul it out of my room just as Blake rounds the corner. His eyes soften when they see me, then flick to the bag and his jaw hardens. "Moving?"

I nod. "The rental's ready for us."

"That's good," he says, not sounding like he thinks it's good at all.

This is my chance. I can walk away from him and not look back. I can keep things casual, just like I vowed. I can relegate this relationship to be sex only, and forget about the intensity, the beauty of what happened between us last night. But when I open my mouth to say that, something else comes out instead. "Do you want to join Allie and me for dinner tonight?"

The tension in his jaw melts away, and he gives me a warm smile. "Yeah. I'd like that."

"We're ordering pizza and probably eating it in front of a movie since we have no dining room table. That's probably not

what you had in mind when you asked me out to dinner, but..."
I shrug.

Blake chuckles, then crosses the distance between us and lays a soft kiss on my lips. "Sounds perfect. Give me the address and I'll meet you there. I've just got to wash off my day first."

I nod, heart thundering, and give him the address. Then I head to Fiona's, pick up my daughter, and take her to our new home.

When we walk inside, I expect her to give me lip about the old decor or the fact that this place is far smaller than our old house. But she just drops her bag by the door and goes exploring, then comes back with a smile on her face. "There's a jacuzzi in the bathroom!"

I grin. "And here I was worried you wouldn't be happy to live here."

"A jacuzzi is *awesome*! Where's the pizza?"

Shaking my head, I grab my phone to make the order. I don't know why I was worried. All Allie cares about is makeup, boys, track and field tryouts, school, and Clancy. And jacuzzis, apparently.

Then I freeze. "Do you mind if Blake joins us for dinner, honey?"

She shrugs, already opening the refrigerator to check whether it's stocked. She grabs a cheese stick from the pack my mother bought in her massive grocery run today and turns to look at me, shrugging. "That's fine. Is he your boyfriend?"

"No," I answer, panic gripping my chest. What was I *thinking* inviting him over? Allie isn't ready for that! Last time I went on a date she started crying. "He's..."

"Mom, it's okay." Her lips curl. "I like him. Plus, everyone at school is *totally* jealous that you're dating a movie star."

"I'm not dating—"

The doorbell sounds, and Allie turns toward it. "I'll get it!" She hops down the tiled hallway and a few seconds later I hear a chirpy, "Hi Blake!"

The panic gripping my chest eases ever so slowly, second by second, until I see Blake in the mouth of the hallway with a bottle of wine in one hand and a six-pack of beer in the other. "Beer goes with pizza, but I've never seen you drink it, so I thought I'd be safe and grab a bottle." He lifts it up. "It's the one you liked from dinner last night."

He remembered. Not only that, but he also *noticed*.

Cheeks warming, I nod. "Thanks, Blake." I lift the hand where I'm holding my cell phone. "I'm just about to make the order. You have any requests for pizza?"

"No olives," he replies automatically.

"*Thank you!*" Allie shouts, then pokes her head into the kitchen to give Blake a high-five. "Two against one, Mom."

I roll my eyes only to see her flash her beautiful, crooked grin at Blake, and another piece of my heart clicks into place.

Maybe this could work...

If Blake weren't leaving in two weeks.

And if I were able to move on.

THE DAYS that follow are some of the best days of my life. Blake and I fall into a routine. He either has dinner with Allie and me, or we have dinner with our new-best-friends parents, or, if Blake is filming late on set, I'll meet him at the hotel for a nightcap.

I do enjoy those nightcaps.

Over the course of those days, I rediscover my body. Whether we're alone in his room—or twice, mine, when Allie is at school and Blake has stolen away from set—or just casually walking hand-in-hand, I find that his touch awakens something inside me I hadn't realized I was missing.

I *feel* my body. Blake sweeps his hand over my skin, and goosebumps rise in the wake. He kisses my lips, my neck, my collarbone, and my attention travels with his mouth. He spends time with his tongue between my legs, and I sink into the mattress with my fingers tangled in his hair, worried about nothing and no one but the way he worships my body.

It's...heaven.

Over the course of the week the insurance payout comes through, Allie and I settle in to our rental place, and I work out a formal rental agreement with the twins. Allie looks no worse for wear, more concerned about her sprinting times than the loss of her childhood home. The part of me that should have been devastated by the fire has just...moved on.

And I float through my days, teaching yoga, working the café, dealing with insurance and fire and all the thousand other things that make up my days...and I always end up in Blake's arms.

Guilt and grief fade away. When I think of Paul it doesn't sting, and I wonder why I ever felt like I couldn't love the memory of him *and* love someone else at the same time. My affection for Blake doesn't dim the love I had for Paul. They can both exist side-by-side in my heart, if I let them.

Blake and I don't talk about what will happen after. The Saturday night one week after Simone and Wes's wedding, when Allie is sleeping over at Clancy's, I find myself tangled up in bed with him, sated and sleepy, loving the way his fingers trail over my back.

"Why did you tell me you hadn't had a girlfriend in a long time?" I ask, eyes closed as I enjoy his touch. "You seem to have a healthy love life."

"I wouldn't call those flings a love life," he replies, his lips near my temple. With my head on his chest and my arm across his abs, I listen to his heartbeat, his voice rumbling against my ear. "Sex life, maybe. Love life? No."

I nod, lulled by the movement of his hand on my back. He slides his palm up and into my hair, turning his head to kiss my temple. Tender—he's so tender with me. "I've been married twice."

"I know. I googled you." I turn my head to grin at him, then relax back to my position on his chest.

Blake's chuckle vibrates through me, drawing another smile from me. "My first wife's name was Mikaela. Mickey. She was beautiful. One of those people that lights up a room. Wherever she'd go, all eyes would turn to her. I fell in love with her within minutes, and I fell hard. Asked her to marry me when we were both nineteen."

We're quiet for a while, and I don't push him. That didn't happen with me and Paul. I actually wasn't interested in him at all, but he pursued me and charmed me and made me laugh in his gentle, quiet way, and I slowly but surely fell in love with him. Love at first sight never happened to me. Well, not until...

No, I'm not thinking about that. Whatever's happening between me and Blake isn't love. I can still lie to myself and say it's just sex, even though I'm tangled up in his arms with no desire to leave.

After a pause, Blake continues. "Me and Mickey... I thought it was it for me. I was happy. I loved her. I wanted her to have my kids. But two years later, she sat me down and told me she was attracted to women."

I stiffen, then turn to stare at Blake.

He grins. "That didn't come up in your Google search?"

I shake my head, then feel the pressure of his hand on the back of my neck asking me to lie back down on his chest. I do, because lying on top of him is the most comfortable place I've ever been.

Chuckling, Blake brushes his lips across my forehead. "It was before I started acting, so it's more of a footnote on my Wikipedia page. She's not in show business, never was. Only diehard fans and intrepid journalists ever dig that little piece of my past up."

"Are you still in touch with her?"

"Not really," he answers honestly. "I was mad at her for a long time. I felt lied to, betrayed. I felt like she'd promised me a life together then pulled the rug out from under me. But I couldn't really express those things the way I wanted to because I was afraid of being called homophobic. I didn't care that she was into women, but I cared that she hadn't been honest with me. I cared that I'd planned for a future with her and it just crumbled to nothing."

"I'm sorry," I answer quietly.

"Nothing to be sorry about. I was a kid. Twenty-one. What would I know? Then I spent the next twenty, nearly thirty years fucking around."

There's a subtext to those words. He's saying, *I spent thirty years fucking around...until I met you.*

Ignoring that particular grenade, I move on. "I thought you married again."

"Mm," Blake answers. "In my thirties. It was destined to fail. I was still mad about Mickey, and my ex-wife just saw me as a celebrity, someone to give her the lifestyle she wanted. That marriage crashed and burned when I found out she hadn't been faithful to me for a single minute of our relationship."

"Oh, Blake." I run my hands over his stomach, his chest, lifting my head to kiss his pectoral muscle before meeting his gaze. "You make me feel lucky to have had a good marriage."

His smile is tinged with sadness. "You are lucky, Candice. That's why it's so hard to see you beating yourself up whenever you catch yourself feeling good."

"I feel good now and I'm not beating myself up," I tell him, surprised to realize it's the truth.

His smile is soft, tender, and it warms something deep inside me that I hadn't realized was cold. Then he brings his lips to mine, rolls us over so he's on top, and shows me once again how much he appreciates my body.

Then I push Blake to his back and show him how much I appreciate his.

THE NEXT DAY, after the morning rush at Four Cups, Blake accompanies me back home and we walk inside to find Allie with her head stuck in the refrigerator.

She looks up at the two of us. "Hey. We're out of milk."

"I'll grab some," I say, angling for the shoes I'd just removed.

"I can go." Blake brushes his lips against mine. "I'll be back in ten."

Before I can protest, he's gone. I turn to see Allie staring at me with an arched eyebrow.

"Getting pretty serious, huh?"

I gulp. I've handled this all wrong. Allie shouldn't be seeing me date a man I met a week and a half ago. She shouldn't be meeting *anyone* I date until I'm sure it's serious. The last thing I want is a revolving door of men coming in and out of her life.

But before panic and guilt can set it, Allie walks up to me, wraps me in a hug, and kisses my cheek. "I like him," she announces, then saunters out of the kitchen and into her bedroom.

I stand there, dazed, then shake off my stupor and start tidying up until Blake gets back. He arrives with Gina, Merv, and my mother in tow, and an expression on his face that says, *Sorry, I tried to stop them.*

My shoulders relax, my lips curl into a smile, and I take the bag of groceries from him and ask our new guests if they want something to drink.

We spend that Sunday eating and laughing and talking...as a family. Even after Blake leaves to go to set, his parents stay for dinner, and I find myself enjoying their company.

A thought still slithers at the back of my mind, though...

What happens when Blake is done filming? What happens when he leaves?

TWENTY-FOUR
CANDICE

MORE PERFECT DAYS PASS. Every minute that I spend with Blake, he stitches my heart back together. Gentle touches, tender words, soft looks...I wasn't prepared to feel this way.

At Four Cups, we keep up with the catering for the movie with no hiccups. Jen and Fallon do a fantastic job. I couldn't be more proud. On Friday, two weeks and one day after my kiss with Blake, we fulfill our last order for the set and send Fiona and Simone to drop it off.

I find Jen in the kitchen wiping down her workstation. Allie and Clancy glance over from the sink, then turn back to the dishes. In my good mood, I call out to them and tell them that when they're done, they're relieved of permanent dishwashing duty. Allie pumps her fist in the air as Clancy does a little dance, and I can't help but laugh.

Then I wrap my arms around Jen and give her a squeeze. "Love you."

Jen tilts her head, a smile playing over her lips, her arms stiff at her sides. "You know I'm not a hugger."

"But I am."

Relenting, Jen wraps her arms around my waist and gives me a few cursory pats on the back.

Knowing that's all I'll get from her, I pull back. "You did an amazing job with the catering contract, Jen. And you've done an amazing job keeping up with the café demand, too. Did you see how fast we sold out of your flourless brownies? They should definitely be a regular offering."

Jen waves a hand, ever uncomfortable with compliments. "It's no big deal."

Leaning a hip on the stainless steel counter, I cross my arms. "Are you going to go back to Guillaume and the restaurant after this?"

As Jen opens her mouth to speak, the back door opens and Fallon comes through wheeling a dolly stacked high with boxes of groceries. He winks at the two of us, then whistles as he starts putting the food away.

Jen turns to me. "No, I was thinking I'd stay here full-time. We could expand the pastry offerings, even bake custom cakes. I've been wanting to ask Simone about doing a website for me."

My chest warms, and I can't stop myself from hugging Jen again.

She stands there and takes it, then gives me a flat look when I pull away. "Got it all out of your system?"

I ignore her. "That sounds amazing, Jen. I love it."

"I know a woman who works in publishing," Fallon says from the other side of the kitchen. "An old friend. I could speak to her about a recipe book. I'm not saying she'll be interested, but at least it would start a conversation."

Jen's jaw goes slack. She stares at Fallon for a beat, then launches herself across the kitchen and throws her arms around his neck. He laughs, his beard brushing her shoulder as he ducks his head toward her, swinging her around in a circle as she hangs on tight.

Guess she is a hugger after all, under the right circumstances.

Like, for example, if a very attractive man just offered to help her fulfill a lifelong dream.

Grinning, I slink out of the kitchen and start bussing tables, only to look up when the door opens. Blake pauses in the doorway, his broad, beautiful shoulders tapering down to a trim waist. With the sun shining behind him, it takes me a moment to snap out of my admiring of his shape to look at his grinning face.

"Where's Allie?" he asks.

"Here!" Allie appears behind me.

Blake jerks his chin at her, then returns his eyes to me. "I rented a yacht for the afternoon. You two want to join me for a few hours on the water? Dinner, sunset, the works?"

"Um, *yes!*" Allie cries. "Can Clancy come?"

"Sure." Blake shrugs.

The two girls squeal, and I barely have time to hold up a hand. "What about Fiona? Grant? Call your parents and ask them if it's okay. And hold on, what's this yacht? Where are we going? How long?"

"Baby," Blake says, eyes soft as he reaches for me. His hands slide over my arms and tug me close, his mouth meeting mine for a quick, soft kiss. "We just wrapped up on set, and I have a day and a half before I have to be in L.A. for another project. I want to spend time with you and Allie."

My heart simultaneously melts and spasms. He's so flippin' sweet, and also...he's *leaving*.

"Let me take you out on a boat. I've got food planned, champagne, sunset... I want to spoil you."

Well, I can't say no to *that*, can I?

It takes Allie and me an hour and a half to close up the café, go home, get changed, and meet Blake at the hotel. He grins when I patently refuse to give him the car keys, then directs us to a marina on the coast, where a massive, luxurious yacht is waiting for us.

Oh, my.

The gleaming white hull looms over us, a walkway stretched out to the dock. Three crew members are busy on board, slinging ropes and equipment around. A man in a captain's hat descends the walkway and shakes Blake's hand. "Should be a beautiful evening. Glad to have you on board."

Allie and Clancy waste no time. They run up the walkway and start exploring the decks, then disappear to the interior cabins.

Blake smiles at me and intertwines his fingers in mine. "I haven't had a chance to spoil you the way I want to, Candice. This is my way of showing you how much I've loved the past couple of weeks."

Another spasm in my chest. I gulp, nodding, and let him lead me on board.

. . .

THE CAPTAIN IS RIGHT. The evening is spectacular, with an unforgettable sunset. Pinks, oranges, tangerines bleed across the sky as a few fluffy clouds set the scene. The low sun glitters over the water like a thousand twinkling lights. Sitting on the upper deck on a long bench, a thick blanket draped over my legs and a flute of champagne in my hand, I watch the beauty before me and forget about everything else.

Dinner was wonderful. A four-course extravaganza served to us on fine china, the water lapping at the sides of the yacht all around.

I sigh, taking a sip of champagne, and lean my head against Blake. He has his arm around my shoulders, his body warm at my side.

I'm...happy.

I'm thinking of nothing but the warmth of Blake's body, the comfort of his arm around me, and the serenity of the scene. It's like Simone said—I'm totally present, totally in the moment, totally at peace.

Then I hear Allie yell excitedly and I straighten up, glancing down at the deck below us to see her hanging over the railing at the back of the boat, Clancy by her side. They're watching something in the distance—

"Mom! Beluga whales!"

I follow Allie's finger to see half a dozen white humps moving through the water, getting closer. Standing, I put my champagne down in a cup holder and make my way down the steep steps, Blake at my back, and join the girls at the bow of the ship.

Allie cries out excitedly as the captain cuts the motor, and the whales approach. "I've never seen them so close," she whispers reverently. She turns to Clancy. "Those are belugas. They're in the same family as narwhals."

"They have such a big bump on their heads," Clancy says, leaning over the rail.

"It's called a melon," Allie replies, beaming. "It's used for communication and echolocation." Allie hooks her arm through mine, her whole body vibrating with excitement.

I tear my gaze from the graceful dips and curves of the whales to watch my daughter, my whole body growing soft when I see the rapt expression on her face. She doesn't look nearly seventeen right now. She looks like the little girl that stole my heart at first sight.

She's always loved whales. Actually, "loved" is too small a word. She was *obsessed.* She and Paul used to—

Blake slides his arm across my shoulders, and suddenly it feels wrong. My mouth goes dry and I freeze, my daughter on one side of me and a man who isn't Paul on the other.

We were supposed to do this with Paul. He and Allie talked about whale watching, but he never got around to organizing it. I was always the one to organize events and appointments and activities, but the whales were their thing.

And it never happened.

Until now... Now, with a man who isn't Paul. On a yacht that we could never have afforded, with a sunset I shouldn't be enjoying.

I've betrayed my husband's memory. I've moved on in the blink of an eye, falling into a movie star's arms like it was nothing.

And now Allie will forever associate these beluga whales with Blake, not Paul.

It's wrong. Wrong, wrong, wrong.

This shouldn't be happening. Everything is *wrong*.

Pulling away from the two of them, I try to extricate myself from Blake's arms, but his hand tightens on my shoulder.

"Hey," he says gently. "What's wrong? Are you seasick?"

The warmth and worry in his gaze spears through me, another sign that this isn't supposed to happen. No other man should be feeling warm and worried for me. No other man should be sharing my bed. I'm not supposed to move on! I'm supposed to be like my mother. Dedicated. Devoted. Chaste.

"Mom?" Allie says, her fine blond brows pulling together. "Are you okay?"

Gulping back my panic, I nod. "Seasick," I force through stiff lips. "I'll go sit down up there, get some air." I point to the upper deck. Blake makes a move to follow me, but I shake my head. "Stay with the girls."

All three of them are staring at me, and all I can do is turn my back and hustle away, back up the steps and onto the seat where I was a moment before.

I hear Blake speaking to Allie—a familiar, comfortable tone to his question about belugas that Allie responds to with muted enthusiasm—and my heart turns to a hard stone in my chest.

This isn't right. It isn't supposed to happen this way. I'm not supposed to move on. I'm not supposed to take my daughter whale watching with anyone other than Paul. I'm not supposed to have sex with anyone else, or fall in love ever again.

It's wrong. *I'm* wrong. Everything is wrong.

As I sit on the seat on the upper deck, a blanket wrapped tight around my body, a shiver of guilt rakes through my body, freezing out all the warmth Blake had so carefully tended.

IT DOESN'T TAKE a genius to figure out that something happened with Candice. Somewhere between sunset and belugas, she changed. She won't look me in the eye, and when I try to put my arm around her when I sit down next to her, she flinches.

That hurts.

"You okay?" I ask quietly, my eyes on the horizon. The sun is just an orange sliver now, hanging low on the edge of the world.

Candice nods. "Fine."

I grit my teeth at the four-letter word.

Allie and Clancy glance up at us, but they don't seem too worried. The two girls giggle, then walk down along the side of the yacht toward the interior cabins. We sit in silence, Candice stiff beside me, my hand making slow circles over her shoulder as I try to get her to soften.

She's locked herself in her body, pushed me away, and I don't like it. I need to fix it, but I don't know what needs fixing. She's shutting me out.

When the captain pulls into the dock, Candice just stands and walks away from me. She doesn't protest when I take the keys and start driving, and we head to town to drop Clancy off. When we pull up in front of the big farmhouse on the edge of Heart's Cove, Clancy climbs out as Candice turns to her daughter in the back seat.

"You mind going inside with Clancy, honey? I'll take Blake back to the hotel and come back in an hour to pick you up."

Allie nods and jogs after her friend, the two of them beaming as they disappear into the house.

"Not even a goodbye," I note, then snort. "Teenagers."

Candice gives me a tight smile, and I start driving. With every second that passes, my dread creeps up until I'm gripping the steering wheel with a white-knuckled squeeze. I suck in a breath and hold it inside my lungs as if I can stop time on an exhale. As if I can stop Candice's mind from freezing me out.

We pull into the Heart's Cove Hotel parking lot and I park the car, pull the hand brake, and turn to look at Candice.

She's white as a sheet, staring out the windshield, seeing nothing.

"Talk to me," I say in a low voice.

Candice takes a deep breath and meets my gaze. Nothing—there's nothing in her eyes. None of the warmth, the softness, the affection that was there before. Pain throbs across my chest, but I force myself to hold her cold gaze.

"Blake," she starts, and the tone of her voice makes my blood turn sluggish. Candice gulps. "I can't do this."

"Do what?" I grit out.

"Us." She blinks, looks away.

"Candice—"

"Look, you'll be going home soon. Let's just leave it at that."

My body goes still. I want to scream. I want to rage. I want to shake her and tell her that I can't just *leave it at that*. Leave it at what? At a point where I see a future with this woman? At a point where for the first time in decades, I feel like there's more to life than I thought? A point where I actually might heal from what happened before?

At a point where "home" isn't my mansion in Southern California; home is with her. Home is here, in Heart's Cove.

Instead, I pull a breath in through my nose and let it out through my mouth. "I'll cancel my commitments for the next while. I'll stay."

"No!"

I frown. "No?"

"This was supposed to be just sex, Blake." Candice meets my eyes again, her voice hard. She grips the edge of the door, her pulse fluttering in her throat.

My jaw clenches hard enough to hurt. "It was never just sex."

"It was."

"Stop lying!" It comes out louder than I wanted it to, so I grip the steering wheel and squeeze my eyes shut. Inhaling hard, I force my voice to settle. My lungs are heavy, hard as iron. I try to breathe in, but the air gets stuck, chokes me. I can't stop this from happening. I can't keep her from pushing me away. Still, I try. "You know from the moment we kissed on set, it was more than sex, Candice."

"I have nothing to give you."

"You...what?" I turn to stare at her again. "You think you can't offer me anything? Is this because I'm an actor?"

"What?" She frowns. "No. It's because you think I can be a partner to you, when I can't. When my husband died, a part of me went with him. That's the way it's going to be."

"That's the way you're *choosing* to be, Candice."

"Don't you dare tell me how to grieve," she snaps, her eyes flaring. A part of me is relieved to see something, anything in her gaze.

"I'm trying to tell you how to *heal*, Candice."

"Oh, and I guess you're the one who's going to save me? Give me a break, Blake. You'll leave Heart's Cove and remember how your life was a few weeks ago. You'll have beautiful women crawling all over you, and you'll laugh at what you thought was happening here."

"Is that what's going through your head? You think I'm not serious?"

"I think you're being a *fool!*" Candice heaves in a breath, then squeezes her eyes shut. "We had sex. Lots of it. We got too close. You're leaving. It's for the best."

"The first part of that is true. The rest is total bullshit."

Candice's jaw clenches.

Silence stretches.

I'm losing her. The first woman in seventeen years—maybe even since Mickey—to pierce the hard shell around my heart is pushing me away, and why? For what? Because she thinks she doesn't deserve to love again?

It feels like I'm scrabbling on the edge of a cliff, my legs dangling in the void. My fingernails are cracked and bloody as I hang on, trying to make her understand, make her see—

"I'm falling in love with you, Candice." My voice is quiet, soft.

She jerks, then shakes her head. "You've known me a couple of weeks."

"So?"

"So, you don't love me. You don't *know* me!"

"But I know my heart."

Her breath catches, hands gripping the sides of her seat.

I watch her for a beat, then turn to look out the windshield. Agnes exits the bookstore, locking up behind her. She throws a withering glance in the direction of the hotel before walking away. An old truck rolls by on Cove Boulevard, and pressure builds inside my chest.

This place feels like home. It feels like the first place I've been able to lay my head and *rest*—truly rest—in years. But as I sit in Candice's car, feeling the chasm between us rip wider, I wonder if I'll have to mourn the loss of this place, too. The loss of somewhere I could have called home. The loss of a woman I could have called mine.

I just want to know why. "What happened today?"

Candice shakes her head, teeth gritted.

"Candice."

She sucks in a breath and lets it out, eyes shut.

"Candice, tell me. What happened on the yacht?"

"What happened was that I realized I was replacing him with you!" Candice cries, hands slamming onto the dash, fingers gripping the hard plastic. Her breath grows ragged, eyes wide and unseeing. "Paul was supposed to take us out whale watching. Allie was supposed to do it with *him*. But he didn't, and she had that experience with a man who isn't her father. A man I stupidly, stupidly brought into her life after knowing him a couple of days. A man who's leaving, who will forget about us the moment he leaves. A man *who isn't Paul*."

Her voice is shredded, painful. I try to reach out to her, to pull her into my arms, but she shies away. Every time I try to get close, Candice flinches, jerks, shifts so we don't touch.

I can't take it.

I can't take this, her freezing me out, pushing me away. It feels like my heart is being slowly but surely shredded after having a shining glimpse of hope for something better.

With a shuddering breath, Candice straightens. She turns to look at me as she squares her shoulders, grim determination in her gaze. "This was a mistake. It isn't what I want. I don't want you to stay, and I don't want to pursue anything with you. I'm releasing you of any commitments, encouraging you to...to do what you were doing before. Date all the models and actresses you want, Blake. It's better that way. Enjoy your life."

She blinks at me, then opens her car door and circles around the back of the car to open mine. Then she stands by the driver's side and stares sightlessly at the hotel looming in front of us as I get out.

I stand in front of her and wait until her eyes flick to mine.

For a brief, fleeting moment, I see the depth of her pain. The broken parts of her swirling in her gaze.

She slams down her shields, and all I get is blank, frigid nothing.

God, it hurts. I want to wrap her in my warmth and make her melt. I want to tear those monsters from her eyes and rip them apart with my hands.

I want to make her see that she *deserves* more. Just because she's lost someone she loved doesn't mean she's lost the *capacity* to love.

But the woman who melted for me is gone. And that makes me angry.

Once again, I'm caught by my own fool ideas. I saw her and jumped, and now the ground is rushing up to meet me. How *stupid* of me to think that this would work.

I've been through this before. I got stung when I was twenty-one years old, and I learned that people, no matter how close you feel to them, have their own shit going on in their heads. I was such a fucking fool to think that simply because I feel this connection, this potential between us, it means Candice feels it too. I might as well be a naive nineteen-year-old again for thinking this could work.

She doesn't want me. She told me flat out that all she needed was sex, and I was all too happy to oblige. I was blinded by whatever piece of me is missing, thinking she would slot into it. Thinking she was the one.

I've known her two weeks. How dumb can I be?

No, let me rephrase that: How dumb can I be, *again?*

The woman doesn't want me. She has her own demons, and me waltzing into her life isn't going to fix them.

I can't trust anyone but myself. I was right to block myself off from relationships. I was right to chase tail and kick women out of my bed before sunup.

The alternative is this. Feeling my chest get shredded to ribbons over a woman who never wanted me in the first place. A woman who might not even have the capacity to love me the way I want to be loved.

Maybe no one does.

Maybe I've been a fool to hold out whatever wisp of hope survived Mickey. Survived the hell of my second marriage. Survived the empty, hollow nothingness of what came after.

Maybe this is it. This is life. You just stumble along, meet people, fuck people, grab whatever scrap of comfort you can take from the encounter, then move on.

But Candice's eyes focus on me, and for the briefest of moments, I see something that looks a lot like regret. Then, as quickly as it appeared, it's gone.

She looks away from me, jaw tight, and my own heart crumbles to ash behind my ribcage. So, I let out a slow breath and nod. "Be well, Candice."

Then I turn around and head to my room to pack up and leave.

TWENTY-SIX
JEN

CANDICE DOESN'T LOOK RIGHT when she walks up to the library above the Four Cups Café. Her eyes—

They're dead.

Seeing the concern on my face, she makes a valiant effort to force her lips into a smile, but it fades almost as quickly as it appears, then she slumps down onto the armchair next to mine.

"Well, it's over," she says.

"What's over?" I ask slowly, lifting my foot to rest it on the edge of the coffee table.

Candice opens her mouth then closes it again. "The catering contract. We did it." Her eyes shift to meet mine. "You did it. You and Fallon."

It doesn't sound like she was talking about the catering contract, but I decide not to push it. "We all did it together."

Candice nods, her eyes going unfocused again.

I clear my throat. "Where's Allie?"

"Just dropped her off at home. Fiona and Simone?"

"On their way."

We organized this meeting earlier in the week to go over the movie catering contract. What worked, what didn't, what we could do differently, if catering is something we want to pursue. Business talk.

But the way Candice looks, I can tell her mind isn't on the café.

"How was the yacht?"

She shakes her head. "I shouldn't have gone. Shouldn't have done anything with Blake. Shouldn't even have stayed at the hotel for those few days."

"Your house burned down."

Candice waves a hand. "An air mattress at Fiona's would have been a better idea, even if my back wouldn't agree."

The door opens, and Simone's fiery-red hair pokes through. "What's this? I hear something that sounds a lot like wallowing."

Candice leans her head back on the chair as Simone and Fiona come in, taking their seats across from us. She takes a deep breath. "I wanted to say how grateful I am for the three of you. The catering contract wasn't easy, but we did it, and—"

"Hold up," Simone says, lifting a palm. "You look like someone just ran over your new puppy, and you want me to believe we're here to talk about the catering contract? Old news! We did it. It was great. We'll get more of them. Done. Next." She leans forward. "I want to know why you look like someone just punched you in the throat."

Candice closes her eyes. "I'm fine."

"Honey," Fiona says gently, "you don't look fine. Did something happen with Blake?"

Candice winces. I've known her for a long time, and I've never seen her do that. Like her whole body was jolted with pain at the mere sound of Blake's name. Even when Paul died, she took the brunt of her grief on her shoulders and carried her family through it.

She didn't wince when someone mentioned his name.

"He's leaving," Candice finally says. "It's for the best."

Fiona, Simone, and I exchange glances. It's Fiona who speaks. "That's surprising. He seemed to really like it here. And his parents are talking about retiring here with Lottie."

Candice groans, throwing her hand over her face. "Please, don't remind me about my mother's new best friend. Gina is great and all, but she had the wrong idea about her son and me. You all did."

Simone opens her mouth to speak, but I lift a hand and shake my head. She settles back.

Candice lets out a long sigh, straightens up, and takes a deep breath. "It's better this way. I'm not ready for anything serious." She gives Simone a weak smile. "A box of vibrators would have been a better option."

Simone smiles back, but says nothing.

Sensing Candice needs time with her thoughts, I nod to Fiona. "Did you bring the Fringe Fest sales estimates? We'll need to place orders now if we want to have everything delivered on time."

The Fringe Fest happens every year in Heart's Cove during the first week of June and draws huge crowds. Local artisans display their wares, Candice holds huge yoga seminars and free classes, and the town council puts on free concerts every evening. Lots of people in Heart's Cove means lots of coffees and just as many pastries. We were overrun last year, so we need to be ready.

Fiona nods, and the four of us go over a few details. Candice sits quietly, stewing in her own thoughts, and doesn't stir until we break up the meeting for the evening.

I put a hand on her shoulder as I stand up to leave. "You want me to drive you home?"

She shakes her head. "I'll walk. The fresh air will do me good."

Nodding, I squeeze her shoulder and head downstairs.

Fallon is waiting for me in the Four Cups kitchen. His face relaxes into a smile when I enter, and he gives the counter one last wipe before throwing the towel into the laundry bin. Then he crosses the distance between us and wraps me in his big, beautiful arms.

I wrap myself around him, squeezing tight. I've never enjoyed hugs, but being in his arms feels like home.

He smooths his hand over my hair in soft, gentle movements. "What's got you looking so worried, Jen?"

"Candice."

He makes a low, rumbly noise, then nudges my chin up. His lips are soft, warm, perfect when he touches them to mine.

We haven't done much more than kiss since that first night. I know it's because of me. I'm the one who pulls back, who retreats. It's not that I don't want to take it further, it's just... I don't even know! I'm afraid things will change and this feeling will end. He'll realize that I'm just a dork and not some mysterious, intriguing woman, and he'll move on. I don't want him to move on. I want him to kiss me like this every day for the rest of my life.

When I end the kiss, Fallon's lips curl into a smile. "Will you let me take you home?"

"I drove."

"Mm." He nudges his nose with mine. "Will you text me when you get home safe, then?"

I frown. "Fallon, we live in Heart's Cove. Why would you be worried about me getting home safe?"

"Humor me."

"Seems illogical."

"What if I just want you to have an excuse to text me later?"

Warmth spreads through my chest. No one has ever said something like that to me before. I've dated, obviously, but the men I've been with haven't been so clear about their feelings for me. It was always up to me to guess, to wonder, to overthink.

Fallon makes it easy.

Before I can answer, the bell above the café door jingles.

"We're closed!" Fallon calls out, his eyes on my lips.

"Fallon Richter? Is that you?" a female voice calls out.

Fallon goes solid against me.

I frown, turning my head to glance through the doorway to the front of house, then I freeze, too.

The woman is beautiful. More than beautiful. She looks like she just walked off an advertisement for luxury perfume and into the Four Cups Café. Dressed in a tight, perfectly tailored white dress, with sky-high nude heels and long hair falling in soft curls, she has a navy suit jacket draped over her shoulders like a cape.

When she sees us, shock flits over her face.

Fallon steps away from me, and I feel that distance in every part of my body.

I shuffle to the side, glancing between them.

"Amanda," he says, voice tight.

She walks—no, *glides*—toward us, slim body swaying with every step, and pauses in the doorway leading to the kitchen. Flicking her eyes to me for a brief moment, she then turns to face Fallon. "This place is cute."

It doesn't sound like a compliment. I bristle.

Fallon combs his fingers through his short beard, throat bobbing as he swallows. "What are you doing here?"

"You invited me." Her laugh is delicate, feminine. "The taxi driver left my bags just inside the door"—she points over her shoulder at the entrance to the café, where two large Louis Vuitton cases rest on the floor—"so I'm hoping you have a car to bring them to your place."

Fallon frowns, eyes darting to me. "My place?"

"Isn't that what you said in your email? That you had more than enough room?" She tilts her head coyly, putting a hand on her slim hip. "Are you telling me you forgot that you contacted me out of the blue five years after we broke up, said you missed me and wanted to talk, and when I asked where you were, you told me to come see you in Heart's Cove?"

"I didn't mean—"

"Who's this?" She turns to me, bright eyes assessing.

"I'm Jen." I glance at my bare wrist. "Oh, look at the time. I better go. Bye!"

"Jen, wait!" Fallon finally moves from his frozen position, catching up to me in three long steps. "Wait, this isn't what you—"

"I'm tired," I interrupt, eyes on the wall over his shoulder. "I'll see you in the morning."

He puts his hands on my arms and I stand stock still, eyes on the wall. His voice is like silk over my skin. "Jen, look at me. Please."

"I'll see you in the morning," I repeat. "Enjoy your night." I pull my arms away from his grasp, spin on my heels, and walk out the back door. Once outside, I let out a long breath, eyes adjusting to the darkness as I clasp my hands on top of my head.

I want to laugh and cry and rage. He kissed me and I believed him when he said he liked me. I thought he was being clear with his intentions because I was special. Meanwhile, he was inviting other women to stay with him?

I should stick to awkward men with clammy hands I meet on the internet.

Rubbing my hands over my arms, I hunch my shoulders and walk down the alley. My car's parked out front, so I have to take the long way around to avoid going through the café again. When I get to my car, I glance at the café and see two shapes inside, standing close. Very close.

Amanda's hand is on Fallon's shoulder, and a jagged line cracks through my chest.

Then I turn my back on them and go home. Alone.

I don't text Fallon when I get there.

IT'S ten to seven in the morning the next day, and I'm unlocking the yoga studio. A couple eager students wait outside with sleepy eyes and soft smiles. I nod, say my hellos, and let them in.

Once inside the studio, I start some gentle music and set up my mat at the front of the room. Then I glance at the back corner where Blake was just a short while ago, sweating and struggling to move his body in a new way. Shaking my head, I turn back to the class.

An hour of sweat, movement, and breathing later, I say goodbye to the last student and spin a slow circle in the studio.

And I realize I was wrong.

Wrong to push Blake away. Wrong to panic about whales, of all things. Wrong to tell him that it was only sex.

It hits me like a punch in the gut, my eyes flying to the wall of mirrors. Hair wild, face lined, and body clad in tight spandex, I inhale hard and look at the woman staring back at me.

A woman who insisted on torturing herself, on holding herself to an impossible standard. A woman who turned her back on something beautiful just because she didn't think she deserved it. Because she thought she couldn't possibly get a second chance.

It wasn't the yacht, the whales, or Blake that was wrong. It was *me*.

Barefoot, breathless, I tear out of the studio and sprint to the cabanas. I fly past the ice machine, through the whisper of memories of what happened there, and round the corner to the pool.

His door is open.

I'll catch him before he leaves. I'll throw myself to my knees and beg him to forgive me. I'll tell him I was afraid; I was a fool; I was *wrong*.

I'll tell him he's the first person in nearly a decade to make me feel like a woman. Not just a mother. Not just a wife. Not a widow.

A *woman*.

He's the first person I've met who has shut himself off from love, then after a single kiss, decided to jump in with both feet. He's the most courageous person I've ever met.

And I turned my back on him. I told him it wasn't enough.

He gave me his faith, his belief, his heart, and I threw it back in his face.

He told me he was falling in love with me, and I froze him out.

My bare feet slap along the concrete as I run toward Blake, toward my future, toward the one person who's taken the broken bits of me and handed them back to me whole.

His door yawns open, spilling yellow light onto the stoop, and my heart hammers in its cage, trying to break free. Needing to break free.

"Blake!"

I grip the doorjamb and whirl into the room, only to come upon a maid flicking fresh sheets over the bed.

She yelps at my sudden entrance, stumbling back, then lets out a huffing laugh. "You scared me, Mrs. Viceroy."

Wide-eyed, short of breath, I stare. "Where's Blake?"

"Blake Harding? You know him?" She frowns, grabbing the edge of the sheet again. She must be the only person in Heart's Cove that hasn't heard the gossip.

"Yes, I know him. Where is he?"

She straightens, biting her bottom lip. "He checked out early this morning around four. I'm assuming he's either on a plane or home by now."

Fractures split across my heart as I stumble back, bumping into a table, a chair, the edge of the door.

"Are you okay?" The maid advances toward me, brows drawing together.

I shake my head, eyes wild. "He left?"

She nods, pausing in the center of the room.

"Did he leave anything behind?" A letter. A note. An address. Anything.

The maid frowns. "Not that I've found. Maybe at reception?"

I shake my head and stumble outside.

He left.

After everything, after telling me he was falling for me, he let me push him away.

He *left*.

I know this is my fault. I know I did this. But it hurts too much to breathe, let alone think.

I stumble back to the studio and find my phone in my bag, hands trembling as I find Blake's number. *You're gone*, I type, not thinking straight, not knowing why I need to say that to him. *You left without saying goodbye.*

The screen stares back at me, bright and unyielding, a sterile, sorry substitute for the depth of feelings I have for Blake.

When three dots appear below my message, my heart leaps.

I thought yesterday was goodbye, he writes.

I wait, and wait, and wait, but no other message comes.

Leaning my head against the studio wall, I drop my arms to my sides and let the first of my tears fall. They come slowly at first, sliding down my cheeks one by one, then faster and faster until I can't keep up with brushing them away. Sinking down on the floor, I lean my head on my knees and curse myself for being me. For pushing him away. For not realizing that he might have been my only chance at happiness. My only chance to start over.

But he's gone, and he's not coming back.

. . .

JEN FINDS me in the studio a while later. I don't know how long. An hour? Two? My butt is numb from sitting on the floor, but I don't move when she enters. She just slides down the wall beside me and hands me a coffee, her head bowed as she pulls her knees up.

"I made a mistake," I tell her.

"With Blake?"

I nod. "I pushed him away."

"Yeah. You did." Jen stares at a spot on the floor. Never one to speak much, Jen has always been brutally honest. Logical. Rational. But her voice is soft, and I don't think she's just agreeing with me to be logical. I think she understands why I felt the need to push him away.

Because I'm broken. Because I'm hurt. Because I thought my life was laid out before me, and I was resigned to live it alone. Then Blake walked in and broke that illusion, showed me just how much I was holding myself back.

And I got scared.

Her shoulder nudges mine. "What are you going to do?"

"I don't know," I answer, and it's the truth. "The Fringe Fest is coming up, so I need to make sure all the orders are made and my yoga sessions are planned. Allie made the track and field team. My mother is moving to town and will need help unpacking. Trina will need somewhere to stay for her and the kids. She'll probably need a job. My house is still charred to bits, and I need to find a contractor to fix it up." I snort, shaking my head. "I guess I'll deal with all those things while I figure out where the hell it all went wrong."

Jen sighs.

I turn to look at her. "What's going on with you and Fallon?"

Her face screws up, throat bobbing as she tries to swallow. Then, she gives me a one-shoulder shrug. "Nothing."

"Nothing?"

"His ex-girlfriend showed up in town last night. She's staying at his place."

I start. "What?"

My best friend lets out a humorless laugh. "Yeah. We kissed, you know. He told me he liked me. He helped me fix Simone's wedding cake. But I guess meanwhile, he was emailing his ex and inviting her to come to town."

"What an ass."

"Mm."

I frown. "Are you sure that's what happened? Have you spoken to him?"

"I ran away."

A snort slips through my nose. "Can't blame you for that."

"We're some pair, aren't we?"

"Very well-adjusted." I grin at Jen, who grins back. Then I start laughing, leaning my head against hers, until more tears are flowing down my face.

Then, with Jen's help, I get to my feet, pack up my things, and make my way home. It's not until I'm in the shower, alone with my thoughts, that heaviness settles in my chest.

I thought yesterday was goodbye.

Those words echo through my heart. Soft, cruel words.

It hurts too much to think about, so I push all thoughts of

Blake aside. By the time I'm out of the shower, dressed, and headed to the café, my heart is hardened. My jaw is set.

I have a festival to plan for. Yoga sessions to coordinate. A house to fix. A daughter to raise.

Maybe this is for the best. Blake was fun, but now he's gone. It's time to move on. For good.

TWENTY-EIGHT
BLAKE

VERONICA TAYLOR PUTS her hand on my thigh and giggles, leaning against my shoulder at something the interviewer said. She bats her eyelashes, an expert at flirtation.

I grit my teeth.

I'm on camera, which means I can't pull away and remove her hand without a million gifs of the movement popping up online within the hour. As it is, people might miss whatever she's trying to sell.

The bulk of our promotion work for this movie will happen months from now, when the release is imminent. This interview is just a tease, a precursor of what's to come—and Veronica is using it to its full advantage.

It's not until the cameras are off and I find myself backstage that I round on her. "What the hell was that?"

A coy smile tugs at her lips. "What the hell was *what?*"

"I told you I didn't want to pretend to have an affair with you, Veronica."

She waves a hand. "Oh, please. We're co-stars. We've gotten close." Her phone rings, and someone arrives to take her away, whisked off to her next appointment for the day.

I lean against a table in the dressing room, letting my chin sink down against my chest. My jacket lays across the back of a chair, and I can see the outline of my phone in its pocket. Teasing me. Taunting me.

Two days ago, I left Heart's Cove. As soon as I landed in L.A., Candice messaged me. Her message sounded... It sounded like she didn't want me to leave. Like she'd gone looking for me.

After I sent my initial message, my fingers flying over the screen before I could stop them, I stared at the phone, willing her to answer. To rise to my bait. To *tell me* that she hadn't wanted me to leave.

It was stupid to say that to her. I should have sent an apology right away, told her that I've thought of her every minute of the day since I left, but I couldn't bring myself to say it. All I could think about was the blankness of her face the last time I saw her. The finality of her words.

Why should I run back to her? Shouldn't I have learned my lesson with Mickey? With my cheating second wife? With all the women who are in my bed for a few hours and leave without ever wanting more?

I stopped myself from sending another message, wanting to see if she'd push it. If she'd show me that she wanted this, wanted *me*. I wanted her to prove to me that I wasn't being a fool, that she wasn't another Mickey just stringing me along when she's incapable of loving me the way I wanted.

But Candice said nothing, and I've been waiting. Thinking. Wondering.

Maybe I should go back. I should talk to her just one more time—

But the door opens, and my assistant stands in the opening. "Photo shoot starts in forty minutes. The Calvin Klein creative director for the shoot just called asking where we were."

Nabbing my jacket from the chair, I throw it over my arm. "Let's go."

The thing about Candice and Heart's Cove is that it feels like a different world. It's easy to slip back in to my life in Los Angeles, back to the thousand and one projects I'm working on right now, back into the phone calls and cocktail hours that filled my calendar before.

But it feels...empty.

From the front seat, my assistant turns her head. "People have been wondering," Christine starts.

"About what?"

"You're not acting like you usually do."

Shifting my gaze from the window to Christine's face, I frown. "What's that supposed to mean?"

"You haven't been seen with anyone since you got back."

"I've been back two days."

"That would have been enough for at least two dates, if not three for the man I knew before." She arches an eyebrow, eyes razor-sharp. "Maybe I should have come to Heart's Cove with you."

"You asked for a vacation, Christine, and you deserved it."

Her gaze narrows. "What's going on with you?"

I shrug. "Nothing. Just not in the mood for vapid dates. Needed a break from it."

"I've known you twelve years, and you've never once needed a break." Her tablet dings, and she turns back to the front to tap on it, but I can tell her attention is still on me. She sets the tablet on her lap and turns her head slightly toward me, head facing the driver. "This thing between you and Veronica..."

"There's nothing between me and Veronica."

Christine nods. "Okay. Does Veronica know that?"

"There's never *been* anything between us. She's trying to manufacture it for publicity."

"Right. I'll deal with it." Christine clears her throat. "Just got the confirmation for *The Tonight Show*. You're appearing on Wednesday night. I'll get the flight confirmation to JFK sent over shortly."

"Thanks," I mumble, my attention on the world passing by outside my car window.

AFTER A LONG DAY, I walk through my front door and nod to my housekeeper, Flores, who greets me with a wide smile. She's like Christine—been by my side for years, has always been loyal, and isn't afraid to tell me exactly what she thinks.

And when she sees my face, she sets down the cloth in her hand and walks toward me. "Mr. Harding, something happened. Tell me."

I shake my head. "Just tired, Flores. Why don't you take the rest of the day off? Go see your grandson."

Her brows inch together, eyes searching, but she says nothing. She just nods, and as I walk toward the kitchen, I hear her humming to herself as she gathers her things to leave.

Minutes later, I'm alone. With a sigh, I open the perpetually fully-stocked fridge, grab a beer, and lean against the wide marble counter as I tip half of it down my throat. My eyes travel around the room, to the double ovens, the massive island, the perfectly curated artwork chosen by a very expensive interior designer...and it feels so cold.

I miss her. I miss that cramped, outdated house she was renting. I miss the way she'd smile when she saw me. How, even though she made fun of Simone for it, she left a candle in my hotel room and lit it whenever we had an evening there together. How her house was small, intimate. How our mothers filled every silence.

I miss her body, too. The way she'd give herself to me fully, completely, without any hesitation. All it took was one touch, and Candice would melt into me.

It was a gift. A precious, beautiful gift—then she took it away.

My beer's empty. I stare at the bottle, sigh, toss it in the recycling bin, and grab another.

My phone buzzes, and my heart—just as it's done every time my phone goes off unexpectedly—bangs against my ribs. I force myself to move slowly, to pretend my mouth hasn't gone dry.

But it isn't Candice. It's a flight confirmation. The jet will pick me up on Tuesday morning and bring me back the next day. Christine has organized my usual hotel room in Manhattan.

Heart sinking, I toss the phone aside.

It's over. Candice didn't want me. If she did, she would have spoken to me. She would have asked me to stay. I was an idiot to think that two weeks together meant anything to her. Maybe I imagined the whole thing. Now that I'm standing in my big, empty house, I wonder if the warmth she gave me ever existed at all.

I'VE BEEN AVOIDING the café.

Okay, that's a lie.

I've been avoiding Fallon. I've been to the café, usually around three o'clock in the morning, to bake until my eyes got blurry as the sky turned grey with watery light. Then I've scurried away, back to my home. My phone has remained off and buried at the bottom of my underwear drawer. Don't ask me why I had to hide it, but I did.

I can't avoid him today. The biggest Fringe Festival order came in yesterday, and I need to get started on cookie dough to be shaped and frozen in preparation for the week-long event. It'll take all day. There are thousands of cookies to prep.

So, sucking in a deep breath, I enter the café.

Fallon looks up as soon as I enter, putting down his knife then wiping his hands on a cloth. "You've been avoiding me."

"Yeah," I answer, because what else is there to say?

That makes him smile, and a sharp pain slashes across my chest. I love his smile.

"You haven't let me explain."

"It's fine, Fallon. There wasn't anything happening between us and you're free to do whatever you want. I just wish you'd told me."

"I'm not getting back together with my ex," he tells me.

"She's staying with you."

His eyes slide away, lips pinching. "Yeah."

"So..."

With a deep breath, he meets my eyes again. "She's the one I was telling you about. The woman who works in publishing who might be able to help you with developing a recipe book. I never invited her to stay with me."

"But you told her you missed her?"

He cringes. "I..." He shoves a hand into his hair. "It was before you and I ever..."

Something rotten curls in my gut. Jealousy, but uglier. I'm not naive; I know that Fallon's been with other women. Probably lots of other women. After all, I'm the weirdo who never got married, who never even had a boyfriend for more than a year. I'm the weirdo who worked in computer science because I thought it would make me happy to have a stable job, then on a whim, stood up from my desk, marched to my boss's office, and quit to become a pastry chef.

My boss called me the wrong name when he tried to stop me. I'd worked for him for seven years. That's how memorable I was to him.

I guess I just thought... When Fallon told me he liked me, I thought maybe there was something special. Like maybe he saw *me,* and not just the quiet, awkward woman that everyone seems to forget.

Fallon's hand slides over my arm, all the way down to my hand. He intertwines his fingers through mine, pulling me close. His eyes are warm, so dark they're nearly black. "Do me a favor and talk to her, okay? She's really good at what she does, and she's got all kinds of contacts in publishing. She could make your recipe book a reality."

"What if she doesn't like my recipes?"

"She does. She's been asking about you every day. Particularly likes your lemon squares. I showed her pictures of the wedding cake you made for Simone and she couldn't believe you did it in a day." He tugs me even closer, his other hand sliding over my hip. "Just talk to her, Jen. Please. She's leaving the day after tomorrow, and she came all this way to meet you."

"I think she came all this way for you, Fallon."

"Jen..."

He's so close. So big. So warm. My eyes drop to his lips, then away. Instead of answering, I just nod. I'll talk to her. If I have to choose between a lifelong dream and a man, how could I choose anything but the dream?

Fallon gives me one last squeeze, then lets me go.

We work in silence for the rest of the day, and I can't shake the feeling that if I work with Amanda, it'll ruin whatever fledgling thing is happening between me and Fallon.

THIRTY
CANDICE

SOMETIMES IT'S a blessing to be a busy single mom with two businesses. Like, for example, when a man scrambles your brain and body for two weeks, then leaves without looking back.

Days are easy. There are school runs to do, meals to plan and prep, chores to complete, insurance claims to chase up, coffees to make, festivals to coordinate, yoga sessions to teach. I just go, go, go and I don't stop.

Nighttime is harder.

When the world slows down, when no one needs me—that's when I think of him.

Blake left on Saturday, one week ago. Since then, Jen has started talking to Fallon's ex-girlfriend about developing a recipe book, Clancy and Allie have been running track every day, and things at the café are in full swing in preparation for the Fringe Festival in a couple of weeks.

I've confirmed my yoga schedule and set up guest teachers.

I've got a full schedule booked for the week of the festival, the busiest I've ever been.

But I miss Blake.

It sits like a weight in my gut, this heavy emptiness that just won't go away. No matter how much I practice yoga, how much I meditate, how much I run around trying to take care of everyone else, I don't have his arms to go back to at the end of the day.

And it's my own fault.

He told me he loved me, and I pushed him away. He was ready to move here, to make a future, and I turned my back on him.

In the dark of night, when the world is still and my mind starts spinning, I wonder if it's for the best. There's so much going on in my life that I can't afford a romantic relationship. It takes up too much time, too much energy.

Plus, there's Paul. There's still that knot of guilt for even wanting to move on to someone else. I still feel like it's too soon.

But on Sunday morning, I find myself waking up before the sun spills yellow rays over the horizon, standing barefoot in my kitchen as the coffee machine drips into my waiting mug.

"Morning," Allie says, rubbing her eyes.

"You're up early."

"Meeting Clancy for a training run," she explains, then yawns. My daughter is turning seventeen in just a couple of months, and I can't handle how quickly she's growing up. I watch her go to the laundry room to the pile of clean clothes neither of us have folded yet. She plucks two mismatched socks from the hamper and tugs them on.

When she lifts her gaze, I give her a tight smile. "I remember when you were only about this high"—I put my hand to mid-thigh—"and you insisted on dressing yourself. The outfits you'd put on, Allie, I swear..." I shake my head.

Allie laughs, wiggling her toes. "Still can't match to save my life." She unfolds her body to stand up, my beautiful daughter. She must see the look in my eyes, because Allie comes over to wrap her arms around me. "You okay?"

"I'm okay," I answer. "You're just growing up so fast. You'll be gone soon."

"I'll always come back," she promises.

I smile, because I know it's true but it still breaks my heart. But I guess this is the whole point. To raise a daughter who can take care of herself, even if she can't wear matching socks. To teach her how to work hard, to chase her dreams, to keep laughing. It was my job to get her through the toughest times when Paul passed away and make sure her scars healed as best they could.

And I did it, but...

Now what?

"Have you spoken to Blake?" Allie asks out of the blue.

I frown. "No, why?"

She shrugs. "Just wondering."

Mug full of coffee, I swap it for the empty carafe, then dump a heaping spoonful of sugar in before taking my first sip. Allie leans against the counter, tapping on her phone.

"Can I ask you something?"

She looks up, phone still propped in front of her. "Sure."

"How did you feel about me dating Blake?"

Allie puts her phone down, then lifts herself up to sit on the counter. "I liked him," she finally says with a shrug.

"It didn't bother you that I was seeing him?"

She shakes her head. "Nah."

"But..."

Her legs swing as she tilts her head, a blond curl falling across her cheek. "But what?"

"When I went out with Rudy, you were upset."

"I wasn't upset about you dating Rudy, Mom. I *want* you to date. You're allowed to be happy."

"You were upset," I insist.

Allie cracks a grin, then shrugs. "Yeah. I don't know. I just missed Dad that day."

I nod.

She continues, "But Blake was different."

"Why?" I sip my coffee, trying to act nonchalant. Trying not to let my heart hang on her words.

She bites her lip, eyes focusing on the middle distance behind me. Then her gaze returns to mine. "It's the way he looked at you," she finally replies. "He'd look at you the same way Dad did. It felt right."

Before I can answer, or even process her words, Allie's phone dings and she slides off the counter. She gives me a kiss on the cheek and tells me Clancy's waiting.

Then my daughter jogs out the door, as if she didn't just shatter me with a few words.

She thought Blake looked at me the way Paul did. That he cared about me. That we were good together.

Putting my mug down, I spin around to rest my elbows on

the kitchen counter and I stare at nothing, cupping my head in my hands. I comb my fingers through my hair and fist into it, tugging, as if the pain on my scalp will bring any sort of clarity to my mind.

I was right to push Blake away. I *was*! I'm not ready for a serious relationship, and I don't know if I ever will be. It's *wrong* to jump into something else. I loved Paul!

A knock sounds on the door as it's opened, and my mother calls out before rounding the corner in the kitchen. She finds me straightening up from my position against the cabinets, and her face falls. "Come here, baby," she says, arms wide. "Come give me a hug."

And, because I don't have the strength to resist, I just nod and let my mother wrap her arms around me, cooing soft words in my hair as she holds me close.

"It's okay, Candy Cane," she says quietly. "Everything will be okay."

"I messed up, Mom."

She pulls away, wiping my tears with her thumbs. "You know, when I was in college, I failed an economics class."

I frown. "Okay..."

She gives me a smile. "I was totally overwhelmed. Doing too much. Taking too many classes, working at the campus library, and I was one of the only women in my degree. Your father and I had just had a huge fight right before the exam, and I hadn't slept in three days."

"You and Dad?" My voice is small. Even though I'm a grown woman with a child of my own, I still feel like a kid in my mother's arms.

She smiles sadly, nodding. "My professor listened to me cry and wail and rage, and he just said five words to me: 'Every problem has a solution.'"

Instead of lifting me up, her words lay over me like a weight, pressing me deeper into a hole in the earth. I shake my head. "Not every problem, Mom. Nothing will bring Dad back. Nothing will bring Paul back."

"Honey, I'm not talking about them. I'm talking about *you*." Her eyes soften, and she gives my cheek one last swipe. "It doesn't have to be Blake, sweetheart, but you have to give yourself permission to live. Allie will be gone to college in, what, sixteen, eighteen months? And believe me when I tell you, Candice, when they're gone, they're gone." She takes a deep breath, tucking a strand of hair behind my ear. "So, take it from someone who knows. You need to start thinking of yourself."

"You never dated anyone," I blurt. "You and Dad, that was it. You never found anyone else after he died."

"That doesn't make me better or worse than someone who does." Her eyes soften. "I got so used to being alone that it seemed easier than opening myself up to that kind of vulnerability again. But maybe..." She smiles, shrugs. "Who knows? Maybe I'll never meet another man. Maybe I will."

I've never heard my mother say that. I always assumed that she'd never date again. That she'd never love again. She held a candle for my father, and she was happy to live out her days with nothing but the memory of him. But her expression is soft, and I know she's telling the truth.

My throat is tight, but I push the words through anyway. "It feels like I'm betraying Paul's memory if I move on. Especially so soon. It feels like I'm just erasing him from my past and starting over."

My mother lets out a breath, then moves past me to grab a mug. She pours herself a cup of coffee and drops a bit of cream in it, watching black turn brown as her spoon clinks against the mug. Still staring at her drink, she speaks. "Love isn't some finite resource, Candice. You're not going to run out of it if you use it up too fast."

"I know that, but—"

"Does your love for Allie mean you loved Paul less? Does it mean you love me less?"

"Of course not, Mom, but that's different. A man—"

"Romantic love, family love, friendship...they all originate from the same bottomless well. If you let yourself love someone new, it doesn't mean you love everyone else any less. It's not like giving out pieces of pie, where the more people there are to feed, the less there is to go around. Loving someone new is like making a whole other pie just to share with them. No one ends up with less; you just end up with more."

Her words hit me square in the chest, but I can't... There's still a knot of pain there, something deep and twisted that I'm afraid to bring up to the light.

"Paul was a good man," I whisper.

"I know that, honey," my mother says, her coffee forgotten on the counter.

"He was a good husband. A great father. I don't want anyone to think he wasn't."

"No one thinks that."

My heart thumps. There's a boulder in my throat that

makes my voice come out breathy, choked, but I need to say this out loud. At least once, I need to voice that rotten secret I've kept inside for so long.

So, squeezing my eyes shut, I force my voice to work. "I wasn't happy, Mom. I loved him and I cared about him and he was sick and I wanted to be the one to take care of him, but I wasn't happy. I used to wish..." I shake my head. "I used to wish that it happened to someone else. It was someone else's husband who'd had leukemia when they were little, who had all those complications. Someone else's husband who was in the hospital at least once a month. Someone else's life that revolved around doctors and medication and insurance. I wished that I had had an easy marriage, an easy life. I betrayed him in my thoughts even when he was alive, Mom. And now I'm betraying him when he's dead."

The words leave me in a rush, and the familiar black wave of shame starts breaking over me, tugging me under. But before it swallows me, my mother fills my vision.

She grips both sides of my face and forces me to look at her, to see the intensity of her gaze. "Candice, listen to me, and listen to me good."

I nod, bottom lip trembling.

"Those thoughts aren't a betrayal. They are *normal*."

I sob, squeeze my eyes shut.

"Look at me." Her voice is fierce, low.

I open my eyes to see her nose an inch away from mine.

"It doesn't make you a bad person to hope for something better. You went through hell, Candice, and you carried your family on your shoulders. If you *didn't* feel this way, I'd worry about you. And whatever shit went on in your mind, what matters is what you *did*. How you *acted*. You took care of your family, of your husband. You raised Allie into the beautiful, headstrong, smart young woman she is. You were by Paul's side until the end, and your love for him was obvious to anyone with two eyes and a brain."

I'm crying now, sobbing so hard my eyes are screwy. I shake my head. "I was selfish. I'm still selfish."

"Stop it," my mother snaps. "Stop that right now."

I start, trying to back up, but she's still gripping my face. Tears fall from my eyes onto her hands, but she doesn't move, doesn't let go.

"You're human, Candice. Emotions are messy. Stop punishing yourself for things that aren't your fault. You're allowed to love someone but still wish they could give you more. You're allowed to honor your late husband but still date someone new. You're allowed to be happy."

As my sobs rack my whole body, my mother wraps her arms around me and hugs me tight. She holds me as I empty it all, cry until my stomach hurts, until it feels like there's nothing left inside me at all. Then she holds me longer, combing her fingers through my hair, pressing soft kisses to my temple.

When it's over, we pull apart and I see my mother's face is wet. She lets out a heavy sigh, then looks at the forgotten coffee on the kitchen counter. Touching the mug, she grimaces to find it cold.

"I can't bear the thought of a microwaved coffee right now," she admits. "Let's go to Four Cups. Get Sven to make us something with lots of whipped cream and chocolate shavings."

I snort, nod, then wipe my face with my palms. "Let me just wash my face and get dressed."

When I'm halfway down the hall, my mom calls my name. I turn to see her standing there, leaning against the wall. "If you called Blake, he'd pick up. I'm sure of it."

My thoughts flick to the last message he sent me, and I give her a sad smile. I don't have the heart to tell her I don't think he would.

THIRTY-ONE
BLAKE

"WHAT DO you mean you haven't put an offer on the house?" my mother screeches. She lets out a sigh and glances off-screen.

My father toddles over and puts his hands on his hips, framing his slight beer gut on my screen. "Son, that's the deal of a lifetime," he tells me. "If you won't put an offer on it, we will."

"Don't buy a house in Heart's Cove, Dad."

"Why not?" my mother answers. "Give me one good reason why not!"

"Because..." My voice trails off. For some insane reason, I can't think of a reason for my parents not to buy that house. There's Candice, obviously, but that feels like a reason why they *should* get the house, not the opposite.

"Exactly." My mother harrumphs and crosses her arms. "We're calling Miss Chrome tomorrow morning and hoping she hasn't already sold it. A property like that, on the ocean! It could be gone by now."

"It was a run-down house on an overgrown lot, Mom. And no matter how much you liked it, it's not exactly a hot real estate market."

"And what happens if it's sold, hm?" She widens her eyes at me, then waves a hand. "You messed up with Candice, didn't you? That's what this is about."

"Candice doesn't have anything to do with this. I'm trying to save you from a financial mistake."

Liar, liar, pants on fire.

My mother arches a brow, clearly seeing right through me. "I'm calling the agent tomorrow. You need a haircut, honey."

Then she disconnects.

I sigh, staring at my laptop screen, then lean back in my chair, scrubbing my face. The last thing I need is for my parents to buy property. It'll be another mortgage for me to pay—or another house for me to buy with cash...

But it's not the money.

I want to leave Heart's Cove behind. Even thinking about the place makes my heart clench. I was stupid to go all-in with Candice. Foolish not to listen to her when she told me she wasn't ready. Naive to put my heart on the line.

Closing my laptop screen, I look around my empty living room. I'm back in my place in California, just a couple hundred miles away from Candice, alone.

So, so alone.

The walls press in on me, and I can't take it anymore. I toss my laptop onto the couch cushion beside me and pull myself up, tagging my keys and wallet from the kitchen counter on my way out the front door. Then I'm in my car, driving faster than I should to get away from the silence of that house. Away from my thoughts.

I've spent the past however many years drinking in fancy cocktail bars, being seen with models and socialites. But I don't want to be anywhere near those people. I want to be ignored. Forgotten.

So, I crank my music up and I drive.

For hours.

I drive away from the coast, because the coast reminds me of Heart's Cove, of Candice. I drive until I hit desert, then I drive some more.

With my hands on the steering wheel and my eyes on the road, I let my thoughts drift away. Thoughts of that beautiful property my parents won't let me forget. Thoughts of the life I thought I had in my grasp with Candice. Thoughts of the pain shattering through my chest whenever I find myself alone.

My mind races until I reach Las Vegas. I blink as I slow the car slightly, crossing the city limits and following signs until I get to the strip, alive with lights and people and drunks. It's midnight, and I let out a breath and pull into the Bellagio's valet parking.

I'll be taken care of. They'll give me a room. Sure enough, as soon as I exit, recognition flits across the valet's face and he presses a button on his walkie-talkie. "Mr. Harding," he says with a nod. "We weren't expecting you."

"No," I answer, even though it's no answer at all.

I don't know what I'm doing here. I let him take my car and

I make my way inside, where I'm greeted again and treated like royalty. They give me a room, ask for my bags, keep their faces blank when I say I don't have any, and I just take the key card and wave them away. I need to be alone.

Wandering to the casino, feet stepping over patterned carpet, I pause, bright lights flashing all around. Green velvet tables litter the space to the left, with dealers in crisp shirts sucking money from lonely patrons.

Patrons like me.

After exchanging some cash for chips, I sit down at a black-jack table and let them suck money out of me for an hour, until I feel even emptier than I did before. Then I push away from the table, give a fan an autograph, and wander outside. The night is alive, but I just feel numb.

What am I even doing here?

I walk around to watch the fountain from the promenade, leaning against the waist-high rail as a fine spray of water mists over me. Goosebumps lift over my skin, but still I don't move.

I miss Candice. I miss the way she'd smile at me, the way she made me feel like we belonged together even if we'd only known each other a matter of days. I miss family dinners. I miss Allie's snark, and the way Candice would hold in her exasperation at the teenager's attitude.

I miss Candice softening against me, those moments of beautiful connection that happened whenever we touched. They happened despite our egos, despite ourselves.

Is this going to be my life from now on? Going back to vapid dates with vapid women, gambling, wandering the world aimlessly? Driving to Vegas for no reason other than not being able to stand my own thoughts and my quiet, quiet house?

Candice didn't want me. She still doesn't want me. The fountains dance in front of me, and I stare. I don't know how long I stand there, but it's long enough for my skin to feel damp from the spray, for my legs to feel stiff and cold.

Then, I hear a familiar voice. "Blake?"

My heart seizes, just the same way it did nearly thirty years ago. Turning slowly, I see my first wife dressed in a gorgeous, white, figure-hugging dress, her feet clad in sparkly silver sandals. But my eyes linger on her face, her hesitant smile that spreads even wider when she sees me turn, and my heart jags.

Still the same beautiful smile. It still lights up her face.

It's not until she has her arms wrapped around me that I realize she's with another woman. The other woman is dressed in white as well, holding a small bouquet of white roses.

"You remember Lauren?" Mickey says, her hands on my biceps, eyes searching my face. That brilliant smile still hangs on her lips, then she turns to her wife and introduces us.

"I remember you," I say to Lauren as I shake her hand. My eyes flick to their outfits, to the bouquet. "Um, congratulations."

Mickey laughs, that beautiful musical sound. "Oh, we were already married. It's our official five-year wedding anniversary, and twenty-five years since we unofficially tied the knot, so we decided to come celebrate and renew our vows. I'd always wanted to elope in Vegas."

Despite myself, a smile tugs at my lips. "I remember that, too. You weren't happy that I wanted a big wedding."

"And you expected me to plan it!" She huffs, then laughs again as she gives Lauren an eye roll. "My worst nightmare."

Lauren chuckles, and I'm surprised to find there's no awkwardness between us. She teases Mickey, who blushes, then puts her arms around her wife and kisses her. They lean their heads together, nothing but love emanating from them.

Seeming to remember my presence, Mickey straightens. "What are you doing here, anyway?"

"I'm not sure," I answer honestly.

"Oh." She tilts her head, eyes searching mine. I don't know what she sees, but her face gentles and she gives me another hug. When she pulls away, something sharp softens in my chest.

I clear my throat, but have nothing to say.

It's Lauren who speaks. She glances at Mickey, then at me. "She always said good things about you, you know. How supportive you were when she came out, even though she could tell you were heartbroken."

A lump lodges itself in my throat. I nod. "I was. I didn't feel very supportive."

"Oh, Blake," Mickey says, eyes soft. "I never meant to hurt you. And you were, you know. You were great. You didn't lash out, you didn't make me feel like I was anything less than myself. I'm so sorry I hurt you, Blake."

I shake my head. "Nothing to be sorry about. I'm glad you found someone who can make you happy."

At that, Mickey gives me one of her brilliant smiles, and intertwines her fingers with her wife's. "Saw you on *The Tonight Show*, by the way! Can't wait to see your new movie."

I lean back against the rail, fingers gripping the wet metal. "I didn't know you watched them."

"You know I'm a sucker for romcoms," Mickey says with a smile. "Always have been."

I chuckle and nod. "I'm pretty sure the hours I spent watching romcoms with you is what made me good at acting in them."

"I'll expect my check in the mail any day, then." She winks, and we both grin. Then Mickey gives Lauren a look that says she's ready to be alone with her wife. When she turns back to me, her gaze makes me feel bittersweet. "Well, it was nice seeing you."

"Same to you. Congrats again."

They wave, then wander off, hand-in-hand.

I watch them for a moment, then realize I'm cold and hungry and alone. But when I get to my hotel room and order a meal for myself, my body warms up...and I realize I'm happy for Mickey.

There's no bitterness in me. No pain at seeing her again. That spot in my chest that I always thought had died feels...if not whole, then at least it feels like it's waking up from a long sleep.

And as I lie back on the bed in the huge and luxurious suite in the Bellagio, I make a decision. It involves a phone call in the morning, and it'll make my parents very happy.

Whether or not it makes anyone else happy, only time will tell.

But after seeing Mickey, seeing how happy she is and

knowing she holds no hard feelings toward me, I know I need to try to find that for myself.

And there's only one woman who can give it to me.

Once the decision settles over me, I find myself getting almost angry. I won't let Candice push me away. I won't let her hide behind her scars. She will realize, one way or another, that we belong together.

I just have to prove it to her.

IT'S NOT until the Heart's Cove Fringe Festival is over that I can take a full breath. I had packed yoga classes four times a day every day for a week, not to mention the highest volume of clients to Four Cups since its inception. On top of that, every free moment was spent trawling through contractors' quotes for the repair of my home.

But on the final night of the Fringe Fest, I find myself on Cove Boulevard, sitting at a table in front of Four Cups with Jen, Fiona, and Simone, as we watch the final free show on the pop-up stage down the street. It's a folksy band, with a bearded banjo player and a crooning female lead singer, and everyone is enjoying the music.

Fiona glances back at me and gives me a smile, reaching over to squeeze my hand.

She's been amazing during the festival. She managed all the staff, procurement, and daily operation of Four Cups on her own while Jen spent her days in the kitchen and Simone did all our online advertising. It left me free to manage my yoga sessions. Without the three of them, I would have lost my mind.

The evenings have been easier, since I've been so dead tired that I haven't had time to think about Blake. But tonight, as I sit back and relax for what feels like the first time in weeks, my thoughts drift to him.

He hasn't messaged or called since his last text, and I know how to take a hint. He's been on talk shows, doing promotional tours, doing whatever it is that movie stars do, and he has no time for me.

I haven't had time for him, either.

"What's going on with you and Fallon, Jen?" Simone asks, turning her back on the stage.

Jen shrugs. "Nothing."

Simone arches a brow.

Jen sighs. "His ex-girlfriend works in publishing. She agreed to work with me on a recipe book."

"What?" I gape at my best friend, spinning in my chair to look at her.

Jen shrugs. "Yeah."

"Wait. Back up." Fiona lifts her palms. "You're writing a book?"

"Yeah. Inspired by the weekly specials at Four Cups."

I whoop, then throw my arms around Jen, soon followed by Fiona and Simone. When we pull back, Jen is red-faced, staring at the table. She gives me a tight smile.

"This is good, Jen," I say.

"Yeah. It is."

"What's going on with Fallon?"

Jen's face get tight as both Fiona and Simone get very, *very* interested looks on their faces. Jen shrugs. "Amanda left to go pitch the book to her bosses, but she'll be back in a few months. I know she isn't just coming back for the book. She and Fallon..." She shrugs. "Getting a book deal out of it doesn't seem like a bad outcome."

I frown, but before I can probe further, two large men walk up to the table and put their arms around Fiona and Simone. Wes and Grant bend down in tandem, kissing their women full on the lips before pulling back and greeting me and Jen. I nod, then shift my chair as the two men grab seats of their own to join us.

Not long after, Clancy and Allie join, and we spend the last of the Fringe Fest together, exactly two years after the initial festival that brought us all together.

It's a happy time. Everyone is talking and laughing and loving on each other, but I can't help but wrap my arms around myself to try to warm up.

When I take Allie back to the twins' rental house, it feels like a relief to be alone.

And that's how I find myself in bed, on my own, feeling wired and tired as I unlock my phone and open my messaging app for the millionth time.

I thought yesterday was goodbye.

The words are still there, and they still hurt. But moving past this silence is up to me. I'm the one who pushed him away. I'm the one who told him I wasn't ready. I'm the one who had knee-deep shit to wade through in my grief, and I'm the one who can climb out of it.

So, heart thundering, I position my thumbs over the keyboard and pause.

What the hell do you say to a movie star after a month apart, when you only spent two weeks together? What if I just imagined the whole thing? What if I was just a bump to him, when he's a mountain to me?

Allie interrupts my thoughts when she bursts through my door. Her face is red, jaw set.

I sit up against my pillows, frowning. "What's wrong?"

"Blake Harding is fucking Veronica Taylor," she announces.

I jerk. "Language," is the first thing that comes out of my mouth before my throat closes up and it becomes impossible to speak.

Veronica "let's run our lines" Taylor. The woman who caught me with him in the pool and dismissed me with a blink. The woman who Grant thinks is red-hot.

Of course he's in her arms. What man wouldn't be?

A dagger lodges itself in my heart as I blink at Allie, trying my best to keep from bleeding out on the bed.

She waves her phone at me. "I just saw it online. Everyone is talking about it. What an *ass!*"

Swallowing back the lump in my throat as I do my best to keep my face neutral, I give Allie a one-shoulder shrug. "He's allowed to get involved with whoever he wants," I tell her.

"No, he's *not,*" she retorts.

"We're not together anymore, Allie."

"Well, you should be. And he shouldn't be parading around

with another woman." She stares at her phone and shakes her head. "I hate him. I *hate* him."

"Allie," I admonish, but Allie just huffs and walks out of my room. A second later, my phone dings. She's sent me a link.

Before I can stop myself, I click on the article, which is a long, detailed breakdown of all the public places Veronica has been seen with Blake. A ten-second clip of them on a talk show, where she puts her hand on his knee and he seems to enjoy it. The article points out that Blake had been seen with a new woman every night up until he filmed this movie. Now the only woman he's been seen with is Veronica.

Eyes blurring, I close the article and turn off my phone. I don't want to admit to myself that my heart is breaking all over again, and it's all my fault.

I'm the one who pushed him away.

I'm the one who held my silence.

I'm the one who was too much of a fucking coward to admit to myself that I had feelings for him.

And now what? I go back and grovel? I ask him to come back to me when he can have a literal gorgeous movie star by his side whenever he chooses?

Suddenly exhausted, I turn off my light and burrow under my blankets. Blankets that aren't *my* blankets because everything I own is either smoke-damaged or burned to a crisp. I stare at a wall that isn't my wall, a window with a view that isn't my view. And I feel completely, utterly lost.

I cry until my eyes hurt, muffling my sobs in my pillow, and finally fall asleep as the sun starts to come up again.

. . .

MY MOTHER, who had left town just two weeks ago, calls me the next day to tell me she's decided to spend the summer in Heart's Cove. She, Trina, and the kids will be on their way within a week. Her house is cleaned and tidied and ready to be put on the market, so she'll spend a few months with me while she tries to sell it.

I keep my voice as cheery as possible and when she asks, I tell her I'm coming down with a cold after the stress of the Fringe Fest. I don't mention Blake. I don't mention Veronica. I don't mention my broken heart.

What right do I have to a broken heart? I knew the man two weeks and *I pushed him away*.

So, I bury my pain and I move on. I check on the progress of my house. I check on the café. I teach yoga. I spend time with Allie and make sure she has everything she needs for her final exams.

I don't look at my last messages with Blake. I don't think of how embarrassed I'd be if he'd seen me sprinting toward his room that morning when he'd already decided to move on. I don't allow myself to watch that ten-second clip a thousand times on repeat, even though the weak part of me wants to torture myself by doing just that.

No, I just gather all the scraps of my strength together, and I do what I do best. I put one foot in front of the other and I move on.

Isn't that what I did when my grief overwhelmed me when Paul died? Isn't that what I did when grief was mixed with odd, shameful relief at not having to spend days every month in the hospital? Isn't that what I did when Allie stopped laughing?

I survived all that, and I'll survive this.

I only allow myself one, single moment of weakness. It's when I'm on my way to the airport to pick up my mother, Trina, and the kids. I take a detour down a wooded road, and find myself slowing down when I approach a familiar clearing in the forest.

When the trees clear to reveal a run-down bungalow with a moss-covered roof, I hit the brakes.

A big, red *SOLD* sticker covers the sign on the front yard. I grip the steering wheel tight, eyes bugging, as my stomach bottoms out. I don't know when I start crying, only that my cheeks are wet when I wipe them. I don't even know *why* I'm crying.

Maybe because this property represents something I could never have—a second chance. Another shot at something good.

Flipping my visor down, I groan at the state of my face. It takes me a few long minutes to blot my tears and put a bit of powder on to hide the damage, then I head to the airport to pick up my family.

If they notice my blotchy, tear-stained face, they don't say anything.

THIRTY-THREE
TRINA

CANDICE IS IN BAD SHAPE. I can tell she's been crying, but I know my sister, and I know she doesn't want to talk about it.

"You didn't have to come meet us here, Candice," I tell her as I wrap my arms around her. "We're getting a rental car."

"It's nice to have someone come meet you at the airport," she says, forcing a smile onto her lips.

I exchange a glance with my mother, who nods, and we herd the kids to the car without mentioning her red, puffy face.

When Candice drops us off at our temporary accommodation—that same house we stayed in before—I haul the kids and suitcases inside, make dinner, run a bath, get the kids ready for bed, and put them down. It's dark by the time I have a chance to sit down.

My mother puts the last plate in the dishwasher and turns to me, planting her hands on her hips. "You need a drink."

"I'm fine."

She waves the statement away and opens the cupboards. "There's nothing in this house."

"I'll grab a bottle of wine for you tomorrow." I lean my head against the couch and stare at the popcorn ceiling, sighing.

I didn't think this was how my life would turn out when I married Kevin.

Kevin, the artist. Kevin, the flighty, brilliant painter. Kevin, the funny, creative genius.

I imagined weekends in Paris, gallery openings, beautiful gowns. Instead I got an overgrown toddler who didn't realize I didn't marry him to be his mother. I got a man who was so invested in his art that he forgot I existed, then was shocked when I asked for a divorce. He actually said I owed it to him to forgive him for cheating on me. I mean, what? Delusional much?

I know I sound bitter. It's because I am.

"You *definitely* need a drink," my mother says. "Pronto."

What I need is to *sleep*. Or maybe five minutes to myself without a child or a mother or an overgrown-toddler-ex-husband asking me for something.

I push myself to my feet. "I'm going for a drive."

"There's a cute little bar we passed on the way here from the airport. What was it called? The Cedar Grove? You should try it."

"Why are you so invested in me drinking, Mom?" I look over my shoulder as I grab the keys.

She huffs as her shoulders inch up in a shrug. "You just look like you need to take a load off. You've been through a lot.

Maybe there will be another movie filmed in town soon and you can get a Blake Harding of your own."

"That doesn't look like it worked out too well for Candice."

Mom just snorts and ushers me toward the door. "Head down to Cove Boulevard and hang a left at the lights," she says. "The Cedar Grove's on the way to the airport."

"Mm," I answer noncommittally, grabbing a light bomber jacket and stuffing my feet into my favorite knee-high suede boots with a two-inch heel. Yes, I like clothing. No, I don't feel bad about it. "See you in an hour."

"Oh, don't hurry back, honey. The kids are down and I'm not going anywhere. I'll call you if I need anything." She waves, then slams the door in my face.

I take a deep breath of clean, ocean-salted air, and head for the rental car.

I'm not sure how it happens—the power of a mother's suggestion, maybe—but I end up passing by The Cedar Grove on my roundabout drive that wasn't supposed to take me anywhere near it. Slowing down as I pass it, I grip the steering wheel and, "Oh, screw it." I turn into the parking lot and slide into the first available space, right next to a gleaming, chrome-covered motorcycle.

Stepping out of the rental car, I close the door and click the fob to lock the doors, my eyes still on the bike. With a smooth leather seat and a multitude of crisscrossing pipes and parts, it looks like it would be loud and fast and *fun*.

Okay, and I'll just go ahead and say it—this bike is *hot*.

I know it probably belongs to some old, grizzled biker dude with a beer belly, a foot-long grey beard, and a leather vest that is the opposite of hot, but I can't help staring at the machine in front of me. What would it feel like to ride something like that, I wonder? To just...let go?

With a single finger, I reach over and touch the handlebars, sliding my hand across—

"I wouldn't touch that if I were you," a deep voice says from the darkness.

I yelp and jump back, slamming into my own car as I clutch my chest. "Sorry, I didn't, I'm not, I don't..." My eyes scan the darkness as a figure emerges. The man steps into the light, and he is *not* grizzled with a beer belly and a leather vest.

He's *gorgeous*.

My eyes bug as I take in his height, his breadth, his *aura*. He screams power and confidence. Corded with muscle, he's wearing a black tee with black jeans and black motorcycle boots. His chocolate-brown hair is short on the sides and long on top and messy, as if he constantly runs his fingers through it. With a few distinguished lines around his eyes and mouth, and sexy salt-and-pepper stubble lining his square jaw, he lifts a brow and watches me with dark eyes.

"Is...is this your bike?" I stammer.

He nods.

"I'm sorry for touching it."

"You want to go for a ride?"

I jerk back. *Yes, God yes!* "No thanks."

He takes a step toward me, the light of a nearby streetlamp illuminating the harsh, brutal planes of his masculine face. I've never been this close to a man like that. A man who just screams *man*. He lifts a hand and I watch, fascinated, as he slides it along his square jaw. "I'm not sure I believe you," he finally says with a glint in his eyes.

My heart thunders. "About what?"

"It sure seemed like you wanted a ride when you were looking at my bike like you'd die if you didn't swing those pretty legs of yours over the seat." His voice—his *voice*! It liquefies my insides, and I don't have to be a genius to hear the promise of sex in his words.

My mouth is dry. I shake my head. "I'm good. I was just leaving."

"Let me buy you a drink."

I shake my head. "No. No, that's okay. Have a good night!" My voice squeaks, but before I can open the door, he's beside me.

"One drink," he says. "And your name."

"Please step away from my car." I straighten up, gripping my keys tight.

He steps back immediately, lifting his hands. "I apologize. Didn't mean to get in your space." He jerks his head toward the bar. "If you ever change your mind, just head to the Grove and ask for Mac." Then, with one last, long look that runs down my body then back up again, Mac spins around and heads inside.

I want to follow. I really, *really* want to follow.

Instead, with trembling hands, I get in my car and drive back to Heart's Cove.

I'M HAVING DÉJÀ VU. Fiona and Grant are sitting at the same table in the corner with three plates of cake splayed out in front of them. Jen is dithering. Simone is angling to grab a slice of her own.

And I'm behind the counter with Sven, taking orders while he makes the best coffee in town.

Then, Fire Chief Michael Allen walks in. His eyes cut straight to mine, and a warm smile pulls at his lips.

Uh-oh.

Everything inside me seizes. I'm not ready for this. I'm *so* not ready for this. I don't even know what *this* is!

He walks to the counter, confident and assured, his eyes still on mine. "Candice," he says in a warm, growly voice.

"Michael," I reply. "What can I get for you?"

"Jumbo black coffee, please."

"Which bean?" I point to the laminated sheet with our weekly options, all from local roasters.

He considers for a moment, then points to a green square. "Guatemalan."

As I tap the screen to ring up the order, he pulls out his wallet. I shake my head with a smile. "I told you, Michael, free coffee for life."

He folds a couple dollars up and slides them into the tip jar, winking.

I blush.

Why am I blushing? I mean, yes, he's attractive in a big, burly fireman kind of way, but he doesn't do anything for me. Not the way Blake did. I don't feel like I'm falling through space just by being in his presence.

My mother walks into the café with Toby and Katie in tow. Her eyebrows jump when she sees me with the chief, a knowing smile tugging at her lips.

Oh, no.

"Chief Allen," she croons. "How lovely to see you."

"Lottie." He nods. "Beautiful as always. I know where Candice gets her looks."

"Oh, stop." She swats his arm, and I want to disappear.

I may have been ready to start over with Blake in a moment of weakness, but after seeing that article about Veronica Taylor and reassessing how crazy busy my life is, I've decided that celibacy is the best decision. Permanently.

I can't deal with this.

Sven hands the chief his coffee as I take my mother's order.

She's still flirting with the chief, who's hovering. I cast an eye toward the cake-tasting table, but there's some kind of intense argument going on. I need an out. I need a way to disappear.

"Where's Trina?" I ask, giving the counter an unnecessary wipe with a cleaning rag. Anything to avoid my mother and the chief's eyes.

"She went out for a run this morning. Looked frazzled, like she needed to let off some steam. Probably back at the house by now." My mother and Trina are staying in the same short-term rental they booked before, and planning on moving into my place once the repairs are done. Lord help me.

Mercifully, before the chief can hover any longer and do something like, heaven forbid, ask me out on a date that I'll have to refuse, we get a mini rush of customers. I take their orders as Sven gets busy, and I start running coffees to tables. The chief accompanies my mother to a table, and I do my best to ignore them.

As the last customer sits down, I fill a tray with half a dozen coffee drinks and slide it onto my right hand. Spinning around toward the door, I take three steps, then scream.

The tray starts tipping, and coffees topple. Ceramic smashes, hot coffee splatters, and my tray clatters to the floor, and still, all I can do is stand frozen—because Blake Harding is standing in the doorway, his face looking like thunder.

He clenches his jaw and advances. Three long steps, and he's standing on the other side of the coffee carnage on the floor.

Total silence descends on the café. Even Sven stops making

coffee as conversation dies, my skin growing itchy as I feel a dozen pairs of eyes on me.

"Candice," Blake says, and I melt.

No, Michael didn't make me feel like *that*. Like my whole world shifts when I hear my name. Like the only time it's sounded right was on Blake's tongue.

I gulp.

His eyes drift down my body and back up again, gaze flaring as it meets mine again.

"What...what are you doing here?"

"I live here," he announces.

I start. "What?"

Holding up a hand, Blake silences me. "Don't. I don't want to hear it. I don't want to hear whatever bullshit excuse you've come up with to push me away. I'm here and I'm staying, Candice, and I'll stay for as long as it takes for you to realize we belong together. It could take ten years for all I care. I bought that property, I'm building a new house, and I'm staying."

He crosses his arms, biceps bulging, eyes hard. Challenging.

"You're...wait, *what*?"

"You heard me."

My heart flutters, but my mind won't let me settle. He's here, in the flesh, in front of me. And he's *staying*.

Then, suddenly, Michael is standing beside him. "I think you'd better leave, Harding."

"I'm not going anywhere," Blake growls, eyes still on me.

"Um..." I say, eyes darting between the two of them.

"Candice doesn't look like she's happy with you being here," Michael goes on, "so I'm telling you, you need to go."

Blake doesn't even throw him a glance. "No."

I look at the fire chief and shake my head. "It's fine, Michael. Thank you."

A muscle feathers in his jaw, but he takes a single step back and crosses his arms, watching.

Blake ignores him. "So? You understand what's going on here?"

"But...you and Veronica..." I frown.

His eyes flare again, as if I've said something to anger him. "Nothing has ever happened between me and Veronica. Nothing will ever happen between us, apart from her trying some publicity stunt to revive her career. I'm not here to talk about Veronica. I'm here to make you understand that you're wrong about us, and I'm not going to let you ruin this."

Um, excuse me?

Okay, yes, I did ruin what we had by pushing him away, but I do *not* like his tone. I cross my arms, frowning. "Blake."

"What," he bites off.

My mother wanders over, a soft look on her face. "Blake, honey," she starts. "Don't you think you might be going about this the wrong way?"

"No." His eyes remain on me, hard as ever.

I cock a hip, rising to his challenge. "If you think you can just waltz into my business and tell me how this is going to go, Blake, you're dead wrong."

"Well, I tried being nice. I tried coaxing. I tried spoiling you and taking you out on a luxury yacht. None of that worked, so now I'm trying this."

"And what, exactly, is this? The worst 'take me back' speech in history?"

"I'm not begging you to take me back, Candice," he says, his voice getting ever so slightly louder, the mess of coffee and broken cups still separating us.

"Oh? So what are you doing?"

"I'm telling you how things are going to go."

I scoff. "And how's that?"

"I'm going to come here every day and order a coffee from you. I'm going to build the nicest house you've ever seen on my twelve-acre property just north of town. I'm going to be here, in your face, until you realize that you can't live without me, until you beg me to kiss you, and then I'm going to make you mine. Forever."

A weird mix of outrage, warmth, and red-hot lust spears through me.

My jaw drops. "Yep. This is, indeed, the worst 'take me back' speech in history."

"Yeah, well, I never said I was good at groveling. I told you I was in love with you, Candice, and this is me telling you I'm not leaving till you get it through your pretty, stubborn head." He straightens up and looks at my mother with a nod. "Lottie." Then he walks out the door, gets into a car, and drives away.

I turn around to look at my friends, who are staring at the café door, speechless.

Then Simone bursts out laughing. She points her fork at me and shakes her head. "Girl, you're fucked."

My eyes slide to Michael and when he sees my face, his

shoulders drop. A sad smile tugs at his lips. "There's no point in me trying, is there?"

I let out a long sigh. "I'm sorry, Michael."

He gives me a small nod, lifts his coffee in salute, then he, too, walks out the door and out of sight. Simone laughs harder.

Not knowing what else to do, I go and grab a mop.

I HALF-EXPECT Blake to disappear after his little display in the café, but sure enough, the next morning he's striding in like he owns the place.

The sight of him turns me upside down. He's wearing dark-wash jeans and a black Henley that molds to his body like it was painted on him. I remember being wrapped up in that body, pinned down by it, melting into it.

But his face looks like thunder when he stops on the other side of the counter. "Black coffee and an everything bagel with cream cheese," he tells me, eyes boring into mine.

I tap the screen. "Anything else, sir?" I ask, my voice angelic.

His eyes flare. "Not today." His gaze drops to my lips, then he moves to the other side of the counter to wait for his order. When I hand him the brown paper bag containing his warm bagel, his fingers brush mine and a spear of heat pierces my gut.

But Blake just nods, waits for his coffee, then strides out.

I watch him go, speechless.

Simone wanders over to the counter, eyes on the door before glancing at me. "What was that all about?"

Blinking, I shake my head. "I'm not sure."

The next day is the same. Then again, the same. A third time, the same thing happens. He walks in like he's any other customer, orders, gets his food, then walks out.

And I notice that more and more customers happen to be in the café as the days go on. People come in early and linger, ordering coffee after coffee until the door opens and a certain hot movie star enters. Then a hush falls over the restaurant, and people listen to every word. Blake's particular brand of groveling is good for business, apparently.

On the seventh day, when I've entered his order into the computer, I break down and ask, "Where are you staying, anyway? I know it's not at the hotel."

Triumph flashes across his eyes. "Were you asking about me?"

I huff. "You're insufferable."

His lips tug, and my panties disintegrate right there inside my jeans.

Then he walks out, and I watch him leave, still not understanding what the hell is going on.

After a week and a half of this, with Four Cups nearly as busy as during the Fringe Fest, I start getting impatient. Blake walks in, orders, and I refuse to punch it into the computer. Instead, I cross my arms.

"What's your game plan here, Blake? What do you want me to say? This is getting ridiculous."

He studies me for a moment, then shrugs. "I'm just getting a coffee, Candice."

Exasperated, I thump the screen for his order, then step away from the register and go hide in the bathroom. I don't get it! I don't get what he's trying to achieve. He's coming in here every day, getting in my face, but he won't ask me out. He won't even *talk* to me. He just orders a coffee and a bagel and leaves. What the heck am I supposed to do with *that?*

Every day, the sight of him approaching makes my stomach clench. I find myself replaying every interaction over and over in my head, and spending every hour in between his visits waiting, anticipating, imagining. I keep thinking tomorrow will be the day he asks me out. Tomorrow will be the day he tells me he loves me. Tomorrow will be the day things progress.

But tomorrow comes, and he just orders a coffee and a bagel, then leaves. One day, he orders an apple pie muffin, and I find myself wondering if that means anything. Is it some sort of code? Is it a hint? Am I supposed to understand what he's trying to tell me?

For three whole weeks, my days are mostly consumed with thoughts of Blake. Those few minutes every day take up so much space in my head that I can barely think of anything else. My yoga practice is dominated by thoughts of him. My nights are restless, filled with memories and fantasies and lots of time spent with my hand between my legs.

I can't take it anymore.

When he strides into Four Cups on a Tuesday morning, every seat taken with a few people leaning against the far wall in anticipation of his arrival, my breath catches the same way it always does. His steps are sure, powerful, confident. His eyes find mine in an instant, and he allows himself to run them down my body and back up again, heat flaring before he can hide it.

Is this torturing him as much as it is me? Is he jerking himself off every night at the thought of me? Why won't he just ask me out? Call me? Text me? Why is he freezing me out while simultaneously making me burn up?

As he approaches the counter, I find myself walking around it. I meet him in front of the display cabinet, hands on hips, and his brows twitch in surprise. He stands a few inches away from me, his eyes soft as he looks down at me.

He opens his mouth to speak, and everyone in the café leans toward us like sunflowers trying to follow the sun. I hold my breath, not knowing what to say, what to think.

If he asks me for a coffee and a bagel, I'll punch him in the gut.

But what he says makes my knees go weak. His voice is soft, barely a whisper when he says, "You finally ready to get close to me?"

I blink. "Is that what you were waiting for? For me to walk around the counter?"

"I'm waiting for you to be ready, Candice. You told me it was too soon. You told me two weeks was too fast." His eyes turn molten as he shrugs, palms splayed toward me. "Well, a month away from you was too long for me, so I'm compromising. I'll wait for you for as long as you need, but I'm doing it here. If this is all you give me, then that's all I'll take."

My mouth opens, then closes, then opens again.

He waits as I try to process what he just said. As his words sink in, and I realize being close to him *is* torturing him, but being apart was torturing him more.

Blake watches me, catches every emotion flitting across my face, every thought that he can read in my eyes.

It's been weeks since I had that conversation with my mother, when I emptied myself of the guilt and shame that plagued me so long. But a few weeks is nothing. A few weeks is a blink of the eye. It isn't long enough to fix whatever was broken inside me...is it?

Blake lets out a breath and gives me a sad smile. "Can I get my usual?" He jerks his head to the register.

My heart squeezes. He saw my hesitation and backed off. He saw that I was thinking of Paul, of my scars, of all the things that hold me back from taking the leap with him.

Suddenly, I can't take it anymore. I can't take the thought of selling him a coffee and a bagel and watching him walk out the door, wondering if he'll show up tomorrow. I can't take the waiting, the wondering, the torture of it all.

He says he'll wait ten years if he has to, but is that true? Ten years for us would feel like an eternity! I was with him two weeks and it felt like I'd known him my whole life. A decade would kill him. A decade would kill *me*.

My breath comes fast and heavy, and I find myself shaking my head.

"No?" Blake asks. "I can't have my usual?"

"No." I lift my eyes to his. "No, you can't."

His brows tug together, but before he can say anything, my hands are fisted in his shirt and I'm pulling him down to me. My lips crash against his, arms swinging to hook around his neck.

His surprise only lasts an instant, and then his hands—oh, I missed those hands—are sliding around my waist as he pulls me tight to his body, crushing his chest to mine, taking over the kiss as he devours me.

I wrap my fingers into his hair and press myself against him, kissing him like he's my lifeline, like I'll die if I stop.

Maybe I will.

He breathes life into me, breathes love into me, makes me feel whole for the first time in far too long.

And when his tongue swipes against mine and he lets out a low growl, I realize what he's been doing. He's been waiting for me to realize that what we have is special. What we have doesn't diminish what happened before. It's not about the past.

What we have is about the present. It's about the future.

When we fall apart, arms still wrapped up around each other, his eyes are wide. Vaguely, I hear whoops and hollers from the café patrons, but I don't give a damn. I just stare into his wild, molten-chocolate eyes, and I let go.

"My mother was right," I breathe.

His eyes twinkle. "About me?"

"About love." I loosen my grip on his hair, bringing my hands to cup his face. "Loving you doesn't lessen how much I loved Paul. Loving you doesn't change how I love anyone else. Loving you is a whole new pie, baked specially for you."

He smiles, touching his forehead to mine. "I'll ask for the full explanation later," he says against my lips, then he kisses me again. And again. And again. A thousand kisses for the hours we spent apart, for the times I pushed him away, for the days he spent coming back to me.

When he feels me smile against his lips, Blake tightens his hold on my waist and slides his fingers through my hair, pressing my cheek to his chest so I can hear his thundering heartbeat.

And then I realize we have an audience. Fiona's crying, her hands clasped at her breast. Simone is blotting her eyes, waving Wes away from her. Jen is leaning against the kitchen doorway, smiling, as Fallon stares at her. Twenty or thirty other people are staring at us. Some of them crying, some of them smiling, some of them filming the whole thing on their phones.

Blake pulls away and looks down at me, eyes gleaming, thumbs tilting my chin up toward him. "When do you get off work?"

"Right now!" Fiona calls. "She's done. I'm taking over." She strides toward me and puts one hand on Blake, the other on me, and shoves us toward the door. "Have fun! Bye!"

Laughing, I barely have time to grab the purse Sven hands me from the other side of the counter before I'm rushing out the door. Blake hustles me toward his car, but he doesn't drive to my place. He takes me on a ten-minute drive just north of town, to a bungalow with a moss-covered roof.

Then, hand clasping mine, he walks me inside and over to the kitchen table, where huge architect's drawings are laid out. The plans for his new house.

With his hands around my waist, his chest pressed against my back, he leans his chin over my shoulder and squeezes me close. "I was thinking something relatively small. Three bedrooms with a guest house for visitors." He points to the plans. "A new pier, a small pool, and a huge porch at the back of the house. I also got plans drawn up for a studio that we could put over there"—he points out a window, to the wide lawn and lush trees— "for yoga. Either your personal space or somewhere to hold classes."

My throat closes up. "But...wait. You're building this house for both of us?"

He squeezes me. "Am I moving too fast?"

"Yes. No. Yes."

He laughs and spins me around. "So forget about it."

"What about my house?"

"Keep it. Rent it. Sell it. Doesn't matter. I don't care, Candice, as long as I get to wake up next to you every morning." His eyes are warm, body pressed close to mine.

"My sister could live in it," I say. "Or my mom. They both need places to stay." I chew my lip, hands curling into Blake's shirt.

His hands cover mine, and when his thumb brushes the wedding ring I keep on my right hand, he looks down.

My heart seizes. I'm not ready to take it off. I don't know if I'll ever be ready. "Blake..."

"Keep it on, Candice." He lifts my hand to kiss the jewelry, then moves to kiss the ring finger of my left hand. "You don't need to prove anything to me. You can love Paul and it won't change anything about your relationship with me."

Everything inside me softens, and tears immediately attack my lids. I tell him what my mother said about love and pie, and Blake gives me a soft smile.

"See? He's got his pie, and I've got mine." He kisses me long and deep, as if to show me exactly how he feels about me, and exactly how little he cares that I'm wearing Paul's ring.

I wrap my arms around him and smile against his lips, feeling lighter than I have in years. Then I pull away and let my eyes climb to his. "Were you really going to do this even if I never gave you any sign that I wanted to be with you?"

"You gave me a sign every day, Candice," he says softly, his hands sliding under my shirt, thumbs brushing my skin. "Whenever I left the café, if I ever started doubting myself, all I had to do was wait for the next morning. I knew as soon as you saw me walking through the door, I'd see that look on your face."

"What look?" I arch a brow.

Blake presses a kiss to my neck, then leans back, his fingers sliding up my sides under my top. When his thumbs tease the undersides of my breasts, I shiver, desire flaring to life in the pit of my stomach.

A satisfied male smile. "*That* look."

I don't even have the energy to swat his arm or give him stink for being so damn arrogant, because my hands are already clawing at his belt, and all thoughts of restraint have disappeared from my mind.

And when I get his pants unfastened and slide my hand over his hardness, he groans and cups the back of my neck, crushing his lips to mine. It feels like our first kiss—like every kiss with Blake—that makes my world turn upside down. With his body pressed to mine, his hardness wrapped in my hand, and his lips making a thousand sinful promises, I let go. I soften against him, giving up the last piece of my armor.

Blake growls and pulls back. "I fucking love it when you do that."

"What, this?" I slide my hand over his shaft and smile when he groans.

"That, too, but no. I love it when you soften. When you let go of everything and melt into me." He gathers my top and pulls it off over my head, then kisses me tenderly. "You did that the first time we kissed, and it drove me wild. Remembering how it felt to have you soften for me was the thing that kept me going since you pushed me away." His broad hands are splayed over my ribs, his eyes intent as he speaks.

I walk my fingers up his chest and hook them over his shoulders, then give him a little tug. "So make me melt again, Blake."

With a wolfish smile, Blake wraps his arms around me and lifts me up, marching three steps to the kitchen counter to set me down in front of it, tug my jeans and panties off, then lift me onto the counter. He pulls the pants off my feet and tosses them aside, his eyes flaring at the sight of me. Notching himself between my legs, he fists his hand in my hair and kisses me hard. I wrap my legs around his waist, my hand reaching down between us, suddenly frantic. Hungry. Needy.

When his cock is in my hand and I'm keening, moaning against him, Blake breaks the kiss and pulls me to the edge of the counter with a rough tug. Then he's at my entrance, driving himself home. I gasp at the intrusion, at the beautiful fullness he gives me, and then I'm done. He thrusts into me, holding my legs over his hips as I lean back against the kitchen counter, his body leaning over mine to take my lips in his.

I cling to him as I melt, and he growls, and I get it.

I've been giving myself to Blake since the first moment. I've always been his. It just took me a long time to realize it.

I come in an instant, unable to hold back the tidal wave of emotion that crashes into me as I realize that this is right. It's always been right. I've always been his. And when he finds release, his arms wrapped around me, his breath ragged, he kisses my shoulder and without pulling out, says the words that used to terrify me: "I love you, Candice. I love you so much it should scare me, but it only makes me feel like I'm the luckiest man in the world to have met you."

Fingers sifting through his hair, I let out a sigh as I pull back to place a soft kiss on his lips. "I love you too, Blake. And it does terrify me, but I'm slowly getting over it."

He smiles, gives me one last teasing thrust of his hips, then helps me off the counter. "Let me help you get over it again in the shower," he offers.

I laugh and let him tug me deeper into the house. I have a feeling it won't take me long to get over my fears.

EPILOGUE

CANDICE

ALLIE CROSSES HER ARMS, her jaw hard. "I'm still not convinced."

Blake faces off against her, shoulder leaning against the living room wall as she stands at the mouth of the hallway to the bedrooms.

"You and Veronica—it was a whole thing," she continues.

"That was made-up bullshit by tabloid media," he replies.

Allie glances at me. "Not going to give him shit for swearing?"

"Language, Allie."

She huffs, outraged, then turns back to Blake. "If you hurt my mom, I'll call TMZ and make up nasty rumors about you, and publish your address and phone number on the internet."

Blake's eyebrows jump. "That's...actually a pretty good threat."

Time for me to step in. "Allie, honey, I appreciate your concern for me, but I also want you to give Blake a chance."

She grumbles, then lets out a long sigh. "Fine. I gotta go. Meeting Clancy. Bye!" She turns around and walks out, slamming the door so hard the whole house shakes.

I give Blake a tight smile. "She'll come around."

"I'll bribe her with more whale watching," he says, and I freeze. I wait for the wave of guilt to wash me under, and am surprised to feel nothing but a small twinge in my chest. Blake wraps his arms around me and leans his forehead to mine. "Sorry. Too soon?"

I shake my head. "No. It's good. I need you to push me out of my comfort zone."

"I can do that," he says with a roguish grin.

I blush, and let him take me by the hand and lead me to the bedroom.

CONSTRUCTION STARTS ON MY HOME, and as I walk through the decimated areas with the contractor, I realize I'm ready to let go of this place. Once it's fixed up I'll reassess, but right now, I'm thinking it would be a good place for Trina and the kids to stay.

I've got a beautiful ocean-front property waiting for me, with the design and construction of our new home scheduled to take a year and a half. In the meantime, I ask the twins to extend my lease, and I make my home in the tiny, outdated house that I've grown to love. Blake moves in, and everything feels right.

Summer explodes in Heart's Cove, and with it, my happiness. For the first time in years, I let myself enjoy it. I work hard, I practice yoga, and I let myself fall for Blake.

The café is busy, with Jen working hard to develop recipes for her new book, to the delight of our patrons. When the display case overflows after one of her marathon baking sessions, we have no choice but to give pastries away. Fallon's ex-girlfriend, Amanda, comes and goes from Heart's Cove, and things between Jen and Fallon turn cool. When I ask Jen about it, her eyes dim and she shrugs. "If I have to choose between a lifelong dream and a potential relationship with a man I didn't even know I wanted, I'll choose the lifelong dream."

It makes me sad and proud of her all at once. She's going after what she wants, but I see a few lingering looks that Fallon sends her way when he thinks no one is watching. I wonder if he'd make the same choice as Jen, given the chance. I'm guessing no.

On the twenty-seventh of July, I wake up before Blake and find Allie in the kitchen. She's dressed already, a sad gleam in her eyes.

"Ready?" I ask.

She nods. I leave a note for Blake and head to my car with Allie. We drive in silence for half an hour until we cross the border into a state park, huge redwoods towering over us. It only takes us fifteen minutes to walk along a beaten dirt path to a familiar bench.

I haven't been here since we donated it to the park. Paul's name is etched onto a brass plate in the center of the bench, overlooking the Pacific Ocean in all its glory. Allie runs her fingers along his name, then sits down on the bench. This is where we spread Paul's ashes. It's where he was happiest— among the giants of the forest.

Birds twitter as a soft breeze ruffles the leaves, and Allie and I sit in silence. I breathe in deep, and find myself settling. At peace. My mind is still for the first time in a long, long time.

"I think Dad would be happy for you, Mom," Allie finally says.

I glance at her. "I don't know."

"Before he died, when he was in hospice, he told me to take care of you." Her eyes are on the water, feet burrowing into the dirt and old leaves below.

I arch my brows. "That was a lot of pressure to put on a child."

"He said you had the tendency to put yourself last, and that I should make sure you didn't punish yourself for him dying."

"He said that to you?" I whip around to look at my daughter. She would have been, what, thirteen, fourteen years old? How dare he put that kind of pressure on a child! Anger flares, then fades when Allie leans her head against my shoulder.

"Dad was right, Mom," Allie says. "He wouldn't have wanted you to beat yourself up about dating Blake."

I'm not sure that's true. Paul was human, just like me. How could he have even thought about me moving on?

A cry pierces the stillness, and a beautiful, graceful hawk flies into view over the water. It swoops, ducks, and coasts through the air currents, and finally comes to land on a high branch of a nearby tree. It stares at us, tilts its head, and pauses.

I hold my breath as the bird watches my daughter and me, feeling something profound settle in my heart. It's rare to see birds of prey, and even rarer for them to land so close. The bird stays for another moment, then pushes off with a powerful flap of its wings and flies out toward the horizon, banking out of sight.

"A Cooper's hawk," Allie says, breathless, squeezing my arm so hard I flinch. She lets go, eyes full of wonder.

I huff, shaking my head. "How in the world do you remember all these animals, Allie?"

She chuckles, rolling her eyes. "Long hours studying with Dad. We saw a Cooper's hawk here one day when he brought me for a hike when I was little. Saw it dive down and catch a smaller bird in the forest. I was devastated for the little bird," Allie says, a soft smile on her face, "but Dad just told me it was nature, and death was part of life, and I needed to learn how to accept it." She falls silent for a while, then shakes her head. "I think he knew he was going to die long before a doctor ever confirmed it."

Slinging my arm over my daughter's shoulders, I let a tear roll down my cheek.

Allie hugs me tight, then stands up and extends her hand toward me. "Come on. Blake promised he'd make pancakes for when we got back."

"He knew we were coming here?"

"I told him it was the three-year anniversary of Dad's death today," she admits. "Told him last night, and he said he'd have breakfast ready for us when we got back."

"So I'm guessing that means you've accepted him."

She grins. "Doesn't mean I can't give him stink for the whole Veronica Taylor stunt."

I click my tongue, and Allie just laughs.

Then we go home. As I wrap my arms around Blake, who's standing over the stove with a pancake flipper in his hands, the front door opens.

"Yoo-hoo!" my mother calls out. "We were promised pancakes!"

She comes into view right before Toby and Katie run in, followed by Trina. Then, to my surprise, Gina and Merv appear behind them.

"Surprise!" Gina says, splaying her arms out to the sides. "We couldn't stay away. Saw the plans for the new house and I have a few comments on the guest house, honey."

Blake bites his lip and throws me a glance, an apology and a laugh all in one.

"I'll put out some extra plates," I say with a grin.

Then my movie-star boyfriend puts on another batch of bacon as Allie takes over the pancake flipping, I make coffee, I settle down beside my mother, and I realize everything's going to be okay.

And when Blake kisses me right on the mouth in front of everyone, I let myself think life might turn out better than okay.

TRINA

LOOK, I've been busy. *Really* busy. I had to move the kids to a new town, unpack up all my stuff (again), get ready to move into Candice's old house once it's fixed up, make sure Candice was doing okay, make sure my mother wasn't doing anything too embarrassing (lost cause), make sure my kids weren't traumatized by my separation from their father, make sure Kevin got to see them and talk to them, register for schools for the fall, look for a job, field calls from a crying soon-to-be-ex-husband, talk to my lawyer about a divorce, apologize for moving the kids out of state in the midst of a separation...

It's been...a lot. Too much.

So when, on a warm Wednesday evening in August, my mother pushes me out of the house with stern orders to take some time for myself, I find myself driving aimlessly, until—don't ask me how it happens—I slide into a parking spot in front of the Cedar Grove. Scanning the bar's lot, I spy a gleaming

Harley Davidson leaning on its kickstand, and I almost run away.

But where would I run to? Back home, to laundry and dishes and children tugging at my sleeve? Back to Kevin and his cheating ways? Back to my mother, who I'm living with even though I'm over forty years old and supposed to be a full-grown adult?

Maybe the bike doesn't belong to Mac. Maybe it's some other Harley, and I'll go inside, have a drink, then go home. Maybe I'm misremembering things, and Mac isn't anywhere near as attractive as I remember, even though those few moments are burned into my memory in high-definition.

Maybe he won't remember me. Maybe he'll think I'm desperate.

Maybe...

You know what? Screw it.

The man owes me a ride, and for once in my life, I'm going to go after what I want.

Locking my car with a soft beep and a flash of the lights, I set my shoulders and walk into the bar.

Single mom Trina hasn't been interested in dating since her divorce...until she meets the motorcycle-riding hunk who saves her from a very bad day.

Check out Book Four: DIRTY LITTLE MIDLIFE DISASTER!

EXTENDED EPILOGUE

CANDICE

CAMERAS FLASH as photographers call Blake's name. With his arm around my waist, he gently nudges me to face one pack of photographers, then another, angling his body as he poses in a casual-yet-suave way in his designer tuxedo.

My gown is a vintage Oscar de la Renta off-the-shoulder number that cost so much I want to puke. And swoon. And possibly frame the dress when I climb out of it later tonight. The train is long, the fabric is a luxurious peach color, and the cut is *fabulous*.

I feel like a million bucks, and on Blake's arm, I'm practically preening. Glancing up at him, I'm surprised to see a blank, expressionless look on his face.

This is a side of Blake I don't often see. The sleek, cool celebrity face he shows the world.

I'm not a huge fan of it, to be honest. I prefer the mussed bedhead in the morning, or the warm smile he gives me whenever he walks into Four Cups in Heart's Cove. I miss the furrowed brow that tells me he's poring over the new design of the house, going over some detail the architects can't seem to get right.

It's January, and we're at the Golden Globes. It's been nearly a year since I met Blake, and I can hardly believe it.

He leads me to an interviewer, who bats her eyelashes at him so much I only just barely stop myself from rolling my eyes. I'm sure I'd be turned into a meme within minutes if *that* got released on the internet.

While Blake is being Blake Harding, Hollywood celebrity, I let my head swivel, eyes bugging at the gowns, the tuxes, the sheer amount of wealth and celebrity around me.

Slight pressure on my lower back tells me Blake wants to move. My eyes snag on Brad Pitt. Holy moly, Brad Pitt is *right there*. I stumble, staring, because I remember E-X-A-C-T-L-Y how I felt as a teenager when I first watched *Legends of the Fall*.

Three words: Hot. And. Bothered. I was obsessed with long hair on men for a good ten or twelve years.

Then, Brad Pitt turns his head, looks at me, and *winks*.

I gasp.

Blake laughs. "Do I have competition?" he asks, lips brushing my ear.

I swat his chest and shake my head. "Of course not. But you have to understand, my formative years were spent desperately in love with that man."

"Want to meet him?"

"What? No!" I gape at Blake, shaking my head.

But he doesn't listen. He just gently guides (read: drags) me toward *Brad freaking Pitt*.

Before we can get there, we're intercepted by another reporter. Then another. Then another. I'm simultaneously relieved and disappointed, flushed and embarrassed and excited.

By the time we make it inside The Beverly Hilton, I'm exhausted, and the Golden Globes haven't even started yet. We're led to our seats. I sit back and let myself be entertained.

Ricky Gervais is hosting this year, and when he looks right at Blake in the audience and makes a joke about the sheer number of romcoms Blake stars in, I can't help but laugh.

Blake throws me a sideways glance, then leans over and plants a wet one right on my lipstick-covered lips. On TV!

IT'S NOT until we're back at the hotel and I've carefully placed my gown in its garment bag that I take a deep breath. Blake is looking positively delicious, reclining on a mountain of pillows with one arm tucked behind his head. He's kicked off his glossy black shoes, his bowtie is undone, and his black shirt is unbuttoned all the way down, showing off his glorious chest.

Flicking through the television channels, he glances at me when I emerge from the bathroom, a fluffy white robe wrapped around my freshly washed body. His lips curl into a soft smile. "How did you enjoy that?"

"It was insane. The gowns, Blake! I'm not a fashion person, but I swear to God, Trina will wet herself when I tell her about it."

Blake chuckles. "You'll get used to it."

"I don't *want* to get used to it. I want to be amazed by it every time," I tell him, plopping myself down on the bed. It took me a full half hour to wash the makeup off my face, and I had to jump in the shower to get my hair back to normal. Being glamorous was amazing, and I'll keep the photos for the rest of my life, but I feel more comfortable as myself.

Blake leans over and tucks a strand of wet hair behind my ear.

"Don't get too comfortable," I say, angling my head away. "I have to go blow dry my hair, otherwise it'll be a bird's nest tomorrow morning."

"Who said anything about getting comfortable?" His voice is a low growl, his lips curled into a sinful smile. Then he reaches an arm around my waist and tugs me close with a yank that makes me yelp, and rolls his body over mine. "You looked beautiful this evening, Candice, but I think I prefer you just like this."

My heart warms. I let my fingers drift over his cheeks, his lips, over to his temples. "Not so bad yourself, Mr. Harding."

"It felt good having you by my side," he says, nudging my nose with his before laying a soft, gentle kiss on my lips.

"Are you ready for the tabloids to pick up the story?" I tease. We've had a few intrepid paparazzi come to Heart's Cove over the past few months, and there have been some rumors about Blake dating someone new, but this award ceremony is the first time we've been out together officially.

"It's not a story," Blake growls. "It's real, and it's my life." He kisses me again. "My future."

Oh. Oh, my. My insides clench at his words. Blake's gaze warms right before he kisses me. For real this time. Deep, wet, and hot, his lips devour mine as he works the belt of my robe open. His hands explore my body like he doesn't already know every inch of it, sending beautiful tingles rushing through my veins.

I'll never get sick of his touch. I'll never tire of his kiss, of the soft words he whispers in my ear when he makes love to me.

As if he can read my mind, Blake breaks the kiss and looks into my eyes, his gaze intent. "I love you, Candice. I loved having you by my side tonight. And I love the idea of going back to Heart's Cove with you at the end of the week."

I smile. "I love you too, Mr. Big Shot."

Then he makes love to me. It's soft, sweet, and slow, and it makes me burn up inside. Blake spends a long time with his hand between my legs, then his mouth, until I'm practically begging him for the real thing. And he gives it to me. I run my hands over his shoulders, gaze locked on his, emotions running riot in my body.

I never thought I'd have this. Even long before I lost my husband, I never thought I'd find someone who makes me feel so incredibly special. Someone who doesn't try to smooth my rough edges, but fits right into them. Someone who loves me for me, who isn't afraid to push me, who lets me know whenever I'm throwing up walls that have no business existing.

Over the past few months, I've let myself fall for him. I've slowly but surely let go of the guilt that plagued me for years, and allowed myself another shot at happiness.

These experiences—whether it's a custom-designed new

home, a yacht for whale watching, or a designer gown at an awards ceremony—don't diminish what my life was before. They *add* to it. I'm able to appreciate and love Blake precisely *because* I lived the life that I did before.

I'll always love Paul. And now I know I can love Blake, too.

When we're tangled up in each other in bed, heartbeats returned to normal, I place a soft kiss on Blake's chest. My limbs are heavy, and my eyelids keep sliding down.

"I'm going to wake up with the worst bedhead," I mumble against his chest.

Blake's chuckle is warm and round and perfect as he squeezes his arm around me. "I'll help you brush it out. Or I'll wake you up for round two and make it worse."

Smiling against his skin, I secretly hope for option two.

And, as the first rays of sun peek through the hotel suite window, I get exactly what I wish for. Rounds two, three, and four are only interspersed with room service, a shower, and a much-needed nap. I've never felt so spoiled, so loved, and so alive.

ABOUT THE AUTHOR

Lilian Monroe adores writing swoonworthy heroes and the women who bring them to their knees. She loves making people laugh and is eternally grateful to have found people who share her sense of humor.

When she's not writing, she's reading (or rereading) a book, walking, lifting weights, or attempting to play the guitar with very limited success.

She grew up in Canada but now lives in Australia with her Irish husband. He frequently asks to be used as a cover model for her books, and she's not quite sure whether or not he's joking.

Dirty Little Midlife Dilemma

Dirty Little Midlife Drama

Dirty Little Midlife (fake) Date

<u>Brother's Best Friend Romance</u>

Shouldn't Want You

Can't Have You

Don't Need You

Won't Miss You

<u>Protector Romance</u>

His Vow

His Oath

His Word

<u>Enemies to Lovers/Workplace Romance</u>

Hate at First Sight

Loathe at First Sight

Despise at First Sight

<u>Secret Baby/Accidental Pregnancy Romance</u>

Knocked Up by the CEO

Knocked Up by the Single Dad

Knocked Up...Again!

Knocked Up by the Billionaire's Son

Yours for Christmas

Bad Prince

Heartless Prince

Cruel Prince

Broken Prince

Wicked Prince

Wrong Prince

Lone Prince

Ice Queen

Rogue Prince

Fake Engagement Romance

Engaged to Mr. Right

Engaged to Mr. Wrong

Engaged to Mr. Perfect

Mountain Man Romance

Lie to Me

Swear to Me

Run to Me

Doctor's Orders

Doctor O

Doctor D

Doctor L